YES...
WE HAVE
NO CAMELS

A MYSTERY BY
D.G.HEATH

Publishing services by Hamaca Press
www.hamacapress.com

Design: Lee Steele

ISBN 978-0-9911444-9-5

Introduction

Lady Lynnette Whitcomb and her husband Sir Reginald had grown weary of the gray foreboding skies, the drizzling rain, and ghostly fog that surrounded Mayberry Manor, their country estate in Yorkshire, England. Summer had arrived and vanished in the blink of an eye. Days were getting shorter making the nights longer. The weatherman had promised a lovely and refreshing autumn, but it appears his predictions were about as far off as Iceland.

Mayberry's charming gardens were not a pleasing sight; in fact, they could barely see them when they gazed from the windows through the dense fog. The gray bleakness and bracing winds of Yorkshire had taken the place of colorful summer blossoms and sweet aromas of floral bouquets that had filled their home in August, and were now but a fleeting memory.

It was early September and already the red and gold autumn leaves had begun to turn brown, fall and gather on the ground. The evergreens were covered with a glimmering coat of frost in the early mornings, their limbs drooping with the added weight of solid moisture. Azalea and rhododendron blossoms withered and dropped from the stems.

"If I don't get out of here soon, I'm going to go out of my mind. And, don't bother suggesting the London townhouse. The season hasn't even started, and if these storms continue they may as well cancel the parties and send out the armada instead of carriages." Sir Reginald listened calmly as his wife babbled on. It was cocktail hour and they were enjoying drinks by the warmth of a cozy fire in the smaller sitting room. Lynnette was anxious to be off on a holiday.

"Egypt would be charming this time of the year and I've always wanted to see the pyramids and that lynx or lion thing, whatever they call it. You know, the sculpture with the body of a lion and the head of a pharaoh."

Reginald folded his evening paper and placed it on the small table next to his chair. "If we left this weekend, I might just be able to save my sanity." Lynnette paused with an exasperated sigh and looked at her husband sipping his Scotch and soda with calm reserve as he glanced at his mail from the evening post. "Reggie, are you listening to me?"

He puffed on his pipe and blew a cloud of smoke in the air. "Yes, dear. You've been dropping hints about Egypt all week. I was going to announce my surprise at dinner this evening, but may as well tell you now. We leave on the Orient Express next Saturday to Istanbul and from there we'll sail to Alexandria and motor from there to Cairo and Giza, then cruise up the Nile to Luxor. The tickets arrived in the post just now."

Lynette, eyes sparkled with excitement and for once, she was at a loss for words. But that didn't last long. "Why, you old goat! You arranged everything and didn't tell me. You know how I hate surprises." Of course, she was telling a fib and he chuckled at her attempt to hide the facts.

"I can't imagine that statement comes as a surprise, considering all the spies you have in and around London. Not to mention, I was spotted at the travel office by Molly and Bev, two of the biggest gossips in London society. By now, I wouldn't be surprised if half the people having tea in the Palm Court at the Ritz Carlton didn't know about our planned holiday."

Sir Reginald rose from his comfortable chair, grinned, and winked as he stood by the fireplace. "After twenty years I can read you like a book old girl, and I must say you are not very subtle with the hints. Figs and dates from Nile, and couscous, for god's sake! How African can you get?

"Fortunately, I remembered our trip to Morocco last fall, so I knew you wouldn't want to repeat that again." Sir Reginald was quite proud of himself, standing with his arm resting on the fireplace mantel, pipe in one hand and tickets in the other. He waved them at Lynnette and grinned. "You'd better start packing. And let Minnie know she goes with us. I can manage without a valet, but you need a ladies maid."

Lynnette, gave him her winning smile from ear to ear, poured them each another drink, and joined her clever husband by the fire as he took another puff from his pipe and blew smoke rings in the air. She toasted to her good fortune and her husband's amazing intellectual capability to take a hint. She smiled sheepishly as she said, "Two trunks are already packed. Minnie and I were going to leave with or without you," she joked. "However, I'm delighted you want to join us." Sir Reginald shook his head and chuckled, but Lynnette was not quite finished. "I'm so happy I get to travel with a lady's maid this time. Morocco, she rolled her eyes, was an absolute disaster." He took her in his arms and gave her a hug.

Henry, the butler, gave a knock and entered the drawing room carrying a card on a silver plate. "Sorry to interrupt, sir but you have a visitor. He's waiting in the library."

Sir Reginald glanced at the card. "I'd better see to this, my dear. You go and tell Minnie to pack her swimsuit in case she gets an opportunity to bathe in the Nile waters." He chuckled at the thought of Minnie floating down the Nile, as he glanced at the card once again.

Lynnette hurried off, but turned at the door. "By the way...the Home Office phoned today and they're sending someone out with some information for your review. That's probably who's waiting in the library. Please, darling, don't ask anyone to stay for dinner tonight. I want just the two of us to celebrate this evening and our Egyptian adventure ahead."

"I'll send him away, once I find out what it's all about and what they want. And please, tell cook no more couscous on the menu." She gave a little laugh, blew him a kiss, and closed the door behind her.

Characters

- **Sir Reginald Whitcomb**
  Member of Parliament and investigator for the Home Office

- **Lady Lynette Whitcomb**
  Sir Reginald's wife and part time sleuth

- **Detective Bobby Brennan**
  Scotland Yard detective and Home Office investigator. A friend of the Whitcombs

- **Minnie Sparks**
  Lady Lynette's personal maid and longtime friend and companion

- **Lord Charles Marquis of Menton Abbey in Kent**
  Antiquities collector, museum donor, and excavation sponsor

- **Sir Thomas Treadwell**
  Retired director of MIA—Merriweather Intelligence Agency

- **Lady Grace Treadwell**
  Sir Thomas's wife/chauffer and former bodyguard with MIA

- **Ahmet**
  Turkish Secret Service Director

- **Dashi**
  Egyptian antiquities photographer at the excavation site

- **Mario Regetti**
  Former homicide police detective on Capri—now a wine grower in Tuscany

- **Kathy Stockton**
  Regitti's wife—an appraiser and exhibition organizer for the British Museum. Specialist in artifacts and antiquities.

- **Dr. Roland Stafford**
  British Museum antiquities curator and archeologist

- **Dr. Herit Kasmut**
  Female antiquities specialist with the Cairo Museum

- **Jason Taylor (English), Boris Rykoff (German)**
  Bodyguards for the Home Office in London

- **Timothy Gordon Leeds**
  Chairman of Operations for the Orient Express.

- **Captain Mohamed Kalif Saeed**
  Officer for the Egyptian Police Force in Luxor

Chapter One

The Home Office

S ir Reginald crossed the elegant marble tiled foyer and entered the comforting space of his personal library, filled with tomes and legal works needed for his position in Parliament. The rich aroma of highly polished mahogany glowing like honey in the dim light was soothing and inviting. A fire glowed in the huge fireplace surrounded by sculpted stone with a massive mantle, above which was a portrait of his charming wife, Lynnette.

He smiled a greeting as he approached the gentleman standing by the warm blaze, gazing out the French window and across the terrace at the drizzling rain. He took the man's extended hand in a firm handshake and clapped the shoulder of his wet trench coat. "Bobby, or should I say, Detective Brennan, my old friend, what brings you all the way to Yorkshire in this miserable weather? It must be something terribly important."

"Sir Reginald," he smiled in return, shook his head and mumbled, "I still haven't quite got the hang of using your new title." They both chuckled.

"Don't worry Bobby, you can still call me Reggie, anytime you like. We've both come a long way since Eton and Oxford, but we're still the same mates we were then. Why didn't Henry take your coat?" He stepped toward the bell pull and started to ring for the butler.

"No, no, don't bother Henry. I'm here on business and won't stay long. Besides, you haven't had your dinner yet and I'm sure Lynnette would be upset if I take too long." He paced in front of the roaring fire as he searched for a way to present the information and the Home Office assignment. Sir Reginald was a patient man and didn't wish to pressure his friend.

He placed his drink on the silver tray. "Scotch and soda?" he asked, pouring his guest a drink from the crystal decanters on a small table.

Detective Brennan's face flickered in the firelight, a serious, determined look casting shadows of concern in the deep furrows on his brow. "I really shouldn't."

Sir Reginald gave him a quizzical stare, as he mixed the cocktail anyway. "That serious, old chap?"

"Well—the Home Office seems to think so, and most likely there's bound to be danger. They sent me with instructions to seek your help. Oh, what the heck. I think I'll have that drink you offered." Reginald handed him the glass.

"In that case, you'd better take that coat off and we can sit down by the fire. I'll send word up to Lynnette. She's in a gay mood right now. We're taking a holiday to Egypt, and she's all excited."

"Yes, I know, the Home Office told me. That's why I'm here tonight." Brennan took a sip of his drink, letting the warmth slowly cascade down his throat and take the chill off the rainy night.

Henry had entered and removed Brennan's coat. He seated himself in one of the plush leather club chairs. "Henry, please tell Lady Whitcomb I'll be detained a little longer. She and Minnie can continue packing." Sir Reginald instructed.

"Very good, sir. Will there be anything else? Shall I tell the cook to expect three for dinner this evening?"

Sir Reginald was sure Lynette wouldn't mind if their old friend Bobby stayed, but he knew she would be concerned about having a detective arrive on such short notice; she would want to know what's up, and as yet, even he didn't know the answer to that question.

Reginald gave his friend a questioning glance and Bobby shook his head no. "Detective Brennan isn't staying for dinner, so you needn't bother the cook."

"Very well, sir." Henry exited, closing the library door quietly.

Sir Reginald's hazel eyes held fast to his friend. "Well Bobby? What has the Home Office in such a tizzy? Has someone been murdered? Are we being invaded? And damn it all, what's it to them if I go to Egypt? Is nothing sacred or secret anymore?"

Bobby Brennan set his glass on the table beside his chair. "It's like this," he said, swallowing the lump in his throat. "The London Museum is involved with a new tomb excavation near Luxor, in the Valley of the Monkeys. Unfortunately, there's been a recent rash of mysterious happenings. Antiquities from the tomb disappear then reappear. Two workers have reportedly vanished in the night without a trace, Of course, as usual, no one knows anything about them. Needless to say, they're pressuring the HO to investigate."

Sir Reginald stood and crossed to the fireplace. "Who's pressuring for an investigation?"

"The British Museum and Lloyd's of London, the insurance company that's covering the excavation. They're also sending an undercover private investigator."

"Can't the Egyptian Police look into this incident?"

"The insurance company and the museum are not willing to turn it over to the police entirely. Publicity and all that, you know. You'll of course have their assistance, for what it's worth should you need it. They have been notified and made a preliminary search. However, these artifacts are worth millions at on-site appraisal, and you know how tempting that can be to the "Black Market" operators and the collectors who deal with them. Even the police are easily bribed."

"But you just stated that these artifacts were taken and then returned. Unless someone replaced the originals with copies, there's been no theft. The missing workers might have something to do with the removal and reappearance of these items, or they may not. That remains to be determined. Have the two workers returned?"

"No."

"How long has it been since they disappeared?" Reginald asked.

"I was told they vanished last week, and they didn't return for payroll payments, which in itself is most unusual."

Brennan stood and joined Sir Reginald at the fireplace. "I would go old man, but I'm on another case right now. Your name came up and the decision was made by the top brass. I'm just the messenger. As usual, this is an undercover investigation. He handed Sir Reginald the file he had carried. It has all the particulars, you'll need, contacts, facts, and directions to the excavation site. There's a list of names you'll need on arrival in the Valley of the Monkeys. These are the people in charge."

Sir Reginald placed his empty glass on the mantel along with the file and put his hands on Bobby's shoulders. "Well, old boy, if it can't be helped, I guess I'll just have to mix business with pleasure. I'll want a guard for Lynnette and Minnie and one for myself once we are in Egypt. I'll send the Home Office our itinerary tomorrow."

"No problem. They've already got it," Brennan smiled.

"Of course they have," Sir Reginald chuckled. "They wouldn't be the best in the world if they didn't." He rang for Henry.

They walked slowly into the entry, where Henry helped Brennan slip into his coat and then disappeared.

"Don't ever let anyone tell you that retiring to the country is safe and dull." quipped Sir Reginald.

"It isn't safe anywhere," scoffed Brennan. "In London you could get hit by a bus, run over by a taxi, or mugged in the tube. Out here, you might slip in a pigsty, get chased by a mad goose, or fall off your horse," he chuckled. "But be careful in Egypt. People vanish into thin air."

Sir Reginald laughed out loud. "I've seen that old rope trick a dozen times and still haven't figured out where they disappear to," he chuckled.

Brennan grinned. "I'll take my leave now and see to arranging the bodyguards as soon as I get back to London. Give my regards to Lynnette, once you find the right time to tell her. Or do you plan to keep her in the dark?"

"My dear fellow. You can't keep Lynnette in the dark about

anything. She has eyes like a cat and her mind works like radar. She'll know something's up before you get to the highway. I learned a long time ago, never try to keep a secret from my lovely wife. She has her spies all over, even in London. She knew we were going to Egypt before I told her, but at least she faked surprise. She knows what's going on before I do. How do you think I got into Parliament in the first place?"

Brennan shook his head as they clasped hands. "Take care my friend and keep your pistol cocked."

"I'll leave that up to Lynnette if you don't mind. She's a much better shot than I am." He could hear Bobby laughing as he got in his car.

"Who do I have to shoot to get a drink around here?" came a feminine voice from behind him, where Lady Lynnette stood in the doorway dressed for dinner, one hand on her hip and the other on the door frame. "Wasn't that Bobby Brennan?"

"Yes, dear," Reginald said, closing the door behind him as they entered.

"I must say, this is turning into a rather exciting evening. I can't wait to learn all about it over dinner." She smiled, turned, and glided towards the dining room in her black sequined gown. "Come along, dear. I think you have a story to tell and I'm starving."

The aroma of French onion soup under a cheese crust, roasted rabbit, sesame-braised cucumbers, and oven-roasted new potatoes filled the air in the dining room. A baked apple pudding layered with cinnamon and slivered almonds then topped with whipped cream would be served for dessert.

The sideboard was ladened with selected wines, and chilled champagne. Brandy and Port would be served by the fireplace in the drawing room after dinner. Lynnette had seen to every detail.

Chapter Two

Adventure Begins

Sir Reginald and Lynnette's party of three waited to board their appointed Pullman car at Victoria Station. People stirred like a colony of ants, as station porters maneuvered through the crowd with luggage, and passengers said goodbye to friends and relatives. Whistles sounded and the constant roar of the idling engines echoed in the huge space.

There was a fall chill in the air as thick fog snaked its way through the open station. Soon they would be in France and points beyond. But first they must leave the train at Folkestone, and board the luxury motor coaches that drive you onto the Eurotunnel train and across the channel to Calais, where the Orient Express and white glove-service would be waiting for them.

Lady Lynnette, as usual, was taking a casual survey of the passengers who were gathered to board the train. She tugged Sir Reginald's coat sleeve, "Look, Reggie! I see a familiar face in the crowd. Isn't that Sir Thomas Treadwell standing over there by the post?" She nodded in the direction indicated.

"By George, I think you're right. And that looks like Grace with him. He never goes anywhere without her nowadays."

"In reality, dear, she won't let him," said Lynnette with a knowledgeable grin.

He caught Sir Thomas's eye, nodded, and waved, "They're coming our direction so sharpen your wits and be charming. I know you enjoy their company."

Lynnette gave him a look of exasperation, but didn't have time to make a return comment.

Sir Thomas was the first to speak as he extended his hand in greeting. "I say, Reggie old boy, we haven't seen you in a month of Sundays. You and Lynnette really should come up to Penderleigh and visit us. Not now, of course, we're off to explore Egypt on holiday."

Grace joined in, "My dear, Lynnette, so good to see you. Thomas doesn't mean to ignore you, but we're due to board any minute now.

Where might you be headed?"

"Reggie decided to take me on holiday and out of this dreary wet weather. We're on our way to Istanbul. Then on to Egypt and a cruise up the Nile."

"Bravo!" replied Sir Thomas, "We're all traveling in the same direction. Will you join us in the dining car for dinner this evening? I don't wish to intrude on your adventure, but Grace and I always enjoy your company. We see each other all the time since the accident that forced me into partial retirement from the agency."

"We'd be delighted to join you," said Sir Reginald, before Lynnette could answer. "Shall we say around eight o'clock?"

"That would be splendid," added Sir Thomas with a tip of his hat. "There's the second whistle. We'd best get aboard, old girl. Don't want to be left behind. The Orient Express is always on time, and doesn't wait for anyone—not even the Home Office." He nodded to Reggie and Lynnette then tipped his hat. "See you in Calais."

Thomas and Grace hurried back to the third car in line as a steward assisted Lady Lynnette, Sir Reginald, and Minnie Sparks into the first car. Gliding as smooth as silk, the train moved out of the station signaling their departure with the third whistle.

Seated comfortably in their suite, Lynnette remarked, "Did you happen to notice the tall woman in a turban who boarded car three at the last minute?" Sir Reginald was engaged in reading his newspaper and didn't glance up.

"What was that, dear? You say you want to buy a turban?"

She reached across and pulled the paper down so she had his attention. "I said, did you notice the tall woman in a turban boarding the train in car three? I'm sure I've seen her face before. Perhaps she'll be in the dining car this evening. Maybe Sir Thomas might recognize her. Sorry to bother you." She gazed out the window as they left London en route to Folkestone.

"No bother, love. No bother," Sir Reginald said holding his unlit pipe between his teeth while concentrating on his news.

Holding a pipe between his teeth was a habit he used to comfort himself while reading, and a ploy to keep from answering his wife. You might call it a distraction, but Lady Lynnette was not easily fooled. She learned to gently remove the pipe from his mouth getting his attention, and then calmly ask her question again.

~

Crossing the channel went smoothly. The water and wind had calmed in a combined effort to make the first leg of their journey uneventful. The station at Calais bustled with passengers and stewards preparing for departure to Paris. Once again, Lady Lynnette spotted the woman with the turban as she stepped onto the platform of the third car, a few passengers behind Sir Thomas and Grace.

"There's something strange about that woman in the turban, but I can't put my finger on it. She has a loneliness about her, but at the same time, shows a certain fear, glancing with ferret eyes from corner to corner searching for a face she doesn't want to see. Call it a woman's intuition, but I think she's running from someone. She's frightfully nervous and overly cautious about the two large trunks she's traveling with."

"I believe your active imagination is in overdrive. I was just going to order some tea. Or would you rather join our fellow passengers in the lounge?" Sir Reginald asked.

"Oh, by all means, we should mingle. Maybe we'll find someone who plays bridge. As I recall, Grace is not a bridge player." The lady in the turban did not appear in the club car for tea.

The heydays of the old Orient Express had long since passed. However, the new, sleek traveling cars were well appointed with all the modern conveniences. The art-deco, first-class compartments were decorated in soothing shades of mauve and gray. Highly polished, rich, wood surfaces gleamed in the morning light.

It was eight o'clock on the dot when they joined Sir Thomas and Lady Grace Treadwell in the dining car. The subtle colors of lavender and beige were accented by the starched white linens, sterling silver, sparkling crystal glasses, and custom made china.

Servers in white uniforms with gold braid and white gloves added to the ambiance, as champagne and caviar with chopped eggs were served and food choices were made. Succulent herb crusted rack of lamb and lobster thermidor were the two most popular entrees selected that evening, followed by a melt-in-your-mouth chocolate cake topped with a vanilla Bourbon sauce.

Sir Thomas was delighted to have the company. "So...tell me what's happening in the Home Office these days. I've been out of the loop and on a tight rein since I was shot. I'm sure you remember that "Viper" drug and gambling ring we bagged ten months ago. That's when I got clipped. We didn't want it in print because of the reputation of the agency. Bad publicity for business, you know. What have they drug you out of mothballs to investigate now?"

Lady Lynnette gave him a look of shock. "We're on holiday, Thomas. Aren't people allowed to take holidays?"

Sir Thomas smiled, "Ordinary people, yes, but Home Office people don't get that privilege." He nodded to Sir Reginald and waited patiently.

"It appears there are some issues happening at a new archeological site that the museum is sponsoring—black market, and all that rot. They'll probably have it all ironed out by the time I arrive."

Sir Thomas shook his head. "I wouldn't put too much faith in the Egyptian police if I were you."

Lady Grace chuckled, "You might want to listen to him. He's been around the block a time or two with those police in Egypt."

"There she is!" Lady Lynnette had spotted the lady in the turban entering the dining car. Her long, blonde hair was now braided, laced with pearls and wrapped around her head. She was seated alone.

"Sorry to interrupt you Grace." Lynnette glanced at Sir Thomas, "Do you know who she is? I've seen her photo somewhere before."

Sir Thomas cast his eyes in the direction Lynnette had indicated with a nod of her head. "That's the Baroness Von Karlsberg." He answered after a quick glance. "She was arrested and charged five years ago for theft and substitution of fine jewelry, but due to the lack of conclusive evidence, and victims who shunned the publicity, she was never convicted. When did you first see her board the train?" he asked Lynnette.

"She was at the station in London and boarded the car you're in. Number three."

"I wonder what she's up to now." Sir Thomas murmured. "Once a thief—always a thief. The same goes for murder. Once you've committed a murder, it's easy to commit a second and third murder." Lynnette's head tilted as she gave thought to his statement.

The server arrived with their entrée selections. "Well, on that cheery note, shall we enjoy our dinner while Thomas tells us about his exploits with the drug lords and how he was wounded in battle?" chimed Sir Reginald.

Sir Thomas smiled, "I'm delighted to do so, but you're not going to get out of explaining in detail why the Home Office is sending you off to investigate things in Egypt. I just might be able to assist, if you know what I mean. MIA, our intelligence agency is bound to have one or two field agents stationed in Egypt. As a matter of fact, I was asked by Lloyd's, the insurance company that hires us to protect them, to check things out at the excavation site. My mind is still as sharp as it once was. Even Grace said so just the other day."

"I said you were a pain. I never mentioned the word sharp." Grace quickly added, rolling her eyes.

Chapter Three

The Baroness

As the evening progressed, Sir Thomas and Grace retraced the story of when he was shot. Sir Thomas began by setting the scene in London at the popular French restaurant, Club Gascon. He explained how he was first to arrive and was joined by his nephew Matthew Evans and his fiancé Eve Bond. He had made a toast and leaned over to clink glasses with Eve, when a shot rang out and he was hit in the right shoulder instead of his heart.

"You see," said Grace, "I was acting as his bodyguard that evening and was seated across the room where I had a good view of his booth. However, the shot came through the window from the outside."

Sir Thomas continued, "Matthew and Eve were working together on a special case for MIA concerning the disappearance of George Beckett. They also had two bodyguards stationed at the restaurant—one inside and one outside. I had set myself up, falsely pretending to know who was involved in Beckett's kidnapping.

"Needless to say, I hadn't expected such immediate response. I truly had no idea that the bodyguard outside was a member of the Viper's drug ring, causing all the accidents and murders of the field agents at the agency. You probably read about the arrests in the papers. And I'm sure you received a briefing from the Home Office." He nodded to Sir Reginald.

"Yes. I do recall the case and most of the details. Lynnette and I were traveling at the time, but pleased to know you managed to make a quick recovery."

Lady Lynnette patted Sir Thomas's hand on the table, but stopped suddenly. Eyeing the woman in the turban as she left the dining car, she asked, "Shouldn't we advise someone on the train about baroness von-what's-her-name before jewels start to vanish?"

Sir Thomas nodded, "I'll take care of that, my dear. Timothy Gordon Leeds, Chairman of Operations for the Orient Express, is a personal friend and he just happens to be traveling on this train in his private car. I've arranged to meet him for a brandy after dinner."

Grace sighed. It was her turn to take his hand. "He just can't keep his fingers out of the pie. I'm on guard duty twenty-fours a day. No wonder I'm looking so worn out. "

Sir Thomas placed his other hand on top of hers, "Don't worry, old girl. We still have lots of time ahead of us. Will you join us in a brandy?" he asked his wife.

"Not tonight," said Grace, "I think I'll turn in early."

Sir Reginald turned to Lynnette. "How about a nightcap?"

She yawned. "I think I'll take a raincheck also. It's been a long day. But I'll expect a full report of the meeting with Mr. Leeds over breakfast in the morning."

~

Lady Lynnette spread butter and marmalade on her toast as Sir Reginald attempted to brief her on last night's meeting with Mr. Leeds and Sir Thomas. "According to Leeds, there really isn't much they can do about the old girl traveling on the train until there's been a crime committed. They are aware of the baroness and have been watching her since she boarded the train. We aren't the only ones familiar with her history and she hasn't attempted to hide her identity."

Lynette gave a fake sigh of relief. "Thank you my dear. At least I don't have to hide the diamonds in the lining of my coat."

Sir Reginald gave her a look of exasperation after his rather sleepless night. "You're not traveling with any diamonds, and that was a catty remark," he huffed. "They're doing their job to protect everyone."

"Yes, dear. So where are we staying tonight in Budapest?" Lady Lynnette managed to change the subject quickly.

"At least I've managed to keep that a secret," Sir Reginald smiled, "Your spies haven't spoiled that surprise."

"Oh Reggie...really. You make it sound like I run a private investigation agency. I can't help it if I have a network of connections all over England and France, that's what coming from a large family is all about. However, we'll soon be in Romania, and that means I'm out on a limb without a ladder. So, do be a good sport and give me a hint."

"Not a chance," he grinned. "I love being able to surprise you, which I don't get to do very often."

Lady Lynnette sipped her morning tea and smiled in silence as she returned to her section of the daily paper, tapping her polished fingernails on the white table cloth, just to annoy Sir Reginald.

~

On the afternoon of day four, they arrived in Budapest, for the overnight stop and checked into the luxurious Four Seasons Hotel—Gresham Palace. Reservations had been arranged for dinner that evening not far from the hotel at the Onyx—a Michelin two-star restaurant of the old school, with classic European flare, white-gloved service, and crystal chandeliers hanging in the opulent dining room, creating a romantic setting in the subdued lighting.

The waiter poured their champagne and Lady Lynnette, dressed in green silk and wearing emeralds that matched her eyes, smiled and raised her glass in a toast. "I must say, I could get used to your little surprises very quickly." However, her face suddenly changed from a smile to a frown.

"Unfortunately, another surprise was just seated at the corner table by the window." Sir Reginald started to twist around. "Don't look back, but it's the baroness wearing a magenta cocktail dress, her lovely double string of pearls, and teardrop pearl earrings. I wonder what hotel she's staying in."

"Perhaps Budapest is her destination point. Maybe she won't be on the train tomorrow. Don't let her upset our romantic evening. Ignore her," he said.

Lady Lynnette stared across the table at Sir Reginald. "You're right. She doesn't exist." She raised her champagne glass again and smiled, but her eyes moved past his, returning to the mysterious lady in the corner. "I just wish she would stop staring at me with those begging eyes."

"Then stop staring at her. Your dinner is about to be served."

The food was beautifully presented and the server refilled their glasses. When Lady Lynnette looked up the baroness had vanished. Her untouched glass of wine remained on the table, but there was no sign of the lady. She did not return.

They had time the following morning for breakfast at the hotel and some leisurely shopping with lunch at a charming sidewalk restaurant, before boarding the train to continue their journey.

Lady Lynnette quickly noticed a new passenger entering the dining car. Her curiosity was piqued once again as he was seated at the end of the car facing her direction.

"Don't look now, but we have a rather sinister looking new passenger," she said, tilting her head. She quickly continued before Sir Reginald could speak. "I know...you're going to say I shouldn't make such quick judgments of people I haven't met, but I wouldn't want to meet this person—especially in a dark alley." She twisted her curled hair with her finger. Reginald started to turn. "Don't look... he's watching us."

Sir Reginald chuckled. "You've been reading too much Agatha Christie lately. Must be the dreary wet weather of London that's affected your imagination."

The man in question was tall and dark skinned, with deep, brooding, black eyes under his hooded, wrinkled forehead. The air about him was intimidating even to the servers who approached with caution. His Egyptian profile shined like ebony in reflection as he glanced out the window.

Reginald was now engaged in reading the morning paper, but his wife was not going to be ignored. She peaked over the page he was reading. "I saw him get on the train in Budapest. He's in car number three, along with the baroness. Perhaps they're working together as a team."

Sir Reginald chuckled as he folded the paper and asked for their check. "I wasn't going to tell you this because I didn't want you to get all upset, but the baroness has moved out of car number three. She now has a compartment in car number one. I was standing in the hallway when she arrived."

"But that's our car!" Lynette spoke with authority, as if she owned the rail car.

Sir Reginald stood to leave, "You never cease to amaze me, my dear. You're not only beautiful, but very astute and clever. I'm going back to our suite. Would you care to join me?"

She stood and took his arm as they passed the stranger seated at the end of the dining car. He glanced up and gave her an inquisitive look with a menacing grin that sent chills up her spine and raised the hairs at the nape of her neck. She clung tighter to her husband's arm.

The train wound through the scenic mountainous terrain. Small villages could be glimpsed in the valleys below, smoke circling from chimneys, and Church spires glinting in the sunlight. A light dusting of recent snow laid like lace on the mountain ridges. Winter would soon arrive and cover the villages with a soft blanket of white.

Next stop—Bucharest.

Chapter Four

Missing Passenger

Threw train began to slow and it caught Lynnette's attention. She put down her book and took their itinerary out of her purse. "Why are we stopping in the middle of nowhere?"

"I believe there's a tourist stop in Romania before we reach Bucharest," said Sir Reginald seated across from her. "I think there's a castle tour or something like that."

"Well, don't just sit there. Let's get our coats and go see." Lynnette was up and moving. She tapped on the compartment door next to theirs. "Minnie! Grab our coats and yours too. We're off to see a castle."

Transportation was waiting at the station in the quaint little town of half-timbered buildings with outdoor restaurants and bars, it was only a short drive winding into the Carpathian Mountains to Peles Castle, a Neo-Renaissance structure near Sinaia, not far from Transylvania and Bran Castle, often referred to as Dracula's castle, for those adventurous travelers seeking to enjoy a rather haunting experience.

"I surely hope we don't see any vampires on this visit." Minnie spoke as she was reading the guide's brochure.

"Oh, Minnie, don't be ridiculous. Vampires aren't real, except for vampire bats, of course." Lady Lynnette replied, making herself comfortable in the transportation coach.

Minnie pulled her coat tighter. "I don't want to see any of them either."

Lynnette couldn't help but laugh. "Don't fret, Minnie dear, we aren't going to Dracula's Castle, that's a different tour." She glanced around searching the crowd and turned to Sir Reginald, "Have you noticed anything strange?"

"Now what? Is someone following us?" he jokingly smiled.

"Joke all you like, old boy, but the baroness and her Egyptian friend are not on the tour. They must have stayed on the train, and that makes me very suspicious."

"Don't worry, love." Sir Reginald assured her, "I asked Mr. Leeds to store your emeralds safely in his private car before we left."

"And the pearls your mother gave me?"

"You didn't tell me you brought the pearls."

"Reggie, dear, you didn't ask for an inventory."

Sir Reginald gave a sigh of exasperation and waved his hand in dismissal. "Let's enjoy the tour. I'm sure everything will be just fine. Your nemesis is probably on the tour to Bran Castle to visit Dracula."

"Then that only leaves the baroness I have to worry about," she huffed sarcastically.

~

Once they returned to the train, Sir Reginald attempted to speak with Mr. Gordon Leeds and retrieve Lynnette's emeralds. "I'm afraid he's in a conference at the moment, sir. He asked not to be disturbed. Is there something I might help you with?" said Leeds's assistant.

"Not at the moment. Will you be so kind as to ask Mr. Leeds to find me as soon as he's available?"

The train began to move. "Yes, sir. I'll relay the message as soon as possible. Would you like lunch served in your suite?"

"That won't be necessary. We'll be in the dining car." He met Lynnette at their reserved table and they made their luncheon selections, including a grand cru Montrachet wine. The Orient Express carries only the finest chardonnay.

With a sigh of relief Lady Lynnette announced, "The pearls are safe along with the rest of my jewels. Minnie and I went through the inventory. I even made you a list." She smiled as she handed him a slip of paper. Did Mr. Leeds return the emeralds?"

"No. He was in a conference so I left word for him to contact us when he is free. Shall we see if Sir Thomas and Grace want to join us for dinner this evening at the hotel? I didn't see them on the tour today."

Lynnette was lost in thought as the food arrived, and didn't answer. Why hadn't she noticed the baroness or the Egyptian at the station stop or on the tour?

It was already getting dark as the train pulled into the station at Bucharest. They sent a dinner invitation to Sir Thomas and Grace and made a reservation for four at 8 p.m. in the main dining room of Roberto's on La Strada.

Lady Lynnette began the conversation as they were led into the restaurant and seated. "We missed you on the castle tour today. Did you stay on the train?"

Sir Thomas glanced at Grace and nodded. "My charming wife says that England has more than enough castles to visit. She preferred to rest, read, and have lunch in private."

Grace chimed in. "I've seen more than my share of castles and I'll be glad when we get back to sea level. This altitude is giving me headaches. The rest was just what I needed."

"Did you hear about the commotion on the train when you returned from the tour this morning?" asked Sir Thomas.

Sir Reginald and Lynnette looked at each other in surprise. "No one has said a word," he replied shrugging his shoulders.

"Do tell!" Lynnette eagerly agreed.

"It appears the baroness has vanished." Sir Thomas paused to allow for this announcement to register.

Lady Lynnette leaned forward as she looked at their faces. "What do you mean, vanished? As in, disappeared?"

"Precisely, my dear," Grace nodded. "But there's more to it than that. Give them the details, Thomas. Can't you see Lynnette is waiting anxiously?"

"The lady is gone. However, apparently everything she was traveling with was left behind. Gordon Leeds and I were in conference with the police before the train left the station stop at the castle. The police are beginning a search for the baroness and the strange

Egyptian passenger Abdul Kaliem Hadashi."

"Are you saying he disappeared as well?" asked Lynnette.

"He left the train with his luggage and didn't return. Grace saw him get into a waiting car at the station. We did a search of their compartments with the police." Sir Thomas stopped speaking as Gordon Leeds approached. In his hand he held a black jewelry box.

"I think these belong to you." He handed them to Lynnette. "I believe Sir Thomas has been reporting on the events of this morning. My safe was broken into, but fortunately I had placed your jewels in a secret location I use for valuable items entrusted to me for personal safekeeping. My apologies for interrupting your conversation. Enjoy your dinner."

Lynnette's mouth was open, but no words came forth. Sir Reginald expressed his gratitude and put the emeralds in the breast pocket of his dinner jacket. Mr. Leeds gave a slight bow and moved on to visit with other guests. Dinner was served.

A little wine revived Lady Lynnette's train of thought. "So...they were working together."

"That's one speculation, my dear. However, the lady never left the train. Every compartment was searched, every car was turned inside out, but there was no sign of her. Bodies don't just vanish, but without a body they can't pin a murder on the Egyptian, and without any stolen jewels, they can't arrest him for theft."

"So he drives away, scot-free." said Lynnette.

"Not exactly." Sir Thomas continued to fill in the blanks. "He has a record. They were able to trace some fingerprints in the baroness's compartment and he was the last person to be seen talking with her last night in the passageway. My guess is that something happened during the night while we were asleep, long before we arrived at the tourist stop. There are many river crossings, deep ravines, and places to dispose of a body from the train in the dark of night."

"But there's porters on duty all night. Wouldn't someone have noticed?" asked Lynnette.

"Not necessarily," said Grace, speaking as a former bodyguard. When there's a murder involved, if there's a will to kill, there's a way to dispose of the body. Murder is not accidental. It is planned ahead. I believe premeditated is the proper term to use. I think Thomas is right. She was possibly pushed out the train window or perhaps the body was removed at the last station. Maybe she never returned to the train the afternoon we left Budapest. She was last seen that evening on arrival."

"No! That's not correct. She was at the restaurant Onyx, where we had dinner that night but she left almost as quickly as she arrived. One minute she was there and the next, she wasn't. I distinctly remember her eyes and her face were strained with fear. I knew she was afraid of something or someone. She kept staring at me as if she wanted to say something. May I ask who made the discovery that she was missing?"

"The porter wanted to make the bed but got no response. After several attempts to wake her, he used his key to enter and discovered the compartment in disarray and notified Mr. Leeds.

"Would you be interested in seeing the crime scene tomorrow morning? The police gave it a rough going over, but perhaps you and I might find something they missed. I can arrange it with Leeds. It's still considered a crime scene but we couldn't leave the car behind. It will remain locked until we get to Istanbul and the INTERPOL police take over from there," said Sir Thomas.

"I don't know if I can be of any help, but I'm interested," said Sir Reginald.

"Good! Then we'll plan on it." Sir Thomas smiled.

Grace shook her head, "I told you. He can't keep his fingers out of the pie."

Lady Lynnette grinned, "Me too. I just love pie."

Chapter Five

Varna by the Sea

L ady Lynnette was awake before dawn and had ordered breakfast tea delivered to their suite. She was seated at the table by the window watching the dawn of a new day when Sir Reginald joined her. "Good morning Detective Whitcomb. Shall I pour you some tea?"

"Good morning, old girl. How long have you been awake?" He stretched and yawned in his dressing gown, his slightly graying bed-hair hair all tossed and tussled.

"Long enough to watch the sunrise. How soon do we start the search?" Lynnette's manicured nails were tapping on the white linen tablecloth.

Reginald took a sip of his tea and blinked his eyes at her. "What makes you think you were included in that invitation last night?"

"I have it on the best authority. Sir Thomas winked at me when he offered the invitation. He also knows that I can find a needle in a haystack. I'm like a homing device when it comes to finding things that are lost or misplaced. You should know that by now."

Sir Reginald began to open his mouth, but she put her hand to his lips. "Not another word Mr. Detective. I'm in for the swim and the water's getting cold while we sit and discuss the matter."

Lynnette's attention was drawn to the window and the blue waters of the Black Sea as they headed into the seaside resort city of Varna. "We'd best get dressed or we'll miss breakfast. I already sent word to Sir Thomas and Grace to meet us in the dining car."

Lady Lynnette was not only beautiful, charming, and intelligent, she was a born organizer. Sir Thomas was waiting in the dining car. "Grace is having breakfast in the compartment. She decided that four detectives would be a crowd."

Lynnette ginned as she watched Sir Reginald's face, "See there. I told you I was invited. Shall we order breakfast? I'm starving." She slid into the chair next to the window and the gentlemen joined her. Sir Thomas schooled them on the state of the compartment and cautiously reminded them not to touch or move anything, only to observe and take note of what they see.

They finished breakfast and entered the first car where the baroness had last moved. Sir Thomas had a key and unlocked the compartment door. He handed them slip-on plastic shoe covers before entering.

"Good Lord!" Lynnette remarked. "She must have been traveling with her entire wardrobe. Was it in such a mess when the police saw it?"

Sir Thomas nodded his head. "Yes, my dear. It appears someone was looking for something. They must have found what they wanted or gave up, before they disposed of the poor woman."

"Poor woman!" exclaimed Lynnette. "These clothes must have cost a fortune, and those pearls she was wearing in her hair the night we saw her at the restaurant, those had to be worth a few pounds."

Sir Thomas smiled and agreed. "Only a true lady would notice those details."

"Did they find those pearls she was wearing?" Lynnette asked.

"No. There was no jewelry found during the search."

"Then obviously there's been a jewel theft, unless a dead body, laying in a ravine somewhere, is wearing them," she commented.

Lynnette pointed to something on the bathroom floor. "Did someone spill her face powder?"

Sir Thomas knelt down to inspect. He wet his finger and dabbed at the substance. First he smelled of it, then touched it lightly to his tongue. He quickly spit into his handkerchief. "Opium!" he exclaimed. "I don't believe the police noticed that."

Lynnette was delighted with her find. "And be sure to take note of the tiny bits of glass and plaster around the edge of the powder. I wonder where that came from."

Sir Thomas and Sir Reginald both looked closer. "My, dear!" You have the eyes of a hawk," remarked Sir Thomas.

Sir Reginald smiled at his wife. "I think we have a first rate detective working with us, Thomas."

Lynnette was inspecting the window closest to the banquet seating area. "Did the police notice these small scratches in the paint around the window? I'm sure the Orient Express wouldn't allow paint scratches in a first class compartment such as this."

Sir Reginald was the first to take a look. "She's right."

"And don't overlook the chipped fingernail caught in the groove around the metal frame. She was wearing that color in the restaurant on that last night in Budapest."

"How can you be so sure?" Reginald asked.

"Because I was staring back at her, as you pointed out. I noticed her nails, drumming nervously on the table cloth, were not the right shade for the magenta cocktail dress she was wearing. They were turquoise. Just like the one caught in the window."

"I must make a note of these discoveries. The police in Turkey will be most appreciative," said Sir Thomas.

"Then don't forget the magenta cocktail dress." Lynnette added as her eyes scanned the wardrobe scattered around the cabin. "I don't see it here among her belongings." She pointed at a pair of shoes under the small table. "However, those are the shoes she was wearing at the restaurant."

"Remarkable!" Sir Thomas chuckled as he jotted down his notes. "Hope you lead a cautious life Reggie, old boy. I have a feeling not much escapes Lynnette's talented observations."

"That's right, Thomas. I married a regular Miss Marple, but she's a lot younger and much more attractive."

"Why, thank you, Dr. Watson. Might I suggest we request a conference with Mr. Leeds and bring him up to snuff with our discoveries? I'm sure the Orient Express will want all the details before we get to Istanbul. But right now, I think I'll join Grace for a cup of tea and fill her in on the success of our mission. Unless, of course, there's something I've missed."

Sir Reginald gave her a peck on the cheek. "You've certainly earned your tea this morning, my dear. We'll join you in a moment." He watched as she made her way in the direction of car number three.

"I didn't want to say this in front of Lynnette, because she might get a big head about it, but she's better than most of the agents in the Home Office. She has a photographic mind and a knack for observation that rarely misses anything. She knew we were going to Egypt before I had a chance to tell her. She could tell you the color of someone's eyes after having just met them. Even the Home Office knew we were making the journey up the Nile, but that's to be expected—they know everything."

Sir Thomas chuckled. "Consider yourself a fortunate man, my boy. Women like Grace and Lynnette are a psychological mystery. They should have been men, but something got screwed up in the laboratory before they were popped in the oven and came out all toasty and sweet. It's a scientific blunder, or perhaps I should say wonder, but whatever would we do without them?

"And now, I think we should join the secret agents for tea. I'll send word to Leeds we need to chat. He will be interested to know what we've learned. Don't worry, I'll make it sound like it was a joint discovery to save any embarrassment and I wouldn't want to give away our undercover agent," he winked.

Chapter Six

The Trunks

Lady Lynnette had already filled Grace in on all the details of their inspection. Sir Thomas and Sir Reginald left word with Mr. Leeds' assistant that they requested a conference with him as soon as possible.

You could see the excitement in Grace's face as the four of them sat in the semi-private section of the dining car and discussed the technical points of the morning's search. "I wish I had been there to watch Miss Marple searching like a hungry cat for catnip," she chuckled. "Where would men be today if it wasn't for women with strong intuition?"

"I think of it more as observation than intuition," Lynnette added as her mind appeared focused on something else out the window.

Sir Reginald noticed she had drifted away from the conversation and her eyes were not particularly focused on anything. He leaned over and whispered in her ear. "A penny for your thoughts."

Her eyebrows raised. "They're probably not worth that much, but something still isn't right. It's just a feeling, but nonetheless a feeling that I can't put my finger on. Give me some time to organize the sequence of events in my head. There's something missing and it's as plain as the nose on your loving face; a piece of the puzzle that needs to be found. I can see it, but I can't see it. I know that sounds strange, but it is something that should be there, only it isn't."

"Do you want to see the compartment again? Maybe that would jog your memory," said Reggie.

"That's not necessary," Lynnette said, pointing to her head. "It's already recorded up here. I just need to fill in the empty space with something I noticed, but failed to comment on at the time."

Sir Thomas and Grace had been listening quietly. However, they knew that people with a photographic memory needed time to process their vision like a slide projector...one frame at a time. Whatever was missing would reappear given time.

Mr. Leeds' assistant appeared by their table. "My apologies for interrupting, but Mr. Leeds can see you now if you have finished your tea." Thomas and Reginald followed him to the private car, while Lynnette remained behind with Grace.

"Something's troubling you I can tell. If you don't mind my saying so, I always find it best to talk things out. It works better than making a list. Two heads are usually better than one. Once I convinced Thomas of this, he learned what a good method it is."

"I'm trying to figure out how far back I need to go in the sequence of events leading up to our inspection of the baroness's compartment this morning. There was much that flashed to my mind, but that may not always mean it has anything to do with the disappearance of the baroness. It may be important later, but it doesn't send out a signal until additional information is added." Lynnette began to retrace movements from the restaurant in Budapest as Grace listened intently.

"The baroness was dressed to the nines in a magenta cocktail dress, but appeared in the restaurant alone. I could see her face clearly and it had a worried look of terror written all over it. It was as if she had witnessed a murder and the murderer was after her. I had a feeling she wanted to tell us something, perhaps ask for our help, but fear was holding her back. Our food arrived and when the server disappeared, I looked up and she was gone. Her drink, hardly touched, was still on the table."

Grace held up her hand. "Who paid for her drink?"

Lynnette gave Grace a questioning glance, wondering to herself why that would matter. "I suppose she did. Yes...there was a check and some money on the table next to the glass."

Grace nodded. "I just thought she may have stepped into the ladies room and hadn't returned to the table. If she was there to meet someone, they would have most likely been waiting for her to arrive. Please go on."

"I don't know what hotel she was staying in because we never saw her after that. Not even the next morning when other passengers were boarding the train."

"That's not unusual," said Grace. "People often choose to stay overnight in their compartments on the train rather than move for one night to the hotels. Most of the first-class passengers choose the hotels. Which means the first-class cars are mostly empty. As I recall, she was in the same car with you. It's possible she was the only passenger in the car that evening."

Lynnette gave Grace's suggestion some thought. "You might be right. That would explain why we didn't see her boarding the train that morning. Perhaps someone may have followed her back to the train car. I wonder if they questioned the porters on duty. Surely they wouldn't have allowed someone on the train who wasn't a passenger. Which leads me to speculate that the person she feared was the Egyptian man who is no longer on the train."

"I hope this is being helpful," Grace smiled.

"Oh, yes! Quite helpful. It's putting things in perspective. I didn't give her much thought until we stopped for the tour of the castle. Obviously she didn't venture out to take one of the tours, so she must have stayed on the train, unless she took a stroll around the area while the train waited at the station. You said you were having tea in your room and saw the Egyptian man leave the train. Was there anything strange about his departure that you recall?"

Grace waved at one of the waiters, "May we have more tea please, and a couple of the lemon cakes." She glanced around, and noticed that no one else was around. "I think we have the dining car to ourselves." The waiter returned quickly and Grace refilled their cups. "Now where were we?"

"You noticed the Egyptian leaving the train." Lynnette reminded.

"Oh yes, quite right. There was a car waiting for him and several porters to help remove his luggage. He was traveling with a lot of baggage for a single man."

"Did you notice what kind of car it was?"

Grace tapped the side of her head, "Let me see...having worked as a chauffeur for Thomas, I'm pretty good at identifying automobiles. I'm sure it was a black Land Rover SUV. They tied the two large trunks on top of it."

"Trunks!" cried Lynnette. "Oh my god! That's it!" Lynnette was suddenly excited. "That's the missing piece. I have to find Thomas and Reggie immediately. Come with me, Grace." They hurried in the direction of Mr. Leeds' private car. The meeting was still in progress.

Mr. Leeds's assistant tapped on the door of his office and stepped inside. "You have two more visitors, Sir. They demand to see you immediately."

Lynnette and Grace entered behind him without an invitation. "We have to visit the crime scene once again," Lynnette announced.

The questioning faces of the three men looked at each other. "What's this all about?" asked Reginald.

"Just humor us and you will see." Lynnette had that leprechaun twinkle in her green eyes.

The five of them returned to the compartment in the first car and Mr. Leeds opened the door. "What are we looking for?" he asked.

"Trunks," Lynnette announced.

"You mean suitcases?" he said.

"No. I mean trunks. Just look at the amount of wardrobe this woman traveled with. How do you think she got it all onboard? Certainly not in three or four little suitcases. She had to have trunks. Where are they?"

"Perhaps in the adjoining compartment." Mr. Leeds said calmly as he opened the companion door. But the smaller compartment was empty.

Lynnette was now in her element and everyone was listening. "The Egyptian man left the train at the tourist stop this morning with two large trunks. Grace saw him from the window in their cabin. He was met by a black Land Rover and two trunks were tied to the top of the SUV. I'm sure the porters could verify this. Where did these trunks come from?"

"What are you suggesting, my dear?" Sir Thomas was the first to ask.

"That he was in her compartment when she returned from the restaurant in Budapest. How, I don't know and why is still to be determined. I'm not sure he planned to kill her, but surely he did. Perhaps she was strangled quietly. It appears he was looking for something. Possibly something that contained more opium like we found in her bathroom area. She might have been transporting the 'tears of the poppy' to be sold. She may have had a trunk full of it, very cleverly disguised in plaster or glass containers of some description."

"So, how did he dispose of her body before leaving the train? Was it shoved out the window during the night?" asked Mr. Leeds.

"No," said Lynnette with assurance, "he must have stuffed it in one of the two trunks. The one she had used for her entire wardrobe was probably empty. Look around us. Is there even a suitcase to be found? I happen to know most women don't travel light, but they don't usually travel with an entire department store. There's definitely enough clothes here to fill a large trunk, even without the missing magenta cocktail dress she was wearing. I noticed the lack of luggage on our last inspection, but it just now came back to me."

Grinning, Grace gave her a small round of applause. "I think you gentlemen should listen to the lady. I have a feeling she's on the right track...no pun intended," she chuckled.

~

The porter announced their arrival into Istanbul, noting that they were still in Bulgaria and would need their papers for customs upon entering Turkey. Istanbul is the only city in the world that spans two continents—Europe and Asia. The Ottoman Empire was spread far and wide. Istanbul, or Constantinople as it was originally known, was on the Silk Route from the Orient. A thriving bustling city, full of mystery, intrigue, and trade.

Dazzling spires surround the Blue Mosque and Hagia Sophia in the center of the old city near the Four Seasons Hotel, which used to be a prison. Lynnette's head was spinning to take it all in during their short stay before traveling on to Egypt.

They, of course, had been delayed by the police and secret service to give their reports concerning the events that had taken place while traveling on the Orient Express, but now they were free to explore secrets of the mystical city of sultans, harams, romance, silks, and spices.

Lynnette pulled Grace aside. "We're staying at the Four Seasons near the Hagia Sophia, where are you lodged while in town?"

Grace checked her itinerary. "Thomas wanted to stay at the Sultanahmet Palace. It's just down the street near the Blue Mosque. He wanted a room with a Turkish bathroom. How anyone can enjoy sitting on cold marble, pouring water over their head, soaping up and then pouring water again to rinse it off is beyond me. I much prefer a hot shower."

"Well, if you would like to have dinner with us this evening, just ring the hotel and we'll work it out. Right now, I'm looking forward to a long hot soak in a real bathtub, and a quiet afternoon tea." She heard Reginald calling her name. "It looks like we're going in opposite directions, so I had better hurry and join Reggie." She scurried off to follow her husband.

Check-in at the Four Seasons was quick. Their luggage had arrived before they did and was taken to their suite on the top floor overlooking the fountains in the plaza and a view of Hagia Sophia from a small table in the corner windows. The plush carpet in powder-blue gave the room a soothing ambiance. It wasn't quite as large as their bedroom at home, but contained all the comforts one would need while traveling. "The Orient Express offered a pleasant journey, but I won't miss the confined space of our compartment," Lynnette sighed.

She was standing in the doorway of the bathroom with its gleaming black and white marble tiles. A large jetted tub with a window view of the city was calling her name, as she removed her shoes and began to undress. Minnie Sparks had arrived ahead with the luggage and was still unpacking. She had laid an apricot silk robe across the king bed. "Shall I order some lunch or would you prefer only tea, Madame?"

"Tea will do, Minnie, and there's no need to call me Madame when we're traveling. Just call me Miss Lynn like you do at home. However, there's no rush for the tea, I plan to soak in a hot bath until the water cools," she smiled and slipped into the bubble bath that awaited her.

In a small dreamy voice she called from the bathroom, "Reggie, what was in the message waiting at the desk when we arrived? Please don't tell me the police and secret service still have more questions to ask."

"No, my dear. It was from the antiquities department at the British Museum. It appears we will be joined in Giza by a patron who has sponsored the excavation of the new tomb—a Lord Charles Marquis. Remember when he donated the Orcini Antiquities Collection a few years back after Orcini's son was found guilty of orchestrating his father's murder?"

Lynnette was in a relaxed mood as the waters of her tub began to cool, but her mind was still sharp.

"Of course. I recall attending the opening. Wasn't Orcini murdered at his estate on the Isle of Capri? There was something about drug smuggling, if I'm not mistaken? However, I believe the younger son, who inherited everything eventually moved off to Rhodes or

Cypress, or somewhere in the Greek Isles. That was an interesting case. As I recall there were several murders at the villa?" She stopped talking. "Reggie, where are you?" she said as she opened her eyes.

"I'm sitting here on the side of the tub, patiently waiting for you to finish your monologue," he grinned.

"Well, you did ask me a question." She closed her eyes once again and rested her head on the towel at the back of the tub.

"Yes, old girl, but I hadn't expected an editorial recap. Anyway, we are to meet Lord Charles in Giza. He's making the trip up the Nile on the Nefertiti, the same ship we'll be on, so we'll have plenty of time to get acquainted. I believe Sir Thomas knows Lord Charles quite well."

"I would imagine." Lynnette surmised. "Thomas knows just about everyone in the art community. Doesn't Lord Charles Marquis live in Menton Abbey? That's in Kent, not far from Penderleigh, if I remember correctly. They're practically neighbors," Lynnette pronounced with closed eyes as she soaked in the tepid waters of the tub. Their conversation ended with the sound of the phone ringing.

Sir Reginald departed to take the call and after answering, he returned to the doorway of the bathroom. "That was Grace. She and Thomas will join us for dinner this evening at eight o'clock."

"Wonderful." Lynnette smiled, "Now we'll have something new to discuss instead of the baroness and her sinister Egyptian antagonist."

There was a knock at the door. Reginald stood. "That, my dear will be your afternoon tea." He closed the bathroom door and let the waiter enter their suite.

"Your tea, sir. Where would you like it set?" asked the young man. Reginald waved his hand and directed him to the table in the corner.

Tea had arrived and the bathwater had cooled. Lynnette toweled dry, slipped on the apricot robe, and joined her husband, as they sat quietly at the small table in the corner windows and watched as dusk turned the clouds in the sky pink, peach, and mauve.

"Istanbul is a mystical city I must admit. However, I do miss the charm of our green countryside, the rolling hills, quaint little farms and the fresh air in Yorkshire. Here there's an antiquated, timeworn atmosphere, creating an aged and musty aroma that reminds me of numerous old castles and churches in England, and yet it's different. I can't quite find the words I'm looking for. Perhaps it has something to do with the trade route and the mingling of so many cultures," murmured Lynnette.

A light fog drifted in from the Bosporus, circling the minarets of the mosques. Distant voices echoed across the city, inviting people to their prayers, as a velvet darkness embraced this ancient lady of mystery in a royal Chador with twinkling stars for diamonds.

Chapter Seven

Sir Thomas's Tale

Dinner with Sir Thomas and Grace Treadwell proved to be delightful as well as thought provoking. It was an evening for Sir Thomas to hold court, as he was apt to do so if given the opportunity. The restaurant had been full of hungry passengers, but was now almost empty except for their table, which allowed for less opportunity to be overheard. Sir Thomas was extremely cautious about what he said when strangers might be listening. His training with Scotland Yard and his own secret intelligence agency made it so.

"I believe you mentioned earlier that you would be joined in Giza by Lord Charles Marquis, on behalf of the British Museum, and I'm sure you've had the opportunity to meet him on several occasions. Perhaps you've seen his extensive collection of antiquities and artifacts when visiting the British Museum.

"Lord Charles and I have known each other for years. As a matter of fact, I was still deeply involved with the intelligence agency, MIA, during the murder investigations of Ricardo Orcini, the commercial shipping giant, who was killed at his villa on the Isle of Capri. The Home Office wasn't involved in that case, but I'm sure you were briefed. It was quite a scandal."

Lynnette's eyes grew wide with sudden interest. "How exciting. That was a case that shocked the museums and collectors around the globe." She leaned closer to Sir Thomas. "What can you tell us about it, and how was Merryweather Intelligence Agency involved?" Lynnette queried. Sir Thomas was eager to tell his story; details of which were confidential and never appeared in the newspapers. He didn't require much coaxing.

"I think if I'm to tell this tale, we should order more coffee and perhaps brandies. We may be here for a while." He caught the waiter's attention and their orders were taken.

"As I begin this recap, perhaps I should explain that MIA had been hired by Lloyd's of London, thus we were working on their behalf.

All of Ricardo Orcini's container transport ships were insured by Lloyd's. Scotland Yard, and INTERPOL had been investigating possible drug smuggling into various ports on the Mediterranean, and it was important to Lloyd's that Orcini's commercial investments should not be disrupted.

"Perhaps I should start with the Orcini family. Ricardo Orcini was a man in his late sixties. His wife had died of cancer at a very young age, but they had two sons, Fabio, the oldest, who was head of the company operations, and Adam, the youngest, who was a handsome playboy, gambler, heavy drinker and rumored to be a drug addict. Needless to say, the family was not close like most Italian families. They were always at odds with each other.

"Orcini was associated with the art world as a well-known collector of antiquities. His collection was broad and not focused on any particular part of the globe. He had artifacts from Egypt, Central America, South America, Asia and China.

"Fabio disliked taking orders from his senile father. It was rumored that he was preparing for a hostile takeover of the company. One might say, greed overcame his patience.

"Orcini's body was found floating in the pool of his villa on Capri after an elegant private party to unveil some new acquisitions in his collection of artifacts from Central and South America. He was often suspected of acquiring antiquities through the black market, but no substantial evidence was ever proven. It was all hearsay without the facts to back it up, and most of those items were never offered for public display when his collections were shown in museums.

"However, it was on the night of the party that his son, Fabio, returned by private yacht in the early hours of the morning. Orcini had gone for a swim after his guests had departed around 3 a.m. There were two guards in the gate house at the front of the property and the butler, Williams was still there. A third guard had been hired to circulate among the crowd in the interior during the event, but was said to have left when the guests did.

"Orcini's mistress, the cabaret singer, Carlotta Romero, had turned in early with a headache. She was the first to discover his nude body floating in the pool the next morning when she came down for breakfast. Detective Mario Regetti, of the homicide police division on Capri interviewed the suspects, including all the guests who attended the event. Lord Charles Marquis and his wife Elizabeth were among them and I spoke with him on their return to England."

"Wasn't Orcini killed with a poison dart? I seem to recall that he hadn't been drowned." Sir Reginald was a good listener and remembered being briefed on the murder by reports to the Home Office at the time.

"Quite correct. I was getting to that part. It appears the butler was a dead shot with a blowgun. He had worked as a valet for Lord Charles and often accompanied him on hunting trips to Papua New Guinea and Borneo."

"Then how did he come to work for Ricardo Orcini?" Lynnette questioned.

"According to Lord Charles, Elizabeth didn't much like having Williams around. She decided she didn't trust him and wanted Charles to sack him. For the sake of peace at Menton Abbey, Charles let Williams go, but not without a recommendation to Ricardo Orcini, who hired him as a butler for the Villa Marquesa on Capri. After all, how was he to know that Williams would be drawn into the web of intrigue that Favio was spinning?"

Sir Thomas glanced around the table. His audience waited eagerly for more details about the case. He ordered another round of brandy for everyone. The restaurant was empty except for a few tables, but it was still early in the fall season and Europeans are notorious for enjoying a late leisurely meal.

"So don't keep us in the dark. What happened next?" Lynnette encouraged. Amazing how no one was tired after their journey from Bucharest, but then Sir Thomas was an excellent teller of stories.

"Well, let's see, where was I? Oh, yes...The murder was made to appear as a robbery. All of the newly acquired antiquities on display in the library had disappeared and several glass cases had been broken. Detective Regetti first suspected the interior guard was the assassin and robber. He had disappeared without a trace. The two guards at the gate house had been shot execution style in the back of the head and their bodies were hidden in the bushes.

"Carlotta found the cook's daughter, the cook, and the butler locked in the walk-in freezer. It appears the robber was still in the house early in the morning. He had put them in the freezer, locked the door, and tossed the key in a corner of the kitchen floor. However, he was not seen leaving the villa. The security camera at the only gate showed no one entering or exiting after 3 a.m.

"So, how did he escape? I doubt he had wings," she joked.

"He made his escape off the island through a secret passage hidden in the library wall. A stairway leads down to a grotto at the base of the cliff. There, he was picked up by Fabio Orcini in his yacht and deposited on the mainland. Favio returned to the island by ferry as if he had just arrived, leaving his yacht in Naples to be made ready for his departure after the funeral. He feigned shock that his father had been murdered and notified his brother Adam, who was in Cypress.

"Carlotta was almost murdered when Fabio thought she knew more than she should. She was drugged, chained, and left in the grotto to be washed out with the tide, but Detective Regetti was able to save her once he had traced the movements of Favio's yacht on the night of the murders. Timing was everything and the Marine Traffic Control in Naples had satellite records of all marine traffic in the area of the sea on that evening.

"Favio had some elaborate plans, but how did they determine it was the butler who committed the murder and where did they find the artifacts that were stolen?" Lynnette was not going to give up until she had all the answers.

"A reluctant witness came forward. The cook's daughter, Rosie and her boyfriend were having a secret rendezvous in the pool cabana after the party was over and all the guests had left. It was not the first time he had climbed over the back garden wall. They were afraid to come forward and confess to their secret meetings. However, the boyfriend convinced Rosie it was best to suffer the consequences than live with the guilt.

"They overheard an argument out by the pool and from the darkened interior they could see Favio and Ricardo standing on the edge at the shallow end of the pool, yelling at each other. The underwater pool lights reflected their silhouettes. Then a shadow of a man appeared near the kitchen with a long pipe held up to his lips. Orcini fell backwards into the pool. Favio was not standing close to him. Rosie recognized the man in the shadows as he approached Favio and they shook hands. It was Williams, the butler.

"A poison dart was the cause of death. The dart dislodged when he fell into the water and being lightweight, had floated into the pool's scupper. The pipe was hidden in the corner of a broom closet. Both were later discovered and Williams' fingerprints were all over the blowgun. He had not counted on the sharp eyes of the detectives and the diligent work of the forensic labs on the island.

"As for the artifacts. They were found in a storage compartment on Favio's yacht. Hidden there by the third guard, who later confessed the entire plan. Lord Charles and an antiquities appraiser for the British Museum were quick to note that they were not of great value, prior to his purchase of the more valuable pieces remaining in the entire Orcini collection, which were stored in a basement of the Villa Marquesa.

The youngest son was selling everything. Favio, having been

found guilty of murdering the two guards at the gate, was not allowed to inherit. The shipping company was later purchased by a competitor. And that is how the story ends."

"One more question," said Lynnette. "Did they ever find any drugs being smuggled on Orcini's ship?

"Lynnette, my dear. That is a question that was never resolved with any substantial proof, and without that we have no case. Which, of course, Lloyd's of London was pleased to hear." He glanced at Grace and saw her eyes drooping. "If you will excuse us, I think we should call it an evening. Tomorrow is another day and I know Grace wants to visit the Basilica Cistern in the morning after breakfast."

Lynnette took his hand between hers. "I'm sure I'll have more questions tomorrow, but for now we'll say goodnight. We may see you at the cistern in the morning. I'm planning to visit the main bazar and spice bazar while we're here. Two days is such a short time to cover everything. The palaces will have to wait for another trip."

Sir Reginald guided her to the lift. "I'm going to be dreaming about yachts and blowguns all evening." He yawned.

"I know dear. But there's a lot of water between here and Capri, so you're perfectly safe."

Chapter
Eight

The Cistern and the Mosque

L ynnette was the first to awaken. She slipped on her silk robe and silently made her way to the main room of their suite and ordered morning coffee. "Yes," she said to room service, "Café Americana, not Turkish, if you please." As she placed the receiver back on the cradle, she pulled the heavy drapes aside and a soft light from the first rays of sun began to soften and remove the shadows within the room. It was her personal quiet time of the day. The time when she did her best thinking.

Her shoulder length, curly auburn hair glowed in the morning light and at thirty something, her complexion was still as smooth as silk with a natural radiance. Lynnette was from an old aristocratic English family, had been well educated, attended finishing school in France, and had traveled often to America, where she acquired a less formal approach to life. She was English, but of a new more modern age.

Her green eyes twinkled with mystery. Her analytical mind cataloged and processed data with the skill of a fine-tuned machine, and her photographic memory was better than most inspectors at Scotland Yard. Mystery and intrigue fascinated her ever active brain cells.

There was a soft knock at the door. The coffee had arrived and room service had departed, when she noticed Reginald watching her from the bedroom doorway. "Good morning, dear. Care to join me for a cup?"

Sir Reginald, standing in his dark-blue robe, yawned and stretched. "I smelled coffee the minute they rolled the cart into the room." Lynnette was seated at the table between the corner windows with the sun to her back casting a golden aura around her. "You must be the Roman goddess of dawn or the Greek mythological Eros, surrounded by sunlight." She smiled as he joined her at the table.

"And you must have had too much brandy last night," she chuckled

"Why do you say that?"

Lynnette shook her head and smiled. "Bloodshot eyes my love. Not to mention how you tossed and turned all night, imagining natives with blowguns and trying to swim to the yacht. I had to hop out of bed twice to miss getting a black eye while you bravely fought them off."

He grinned. "Was I really that restless?"

Lynnette giggled. "Let's just say, I'm surprised the pillows have any feathers left in them. Now, do you want breakfast in the room or shall we try the buffet downstairs?"

"Let's have breakfast in the coffee shop, then take a walk through the fountain park and join one of the tours of the Basilica Cistern. Perhaps we can visit the Blue Mosque before lunch."

Minnie had entered quietly from the adjoining room and laid out Lynnette's touring clothes for the day while they quietly enjoyed their morning coffee. Lynnette had made her selections the night before, and everything was pressed and ready.

"Minnie, I want you to take the day off and see some sights. I won't need you again until this evening. Steam the saffron chiffon for tonight and hang it on the back of the bathroom door." Minnie thanked her and disappeared to her own room.

Walking through the Alman Fountain Park after breakfast, they spotted Sir Thomas and Grace sitting on a bench near the large fountain, surrounded by an array of multicolored flowers and low, neatly trimmed, boxwood hedges, enjoying the warmth of the sun.

Lynnette greeted them. "Good morning! You both look well rested. What a beautiful fountain garden," she added, spinning around to take in the entire setting.

"Isn't it amazing?" Grace added. "It reminds me of our gardens around Penderleigh in the spring. However, I'm not missing the cold and fog right now. We're waiting for the ticket office to open for the Cistern. Are you planning to take the tour this morning?"

"Absolutely," said Sir Reginald. "Then I thought we might visit the Blue Mosque before lunch."

"Splendid," chimed Sir Thomas. "I had a message this morning from the Turkish secret service agent, Ahmet, the one who interviewed us at the Turkish Consulate on arrival. It was about the case of the missing baroness. He said, after going through all of her belongings, they found something that might be of interest to us and the Home Office. If it's convenient, he wants us to drop by before lunch today to see what they discovered."

Sir Reginald saw Lynnette's face light up and her green eyes sparkled like emeralds. "Did he say what it was?"

"No. As a matter of fact, he was cautious not to offer too much information over the phone. So we'll have to wait and see. Now, shall we go purchase our tickets and get in line to visit one of the wonders of this ancient city?" The four of them headed in the direction of the ticket booth for the Basilica Cistern, just across the street from the park.

~

Following the crowd of tourists, they descended the fifty-two steps down into the depths of the underground structure with its cathedral or royal palace-like appearance. Marble columns numbering 336, soared over thirty feet high, laced together by stone arches supporting a massive stone ceiling. At over twelve feet thick, the cistern walls can hold over twenty-one million gallons of water when full. The slow dripping sound of water from above echoed off the rock walls and the sticky dampness in the air created a cave-like atmosphere.

Underwater lights at the base of each column changed color from blood red, to yellow gold, emerald green, and sapphire blue, in a dazzling display. The giant, carved, stone head of Medusa rested upside-down, to be reflected right-side-up in the still murky waters.

Lynnette hung onto Sir Reginald's arm and whispered, "Don't get alarmed when I say this, but I have a strange feeling we are being followed." He glanced around quickly just as the lights went out.

There was a collective gasp from the people standing on the wooden walkways. Cell phones began to twinkle in the darkness as people took photos and made eerie, ghostly, sounds in a joking manner. Without any warning, it was a heart throbbing moment, to be surrounded in infinite darkness until lights began to glow in the distance, slowly moving in the direction of the entrance, lighting each row of columns until they reached the main wooden platform.

Sir Reginald turned to Sir Thomas, "Have you noticed anyone following us this morning?"

"Not in particular, but I'm sure if they are, we'll be able to notice more once we are back above ground and in broad daylight. Let's take a leisurely stroll to the Blue Mosque and then have lunch before our meeting with Ahmet. If there is anyone following, we should be able to fish them out by then. I assumed you're not traveling with any bodyguards since I didn't notice any on the train."

"No," Reginald answered with a shake of his head. "However, we will have two guards once we arrive in Cairo. I insisted the Home Office put two on duty for the trip to the tomb site in case we encountered any difficulties."

"Good thinking. My bodyguard rarely leaves my sight. Grace is the proverbial "fly on the wall," he chuckled.

A short walk through the fountain park brought them to the Blue Mosque. Electronic calls to prayer began to sound from the minarets just as they entered. Hundreds of worshipers already inside the huge space began to spread their prayer rugs beneath the multi-domed structure as the sun gleamed through a multitude of small windows casting rays of light and illuminating the haze of dust stirred into the air by the unrolled rugs.

Visitors who were not worshiping stood in the colonnade to the sides of the huge space and listened to the murmured voices that prayed. "It wasn't easy, but I believe I've spotted your followers," whispered Grace. "They're very professional and blend into the crowd as they pretend to be tourists, but I have an idea. There's a vendor's market down some steps to one side of the mosque. Perhaps we can find out who they are before the meeting. We'll follow you out. Thomas and I can stop and look at some rugs while you walk on and enter one of the empty shops. We can then come in behind them and catch them out in the open."

"Excellent plan, Grace." Lynnette was excited. "We'll circle the interior and leave by the side entrance."

Once they were outside, Grace tugged Sir Thomas into one of the fabric shops full of lace and other weavings. They watched as the two men continued to follow Sir Reginald and Lynnette, then slipped in behind them unnoticed.

Lynnette guided Reginald into the shop of a rug merchant who was busy eating his lunch and indicated they should look around at his merchandise. Reginald then turned as the two men stepped into the same shop, followed by Grace and Thomas.

Reginald spoke with authority, "If you have business with us now is the time to speak up. You've been following us since early this morning at the cistern. Who are you and what do you want?"

Both gentlemen smiled and looked at each other. "Shall we tell him?" one said.

"I think you should," said Sir Thomas with a grin. "Why don't you explain, Jason?"

"You know these men?" asked Lynnette.

"I know the bodyguard, Jason Taylor. I haven't been introduced to the other gentleman, but I assume they are both working the same case on behalf of the Home Office."

"It's good to see you Sir Thomas," replied Taylor. "They said Sir Reginald would be able to make us immediately, but we happened to be here in Istanbul when the assignment came through, so I thought we'd see if the Home Office was right."

Sir Thomas shook Taylor's hand. "Actually it was Grace that blew your cover. She's my wife and private body guard."

"Wow! We must be slipping," commented the other man.

"Grace is one of the best at detection and I sensed we were being followed. Never underestimate the powers of a woman," chimed Lynnette.

"My apologies, Lady Whitcomb. I appreciate the lesson." He pointed to the other gentleman. "May I introduce my partner in crime, Boris Rykoff. We finished another mission yesterday and were told to start immediately on your case. No rest for the wicked." He winked. "I'm your shadow, Sir Reginald. Rykoff will tend to the ladies." He turned to Grace, "And I'm happy to know that Sir Thomas is in capable hands. He gave her a slight bow. "Now, if you will excuse us, we'll try to vanish into the scene, but please be aware...you are under our watchful eyes."

Lynnette smiled, "I know that should make me feel safe, but it adds a certain amount of suspense to the rest of this trip. I suppose I shall have to get used to it. Welcome aboard, and now if you will excuse us I'm ready for a light lunch and then we have another meeting to attend with the Turkish Secret Service."

Taylor looked surprised. "Is it anything we should be concerned about?"

"Not unless you have a restaurant suggestion for lunch," Lynnette smiled.

"I was referring to the secret service meeting," he said.

"Actually," added Sir Reginald, "it's in regards to a different case altogether. An incident that happened on the Orient Express on our trip down, but I believe they have it under control. To my knowledge, it doesn't involve the Home Office. However, I'm sure you will want to know that Sir Thomas is investigating the same case at the excavation site in Egypt for MIA. He and Lady Grace plus Lord Charles Marquis will be part of our team while we are at the tomb."

"I'm well aware of Lady Grace's capabilities as a bodyguard. Her reputation in the field of intelligence and espionage is not unnoticed." He gave a nod to Grace. "I don't know if Lord Marquis travels with a guard, but we'll keep our eyes on him as well."

Another couple entered the shop as they moved to leave. "The shadows are about to vanish now that the sun is high. It was pleasant meeting you. Have a safe journey," said Taylor.

Chapter Nine

A Piece of the Puzzle

Sitting at his desk in the offices of the secret service building, Ahmet continued to study the papers they had found among the personal belongings of the Baroness Von Karlsberg, also known as Natalia Kazenski, a suspected Russian spy, jewel thief, and now a missing person under suspicion of transporting opium.

Turkey, and Istanbul in particular, had always figured into the business of drug trafficking with Russia and other ports of call due to their location on the Black Sea and the Mediterranean.

Ahmet had requested a meeting with Sir Reginald and Sir Thomas to discuss the documents he was holding. He was sure the information would be of interest in their pending investigations once they were in Egypt. It was almost 2 p.m., and time for their arrival. He rose and paced the floor in front of the window as he gazed at the distant shipyards, packed with containers waiting to be loaded onto ships. The documents on his desk might be the needle in a haystack; a discovery that could possibly alter the drug trade in this city of mystery and intrigue. His intercom buzzed. "Sir Reginald Whitcomb and Sir Thomas Treadwell have arrived, sir. Shall I show them in?"

Ahmet opened the door to his office and greeted his guests. He was surprised to see that Lady Lynnette and Lady Grace accompanied them. "Welcome my friends." He stood aside and ushered them into his well-appointed private quarters. Indicating a conversation area with matching camel-colored leather sofas and four club chairs in a colorful Turkish design, "Please make yourselves comfortable. May I offer you coffee or tea?"

"Thank you, but no. We've just had coffee at lunch and are anxious to know what your note indicated you have discovered." Sir Thomas was obviously there on business.

"We don't wish to appear rude," Lynnette added, "But all of us are interested to know what you may have found on further investigation of the train compartment and belongings of the baroness."

Ahmet stepped to his desk and retrieved the documents, handing the envelope to Sir Thomas. "The first paper is a map of what appears to be a tomb sight in the Valley of the Monkeys not far from Luxor. I have taken the liberty of making you an enlarged copy, as I recalled your investigations are in that area and perhaps this map might even be the same tomb the British Museum is excavating.

"The second document looks like a set of time tables which tends to be confusing. Perhaps a schedule or cypher, but we have yet to determine what for. We're currently checking plane, train and shipping schedules to find a match, but without the names of places it becomes a difficult undertaking."

Lynnette appeared the most concerned. "I don't understand how we could have missed finding these during our own search. Might I inquire where they were hidden?"

Ahmet smiled. "But of course you may. They were rolled up and stuffed in a pair of ladies tights. I believe you call them pantyhose." He chuckled.

Lynnette's jaw dropped. "How utterly stupid of me. I should have remembered, we were dealing with a woman not a man. Women think on an entirely different plane. I'm sure the Egyptian man wouldn't have looked in ladies undies."

"You're probably correct. They were discovered by one of our female agents going through her wardrobe."

Reginald and Thomas were looking over the map. "We've not visited the tomb as yet, but it will be most interesting to see if the map has any connection, and if so, what that connection might be. As for the second document, the times and numbers might hold some meaning if they are indeed part of the same mystery. May I also have a copy of the second document?" Sir Thomas inquired.

"There is a second set of copies in the envelopes. One for you and one for Sir Reginald. Please keep me informed of your progress. You have my private cell phone number. Do not hesitate to call at any time. If I don't answer, I could be in a meeting or out on a case, but I will return your call as soon as possible. I am at your service."

Ahmet continued, "I will send you updates on our search for the Egyptian man on the train. The Romanian and Bulgarian police are proceeding with the search as we speak. It's very rough terrain and covers much territory, but a black Land Rover SUV is a rare automobile and easily spotted in the rural countryside. Local people in small villages tend to gossip and are quite observant."

"I doubt we will ever truly know what happened to the baroness—whether she's drugged and alive somewhere, or dead and buried," said Lynnette.

"Justice comes in many packages, my dear," said Grace. "Even under the guise of evil."

Reginald shook Ahmet's hand. "We appreciate your assistance from the Turkish government and now, we should be on our way. I'm sure you're a very busy man."

"I'm delighted we've had the opportunity to meet. Perhaps our paths will cross again. Have a successful journey and enjoy your visit to Istanbul." Ahmet closed his office door as they departed. He smiled again as he thought of Lady Lynnette. 'That beautiful woman has a head on her shoulders. She would make an excellent intelligence agent.'

~

Lynnette casually checked her watch. "Oh, my! I didn't realize our meeting had taken two hours. It's time for tea, and I know just the place near the Topkapi Palace. It has a beautiful view overlooking the Sea of Marmara, and after tea, we can pop into the spice bazaar." Lynnette and Grace agreed they were ready for tea and shopping before a rest and dinner.

"That sounds like a splendid idea, old girl. We can take a taxi there to save time." Sir Reginald hailed an approaching taxi. Lynnette offered the driver a handwritten slip of paper with the address of the tea garden she had read about in the hotel magazine and the four of them were whisked away to the Topkapi Palace.

They were seated on a terrace in the shade of a tree, captivated by a view of the dazzling blue Sea of Marmara, its waves twinkling like diamonds in the afternoon rays of sunlight. A soft sea breeze offered a soothing and refreshing moment. Everyone agreed the Turkish tea accompanied by lemon cakes and Turkish Delights covered with powdered sugar, were a gift from heaven.

"How soon do you leave for Egypt?" Sir Thomas inquired.

"Considering what we've discovered today with the help of Ahmet, I think it's important to leave sooner than we had planned. I'll need to make some changes in our original schedule," Sir Reginald stated. He glanced at Lynnette, seeking her support. "I'll make some calls when we get back to the hotel. If possible we'll cancel the longer part of the journey over on the ferry and fly direct to Cairo tomorrow. That alone will save us three days travel time.

"The bodyguards are already on the job and can follow by whatever means they might arrange. The sooner we get to Luxor and the Valley of the Monkeys, the better."

"I totally agree," added Lynnette as she placed her hand over his where it rested on the map they had been discussing. "Hopefully we don't need to cancel the trip up the Nile. Minnie and I are so looking forward to that."

"No, no, of course not." Reginald added quickly to reassure her. "I received word that Lord Marquis is traveling on the same boat. That's where we are to meet him. Remember the letter I received when we arrived at the hotel? He's not due to arrive until Friday. Today is just Tuesday."

Grace quickly added, "We leave for Cairo tomorrow on Alitalia Airlines. Perhaps they still have three seats available." She checked their itinerary on her cell phone and gave Reginald the flight information. "Where will you be staying?"

"Hopefully at the Gardenia Pyramids View—in Giza if they can accommodate us the extra two nights. I wanted to be near the pyramids and the sphinx so we could take a camel tour into the desert," he answered as he watched Lynnette's reaction.

"A camel ride!" she exclaimed. "I never dreamed of riding a camel. What marvelous fun. Simply smashing! I'm sure Minnie will be frightfully excited."

"I think perhaps you mean she'll be frightened," Sir Thomas chuckled.

"Oh no. You don't know Minnie very well. She's a real trooper. Ready for a little adventure at every turn. She even brought a swimsuit so she could take a dip in the Nile," Lynnette announced.

"Before she goes for a swim, I hope someone reminds her that there are crocodiles in the Nile. Perhaps she'll have second thoughts and relax in the hotel pool. It's much safer," added Grace.

Lynnette gave her husband a serious look. "Reggie, you were the one who suggested Minnie bring her swimsuit so she could take a dip in the Nile, but you weren't serious, were you?"

Sir Reginald had a sheepish grin on his face. "Lynn, my dear, Minnie is afraid of water. She wears her suit to the pool but never gets it wet. She won't go near the lake at home, and when we go to Brighton she stands with her feet in the water for two minutes. I'm sure she didn't take me seriously. Just making a boat trip up the Nile will be the closest she gets to the river. She turned almost green crossing the channel." Sir Thomas and Grace both laughed and Lynnette had to admit it was a typical English joke at her expense.

She slowly smiled, "Don't think you're getting off so easy. I hope you're not joking about the camels. Are you?"

"No, my dear," he patted her rosy cheek. "I made the arrangements ahead. Our camels await, once we get there."

Sir Thomas took care of the check for tea. "I suggest we head back to our respective hotels and prepare for departure tomorrow.

We still need to pack and you have reservations to reschedule. Let us know if you can book on our flight and we'll meet you at the airport tomorrow."

Grace took Lynnette's hands in hers. "Cheer up, old girl, we're still ahead of the game. They're just trying to make up for lack of women's intuition." It was time to move ahead.

Chapter Ten

Egypt

Sir Reginald, Lady Lynnette, and Minnie arrived at the Istanbul airport with time to spare. After checking their luggage, they received boarding passes and found their way to the appropriate terminal for Alitalia Airlines and found Sir Thomas and Grace seated near the gate in the empty waiting area.

"How delightful to see you. I gather you were able to make your schedule changes with success," said Grace.

"To be honest, it was a bit of a route, but with only one change, we will be staying in Cairo the first evening. Our hotel was topped out, but they were able to get us in one day early. However, that will give me the opportunity to meet with the Egyptian police in Cairo and see what information they have to offer. Perhaps they've located the missing workers from the tomb sight." Sir Reginald was doing his best to be hopeful in trusting the local police.

Lynnette took a seat next to Grace. "Didn't you mention that you were staying at the Nile Ritz-Carlton, in Cairo?"

"Precisely!" Sir Thomas answered. "Is that where you booked for the first evening in town?"

Lynette smiled in triumph and glanced up at her husband. "You see, I told you it was the Nile Ritz-Carlton, now aren't you glad you listened to me?"

Reginald took the seat next to her. "I've always listened to you, old girl, and look where we are today. Flying off to Egypt on a mission of mystery. This was supposed to be a vacation. However, we are staying in Giza tomorrow and the next day. I've reserved a camel ride out to the pyramids and dinner on a Nile barge at sunset. At least that won't change."

Minnie's eyes got as big as saucers and she squeezed Lynnette's arm. "How are we going to ride camels? Don't they have humps?" she asked.

Lynnette saw the look on her face and patted her hand. "Of course they do, my dear. But they put a saddle between the humps and you climb on—just like straddling a horse."

"Miss Lynnette, you know I've never ridden a horse and I don't have any clothes fit to straddle a camel," Minnie added with concern.

"Of course you don't Minnie, dear. That's why we're going shopping when we get to Cairo. Think of it as adventure," Lynnette said in a comforting voice.

"Unless of course someone has another suggestion," Sir Thomas added with a serious look as he watched a gentleman approach them. "Ahmet, my friend, what brings you to the airport at this hour? I thought our business was completed yesterday."

Ahmet smiled, bowed to the ladies, and shook Sir Thomas's hand and then Sir Reginald's. "I have some news that couldn't wait and wanted to deliver it in person."

"By all means, please have a seat and tell us. I trust the news is good," added Grace.

Ahmet glanced around to make sure they would not be overheard. It was still early and not many people were at the gate. Their flight wasn't due to depart for another hour. He knew they would be early. "The officials at INTERPOL, in collaboration with the Romanian police, have located and captured the Egyptian man who left the train at the station in Sinaia."

"How marvelous! How absolutely smashing! Have they found any trace of the baroness?" Lynnette questioned.

"They traced the man to a chateau in the mountains. I mentioned before that the Land Rover SUV would be an easy car to find in the rural valleys and villages of Romania. It appears the baroness lives, although she was drugged, beaten, and barely coherent after being stuffed in one of the trunks.

"She had been strangled on the train until she passed out, there were marks on her neck, but she was still alive. Currently she's in a local hospital under guard and in time will be questioned.

"The Egyptian is a member of a drug cartel. The rune markings on his chest and back indicate a secret gang in the area near Karnack. It won't be easy to squeeze information out of him. They're bound to an oath of silence unto death."

"Did you find out what was in the second trunk?" Sir Thomas questioned.

"So far, they haven't located the second trunk. He may have hidden it, but they are searching all the grounds around the chateau and every inch of the building. If it is still there, I'm confident they will locate it.

"This was a well-planned drug robbery and in my opinion the goods may be on their way into Russia. The baroness Natalia's part in all of this and how she came into possession of the opium, is yet to be revealed. She may sing a pretty tune once she's able to speak. We have enough evidence to put her away for quite a while. It would be to her advantage to confess what she knows."

"You've brought us excellent news and we want to thank you for all your assistance." said Sir Thomas. "I'm sure I speak for all of us."

Ahmet looked at Lynnette. "If you ever consider taking up intelligence investigation as a hobby, the Turkish government would be delighted to have you join our team."

Lynnette smiled and blushed, "I thank you for the compliment, but I'm afraid Her Majesty would be most upset and surely my husband would agree. However, I will include your offer in my memoirs."

Ahmet chuckled. "In that case, I will bid you a safe and pleasant journey, with much success in your investigations." He bowed and departed.

An airline attendant arrived at the gate and quickly announced that the flight to Cairo would begin boarding in twenty minutes. The passengers began to gather and it was obvious it would not be a full flight.

"Let's have dinner together this evening, unless you have other plans. It will give us a chance to digest this news and see how it affects, or if it affects the investigation we are about to embark on," Sir Thomas offered.

"Splendid suggestion!" said Lynnette, "Shall we say 7 p.m. for sunset cocktails on the rooftop terrace?"

Everyone agreed as boarding was announced and they joined the short line of passengers. The Nile Ritz-CarltonIt was a short two hour and twenty minute flight across the Mediterranean. The hotel limo driver loaded their luggage and off they went to the high-rise metropolitan area in the sprawling, bustling, ancient city of Cairo. A city with a history spanning millennia.

The luxurious Nile Ritz-Carlton was a calm and welcoming oasis amid the bustling traffic of the central city. Their suite accommodations with a view of the Nile River, snaking its way through the city of twenty million people, offered a distant glimpse of pyramids through the gray-brown haze of pollution.

"I feel like we are back in London, but with a change of scenery. The air quality remains thick and heavy. I hope the camels are wearing goggles." Lynnette sighed as she stood next to the window, her mind focusing on the strange large images thirty miles away. "Are you meeting with the police inspector this afternoon?"

Sir Reginald slipped his arms around her as they stood together. "Yes. I was able to arrange a meeting before lunch. You and Minnie should do some sightseeing. The hotel will provide your transportation and a guide. It's all been arranged. I saw our bodyguard Mr. Taylor sitting in the lobby reading when we arrived. I'm sure as soon as the Home Office got wind of our changes, they flew them over in a private plane."

"Oh! I didn't know you contacted the Home Office."

"I didn't need to. They have eyes and ears everywhere. They probably know what we had for breakfast this morning," he joked.

"I wonder if they're watching us now."

Sir Reginald, his arms still around her, gave her a tight squeeze and kissed her neck. "I doubt they have cameras in the hotel room. But you can rest assured they'll be watching our every move once we pass through that entry door."

She turned to face him, her arms on his chest and hands on his shoulders. Her auburn hair shined with rich mahogany tones and her green eyes sparkled like jewels. "I rather like Taylor. He doesn't have the appearance of a staunch, burly bodyguard. To be honest, he has the pleasant personality of a business associate, or someone you could take home to meet your mother.

"Boris, on the other hand, looks like a bodyguard. Do you think we could switch?"

Sir Reginald chuckled, "Lynnette, my dear, I'm the businessman. I need a person who looks like a businessman as a bodyguard. Boris, however, should for all intents and purposes, look like a bodyguard who is keeping an eye on two very charming English women on holiday."

She sighed with a little pout, then smiled. "I suppose you're right, but I feel so strange being followed by a man who looks like a German gestapo, with a face only a mother could love. I think he frightens Minnie."

He laughed aloud. "Minnie is frightened of her own shadow and screams when she sees a mouse, but she's company for you to talk with and a companion when I'm engaged in other matters. Speaking of which, I should be off. Enjoy your lunch and tour of the city. You can tell me all about it over dinner this evening." He kissed her on the forehead and departed. She knocked on the adjoining door and Minnie appeared.

"Minnie, it's time for adventure and I hope you're hungry. Our mission is to discover Cairo in a day. Think we can do that?"

"If you'll pardon my opinion, your ladyship, that appears to be an impossible mission, but we'll most certainly scratch the surface."

Off they went, followed by Boris Rykoff. Once in the lift Lynnette looked at Minnie. "Please ignore the gorilla in the lift, Minnie. He's going to be following us for the next several days to protect us. We're to pretend we don't see him."

Minnie glanced up at Boris and smiled, "I don't mind. I think he's rather cute." Lynnette roller her eyes. Boris actually cracked a smile, but said nothing.

Chapter Eleven

Egyptian Police

S ir Thomas met Sir Reginald in the hotel lobby. "Do you know where the police station in Cairo is located?" Reginald asked.

"I've been there a few times in my life, strictly business, of course. And there isn't a taxi driver in Cairo who doesn't know the location." Thomas joked. The doorman had a taxi waiting for them.

After much horn honking, tires screeching, and strange verbal comments with hand jesters, they arrived at the eight story building that housed the headquarters of the Egyptian National Police (ENP). The department of the Ministry of the Interior of Egypt was not a popular place with the Egyptian people. Armed guards stood at the entry and military security was apparent in all directions.

Sir Thomas looked at Sir Reginald. "Be thankful we are only here for a brief meeting. This place is most intimidating and I doubt they will have much to add to the investigation. It's okay to mention the Home Office, but not a word about MIA. They tend to dislike private security investigators."

"But won't they know who you are?"

"My dear chap, half the time they don't even know what their own mother's last name is, unless she's committed a crime against Egypt or some secretary pulls it out of a file for them. I'm your secretary for all intents and purposes."

They passed through security and were shown into a stark and dismal office on the seventh floor by a rather stern-faced young officer. "The Minister of Police will join you in a moment. Please have a seat." He gestured to two chairs in front of the large desk. This particular room was on the interior for privacy and security, it had no windows.

To say the least, the décor was minimal; one drab wooden desk with a black vinyl chair, two well-worn and cracked vinyl chairs faced the desk, and several metal file cabinets stood along one wall. The walls were devoid of adornment except for framed certificates and various awards scattered on the space behind the desk. Paint peeled off the dirty white walls, stained from years of cigar and cigarette smoke. One stone ashtray sat in the middle of the desk.

Sir Thomas quickly wrote a note on a folded sheet of paper and handed it to Sir Reginald, being suspicious of possible listening devices. The note read, "Say as little as possible. This looks like an interrogation room. We may know more than they do. Keep the questions simple and your answers short. We don't want to stir up a nest of hornets." Reginald's head barely nodded as the door opened behind them, and he slipped the note in his breast pocket.

"Good afternoon gentlemen. Welcome to Egypt. I'm Yusuf Mohamad Mursi—Minister of Police at your service. How may I assist you?" He took a seat behind the desk, but didn't offer to shake hands.

"Thank you for seeing us on such short notice, Mr. Mursi. I'm Sir Reginald Whitcomb and this is my secretary, Thomas Treadwell. We're here at the request of the Home Office in London to see if you might be able to offer any information on the two missing workers at the new excavation site sponsored by the British Museum in the Valley of the Monkeys." Reginald answered.

"Ah, yes." It appears they vanished two weeks ago I believe." He pressed a button on the side of the desk and the young officer appeared in the doorway. "Bring me the missing person's file on the tomb excavation in the Valley of the Monkeys."

"Yes sir," he said, closing the door.

Yusuf Mursi took a casual approach to the disappearance of the workers. "Workers often disappear from the digs for a number of reasons; girl trouble, family demands, or possibly a higher paying job." The officer returned with a file and placed it on the desk then left the room. "Let's see what we have found so far." Mursi reached for the file and thumbed through the pages quickly. "It appears they have not yet been found and have not returned to work. But don't give up hope, we are still searching." The man actually forced a sly grin and his white teeth gleamed against his dark face in the shadow light of the small room.

Sir Reginald nodded his head. "I thank you for your time minister. We won't trouble you further." They stood to leave.

"Are you sure there's nothing else we have to discuss, gentlemen? It seems like the Home Office is going to a lot of trouble and expense to find two missing workers. Perhaps you are here on another mission. Maybe we could offer our services of investigation in that direction."

Reginald wasn't about to mention drugs. He knew that would be an open invitation to jail. "My wife and I had planned a holiday to Egypt and the British Museum had asked the Home Office if I would look into the situation at the project. That's all I know. However, I'll be glad to report your diligence on their behalf."

"I see. And did you enjoy your trip on the Orient Express to Istanbul?" he asked, revealing his knowledge of their travels.

Sir Reginald gave him a curious glance, but didn't ask the question he wanted to. "It was the first time my wife and I had the opportunity to travel on the Orient Express. And to answer your question, we've had a relaxing and enjoyable experience."

Mursi was a master at interrogation. "It's a shame you couldn't spend more time in Istanbul. The city is as mysterious as Cairo and there is much for tourists to see."

Reginald offered a calm smile. "The real purpose of this trip is to see Egypt and take a cruise up the Nile. My wife is looking forward to taking a camel ride. She's used to riding horses so it should be a new experience for her. And now we must be on our way, or she'll be spending all my money at the bazaar." He laughed and bowed politely as they departed without being interrogated any further.

Once they were in the taxi Sir Thomas put his finger to his lips to warn him not to speak of the meeting. Reginald acknowledged his signal and talked about the weather and the architecture in Cairo on the ride back to the hotel.

Meanwhile, Lynnette and Minnie had finished their shopping spree and returned to the hotel, where Lynnette had ordered room service to deliver tea. Reginald, with Sir Thomas at his heels entered the suite. "There you are, I ordered..." she paused when she saw the look on his face. "What's wrong?" she asked, staring at Reginald's red face. "Good afternoon, Thomas."

"What do you mean, what's wrong?" he said through his teeth.

"I know that look. Someone or something has set your fuse alight. Sit down and tell me all about it. Tea will be here in a few minutes." The door buzzer sounded and Lynnette invited room service to enter. "Thomas, would you care to join us for tea?"

"Thank you my dear, but I feel it necessary to check in on Grace. She has possibly ordered tea for two as well. I'm resigned that Reggie doesn't need my help to fill you in on our meeting with the police. I hope you've ordered Chamomile to calm the savage beast." He turned to Sir Reginald, "Remember old chap, you outfoxed a desert rat today. Jolly good." He kissed Lynnette's hand, "A nice cool shower and a shot or two of brandy might be helpful. We'll see you for dinner this evening." He toddled out the door swinging his cane like Charlie Chaplin. Lynnette picked up the phone and ordered two glasses of brandy.

Reginald was already seated at the table when she joined him. Picking up the pot of tea, she smiled, leaning her head to one side with an inquisitive look she calmly asked, "So...how was your day, sweetheart?"

"That pompous ass police minister knows everything." Her eyes blinked, but she knew he wasn't finished. "He knew all about our being on the Orient Express. It was like he had our itinerary."

Lynnette said in her soothing voice, "Well, of course he did."

"What do you mean, of course he did? Have I missed something? Did we send out an announcement?" He took a swallow of tea to calm his nerves.

"Reggie, darling, the Home Office made the arrangements for your meeting with the police here in Cairo. No doubt he requested an itinerary so his secretary could squeeze you in at a suitable time." She continued. "Then of course we made some changes and the Home Office would have notified him to reschedule the meeting as soon as they got word from you." The brandy arrived and they both reached for a glass and took a sip.

Reginald shook his head. "You always have the right answers."

"Well," she said with a sheepish grin, "not always, but I do try to think things through. Perhaps that sinister Egyptian man on the train has some connections with someone in the Egyptian police force. Grace said they couldn't be trusted, or was that Sir Thomas? Maybe they're hiding information about a drug ring operating in the Luxor area. Whatever it is, we are going to find the answers and come out on top. I don't relish being put in an Egyptian prison. One reads such terrible things about people who are put away and never heard of again." She shivered at the thought.

"But then on a positive note, Minnie and I had a lovely day shopping, and I have a new outfit for our camel ride. Wait until you see it."

"Minnie appeared a bit surprised when I mentioned the camel ride at the airport this morning. Did you see the look on her face when you explained how to ride a camel? She'll be as nervous as a worm on a fish hook until it's all over."

"I agree it was a bit of a shock. It was all I could do to control my laughter. Just don't frighten her to death. I still want a ladies maid on the cruise up the Nile," she chuckled.

Chapter Twelve

Giza

Lynnette was dressed in a flowing silk dress and scarf of yellow chiffon she had purchased on her Cairo shopping adventure. A simple golden ankh pendant and matching earrings caught Reggie's attention. "Ah...my little ray of sunshine when all the clouds gather around. Your shopping makes us both happy."

Lynnette smiled and gave him a hug. "And you, sir, could flatter the wings off of a butterfly, so I will take your compliments to heart once I've unruffled and smoothed some of your feathers after your meeting with the police today." She took his hand and tugged him towards the door. "Come with me. It's time for dinner and as usual, I'm starved. A cocktail might be just the ticket."

Dinner on the rooftop terrace of the Nile Ritz-Carlton was relaxing, even though the conversation floated around the rude, inquisitive, and inept ability of the Egyptian police. The air had cooled and a mild desert breeze had magically dispersed the brown haze that hung over the city earlier in the day. The pyramids off in the distance appeared like a mirage glowing in the rays of a red setting-sun. It couldn't have been a more picture perfect evening.

However, Sir Reginald's temper was still on simmer, "That had to be the rudest reception of a Home Office representative I've ever witnessed. These police have absolutely no idea what it is to be diplomatic. I'll be recording it verbatim in my report upon our return."

"I know it's your obligation to make the report, my boy, however I wouldn't put too much hope on it making many waves in the Home Office. Their hands are tied in diplomacy and government red tape. There's nothing they can do about a person's personality or how they handle their business, when no one appears to have broken any laws. Suffice it to say, the man is no better than a clump of camel dung. Wipe your shoes off and carry on. Our investigation tends to expand at every turn," offered Sir Thomas.

"He's right you know. He's seen much worse," replied Grace.

"Grace is correct. Forget the police and concentrate on the rest of our investigation. We can toss out conspiracy theories until the sheep come home, but what we need are facts and evidence that ties things up in a nice little bundle. Between the four of us we should be able to find what we need for the Museum and the Home Office," Lynnette set back in her chair and took a sip of champagne to sooth her dry throat.

Sir Thomas continued, "I believe there will soon be five of us. You mentioned that Lord Charles Marquis will be joining our little party for the cruise up the Nile. It's been some time since our paths have crossed and I'm anxious to hear what he might be able to add.

"He's given over 75 percent of the funds for the exploration of the tomb in the Valley of the Monkeys. Lord Charles, by the way, is an amateur sleuth who enjoys helping his friends at Scotland Yard solve mysterious cases. He weighs things on a psychological scale of human nature. Cause and response, so to speak."

"Well, well—Lord Charles in a nutshell. I can't wait to meet this collector of artifacts and inquisitive man of mystery," chuckled Lynnette. "We've never been formally introduced, but we've attended his marvelous exhibitions at the museum."

"How about some mint tea before we turn in?" Grace suggested.

"I think I'll stay with the brandy," Sir Reginald said, "but order the tea if you like." He seemed to have forgotten all about the police, but his mind was turning like clock-work, filling in the hours and minutes still ahead.

~

Daybreak came early with calls to prayer echoing through the city corridors and across the Nile. The morning sun cast shadows through narrow city streets and wide avenues, as the human traffic below stirred to life. Outside temperatures had already begun to rise. Today they were moving to the hotel in Giza for a couple of days of relaxation before their journey up the Nile.

"Make sure we don't leave anything behind, Minnie. I purchased an extra valise yesterday. I'm sure we'll need it before our return to England."

They said their goodbyes to Sir Thomas and Grace until they would meet once again on the trip up the Nile. "Be sure to inform Lord Charles that we are looking forward to a reunion when the ship arrives in Giza. We, of course, will already be on board," reminded Sir Thomas.

"I'm not sure if we will see him before you do. The Home Office only said he would be taking the Nile cruise on the same ship. Instructions were a little vague as to when and how we were to meet him," Reggie said.

"It wouldn't surprise me if the museum hasn't made all the arrangements for him to contact you. Have a wonderful visit to the pyramids and enjoy Giza," added Grace as they departed.

The Nefertiti would depart from Cairo with its first stop in Giza to add more passengers. Sir Reginald had reserved their suite of cabins forward on the upper promenade of the starboard side for the best views. Minnie would be on the port side. Their Nile holiday had all been arranged in advance.

An hour later, after many detours around traffic congested areas, they arrived at the Gardenia Pyramids View hotel. From the private terrace of their suite, and even from the cloud-soft bed they had a perfect view of the pyramids in Giza. Palm trees swayed lazily and rhythmically in the warm desert breeze. Tomorrow they would set off to explore the three pyramids, and the ancient, stone carved monument of the Sphinx. It would be a day of adventure and Lynnette was striving to do her best to contain her excitement.

"I don't think I'll be able to sleep tonight just thinking about tomorrow." They were seated on their terrace having afternoon tea, while Sir Reginald read his paper and the correspondence from the Home Office that was waiting for him on arrival.

"No doubt you'll be dreaming of camels once your head hits

the pillows," he said as he continued to read a letter. "It appears Lord Marquis is currently in residence at the Marriott Mena House close by, awaiting our arrival. He's invited us to be his guest for dinner this evening at the Moghul Room restaurant and I suppose we should have to accept. There goes my idea of a romantic dinner for two in the land of the pharaohs."

Lynnette reached across the table and patted him on the arm. "Don't sound so sad, my dear. We'll have many more nights for romantic, moonlit dinners together. However, the pyramids do make a charming and exotic backdrop.

"I suppose he learned of our change of plans from the Home Office, and arrived earlier than expected to meet our schedule. I'm sure we will find out tonight. At least it will take my mind off of camels and perhaps we'll learn more about his part in this investigation." Lynnette was most consoling. "And on that note, I think I'll lie down and rest for a while. Are you coming in?"

"I want to finish reading my paper. I'll join you in a moment." She kissed him on the head and slipped into the refreshing cool air of their suite. Meanwhile, Sir Reginald wrote a note accepting Lord Charles's invitation to dinner and had it sent to his hotel.

The Marriott Mena House Hotel is a large complex, surrounded by pristine gardens filled with exotic colorful flowers, palms in all shapes and sizes, and green lawns laced with a multitude of tiled reflecting pools, fountains and swimming pools. Several bars and restaurants offer guests the opportunity of a culinary adventure, and the galleria shops are fun to explore.

While the Mena House was sleek, luxurious, and contemporary, it lacked the charm and simplicity of their hotel—the Gardenia Pyramids View. Although their suite wasn't quite as large as Cairo's Ritz-Carlton, it was comfortable and definitely more spacious than their accommodations would be on board the Nefertiti.

Minnie assisted Lynnette into her emerald green chiffon dress, as Lynnette fastened the emerald necklace around her throat and put her earrings on. "I don't know why I'm so nervous. I've met more lords and ladies than you can count on your fingers and toes combined," she said aloud.

Minnie chuckled. "Just think of him as a man, my lady, not as a saint, even though he does own an abbey. I'm sure he puts his pants on just like any other gentleman—one leg at a time."

"Oh, Minnie," Lynnette said as she fluffed her auburn hair as she stood in front of the mirror, "I don't know what I would do without you. You always seem to know just what to say to make me laugh. I suppose I will look at him tonight and wonder which leg goes in first." Suddenly, they couldn't stop laughing.

Reginald appeared in the doorway. "What's so funny?"

Lynnette glanced at Minnie and stifled a giggle. "You wouldn't understand, dear. It's a woman's joke."

Chapter Thirteen

Lord Charles Marquis

Glowing on the western horizon was a giant red ball of fire as the sun began to sink in the hazy atmosphere of evening; rippling in the waves of heat and casting long gray shadows from the pyramids silhouetted in the final rays of Ra, the Egyptian sun god.

The moon goddess, Sekhmet, was already high in the eastern sky with the promise of moonlight and romance as they arrived at the Moghul Room to dine with Lord Charles Marquis. The maître d' guided them to the table as Lord Charles stood to greet them and shake Reginald's hand.

"I'm delighted to finally meet you. We've been like ships passing in the night at museum receptions and exhibitions; a glimpse across the room gliding past in a sea of familiar faces." He kissed Lynnette's extended hand. "Charmed, I assure you."

Charles couldn't take his eyes off Lynnette. "You, my dear, remind me of the Egyptian goddess Bastet, a lioness with green eyes and a protector from evil. You're most fortunate to have such a charming wife and companion on this investigation, Sir Reginald. I hope you won't mind if we dispense with titles and formalities and allow me to call you Reginald and Lynnette. You may refer to me as Charles, or Lord Charles if you must. Please, be seated."

Sir Reginald spoke first. "We were delighted to receive your invitation for dinner this evening. I hadn't expected to see you so soon."

Lynnette interrupted, "What Reginald means to say is that we were anxious to meet you and hope you didn't have to rearrange your schedule because of the changes made in our plans."

"Not at all, my dear. I've been in Cairo several days now, meeting with museum officials and exhibition organizers planning the opening of my private collection on loan in December. We still have a round of meetings tomorrow, before we make our way up the Nile to Luxor and the Valley of the Monkeys. Everything in Egypt is done at a snail's pace. I won't bother you with any site details tonight. We'll have plenty of time during our little voyage up river to discuss the strange events and our investigation. Two intelligence investigators will surely be able to find some answers."

"Make that three investigators, Lord Charles," corrected Lynnette. "I've been instructed to let you know that a mutual friend of ours, Sir Thomas Treadwell, will be traveling on the Nile barge with his wife Grace, and has already joined us on the case. We traveled down with them on the Orient Express to Istanbul and quite by accident became involved in a strangely interesting criminal investigation while on the train. One never knows what can happen while traveling on a journey, but I rather doubt it has anything to do with the mysterious events at the new tomb."

Lord Charles was eager to hear their story. "I can see this is going to be an interesting evening. Shall we order dinner and begin our tales?"

"Before we do that," Reginald said, "I wanted to let you know we have two ladies who should receive recognition for their amazing observations and assistance in the suspected murder case on the train. Lynnette and Grace managed to find clues that Sir Thomas and I had overlooked. They even surprised INTERPOL and the Romanian police with their women's intuition, as they call it."

Lord Charles nodded and smiled at Lynnette, "Bravo. Before long, the Home Office will need to hire some new recruits. Glad to have you on the team, my dear, and I'm delighted to learn that Thomas and Lady Grace will be joining us. I've worked with him on several cases in the past when he first started MIA—although it wasn't called that at the time."

The Moghul Room restaurant with its contemporary Egyptian décor was comfortable and inviting. Its polished marble walls and arched stone ceiling created a palace-like ambiance. Richly carved wooden chairs, upholstered in garnet and powder-blue, had pointed arched backrests. Tables matched the chairs with their carved geometric patterns reflecting in the mellow tone of satin smooth wood floors.

Lynnette was mesmerized with her view of the Great Pyramids, framed by a backdrop of turquoise blue sky and palm trees swaying in the desert breeze as shades of night approached in Giza. "I feel like I'm in paradise. Can we reserve the tales of crimes until after dinner? I don't want to spoil this special moment."

"By all means, my dear. Egypt has a way of capturing that magical moment at sunset, when all the cares of the world seem to wash away in the waters of the Nile. You should enjoy this experience as the pharaohs and queens of this ancient land once did," said Lord Charles with a wink at Reginald.

The waiter returned with their drinks and they surveyed the menu. Little did they know their delightful culinary experience was about to begin. Lord Charles announced, "I took the liberty of selecting our menu this evening. I hope you don't mind. There are such delicious delicacies in Indian cuisine of which most travelers are not aware. As I've been to Egypt on numerous occasions, I've had many opportunities to experience their specialties. This evening is my treat. I assure you, the tasting experience will be one of exotic pleasure."

Lynnette smiled and her eyes twinkled in the soft light. "I feel like we've arrived at Babbette's Feast and personally, I'm looking forward to every surprise."

"Agreed," said Sir Reginald, folding his menu.

"Then let the feast begin," announced Lord Charles signaling the waiter.

"Did I understand that you are going to open an exhibition of your Egyptian Collection at the museum in Cairo?" Lynnette asked.

Lord Charles chuckled. "Yes, my dear. However, it won't be until December, provided we get through all the paperwork and red tape. Kathy Stockton, a personal friend, exhibition coordinator and antiquities appraiser for the British Museum, was just here helping to present the catalogue of items for the exhibition. I'll introduce you when we get to the tomb site. She's there now, assisting with the museum's curator, Dr. Stafford, making on-site appraisals of the artifacts extracted from the tomb. Her husband, Mario Regetti, is a former homicide detective from the Isle of Capri. After their recent marriage, he retired and is currently a wealthy wine grower in Tuscany. I'll have to tell you their story on our Nile trip."

"I believe we've heard parts of the story from Sir Thomas, but we'd be delighted to learn of your experience first-hand. Is Katherine's husband here with her?" Reginald was anxious to know if a real detective would be at the site.

"Why, yes. As a matter of fact, he's accompanying her until the grape harvest begins next month. The tomb should be emptied by then and hopefully all these mysterious happenings will be resolved. People don't just vanish. Although, in Egypt, that seems to happen more often lately and they dismiss it with a grain of Mediterranean salt. The police apparently have little or no interest in locating the missing workers who were on our staff."

"Oh, Lord Charles! Speaking of the Egyptian police, you just mentioned a very touchy subject of my husband's, which I'm sure you will hear about later. However, I would be delighted to learn more about your adventure in Capri." He noticed how quickly Lynnette changed the subject before Reginald's blood pressure surfaced to the boiling point.

"Truth be known, I had a very small part in that investigation. Mario and his officers did an excellent job in a limited amount of time. Of course, Kathy was a big help. She was the one who mentioned the funicular to the boat dock and the grotto at the base of the cliff, which is where they found Carlotta bound and drugged awaiting the tide that almost drowned her.

"Kathy is observant and noticed how quickly Carlotta, who

is much older than Fabio, attempted to become his lover. When all the time, she was blackmailing him with something she had overheard about the drug shipments he was running. He played her little game up to a certain point, but she knew too much. That's when he decided it was time to dispose of her.

"No one would have known about the secret passage in the library wall that led to a hidden vault beneath the villa where Orcini stored his antiquities collection. Kathy remembered working there several years ago to assist Orcini in cataloguing and appraising his small, but outstanding collection. Unfortunately, she didn't know how to find or open the hidden door to the passage, but Mario and his assistant found it."

"Were the artifacts stolen on the evening of Orcini's party very valuable? I recall they later found them hidden on Fabio's yacht," said Lynnette. "The newspapers never mentioned their value."

Lord Charles shook his head. "That all depends on how you judge the level of value. Were they old? Yes. Were they coherent with his collection? No. They were a scattering of second-rate artifacts from Mesoamerica, possibly purchased on the black market. It was rumored that Orcini would make purchases that were not legal and then offer them to other collectors in the lucrative market of stolen property. Kathy was not at the party and had not seen the exhibition in the library that evening.

"However, Mario's request for an appraiser was made to the British Museum, and she flew to Capri to offer her services. From photos of the pieces she estimated them to be valued at several hundred thousand dollars. Kathy and Mario are from America. She worked for the New York Metropolitan Museum's department of antiquities, arranging exhibitions at various museums around the world and just happened to be in London at the time."

Lynnette looked surprised. "I thought Mario was Italian."

Lord Charles nodded his head and grinned. "Lots of Italians

live in America, my dear. His father is a diplomat from Italy and if I remember correctly, his mother is a surgeon. Mario was educated in the USA, joined the Marines, and attended the police academy after his tour of service, before taking a job on Capri. However, I have rambled on more than I should. I don't wish to monopolize the conversation. According to your husband here, you're quite the detective yourself."

Lynnette blushed and bowed her head. "I can't take much credit really," she offered demurely. "It's just that women are different than most men when it comes to analyzing a situation. I think to myself, and often out loud, 'What would I do if I was the criminal?'

"I don't think I would make a very professional criminal, but if I can follow their thought process on a more academic scale, I feel I've accomplished something without actually committing a crime. Does that make any sense to you?"

Lord Charles gave her a soft round of applause and leaned back in his chair. "Bravo, my dear! If you will pardon the expression, you've hit the proverbial nail on the head. From one amateur investigator to another, it's the psychological approach that often opens the doors to success in an investigation. Know your opponent. The more you can learn about your suspects, the better your opportunity is to solve the crime in an orderly manner."

Time had passed quickly and dinner was over. Sir Reginald folded his napkin and placed it on the table. "Lord Charles, it truly has been a pleasure meeting you in person and we would like to thank you for your generous invitation this evening. Tomorrow is going to be a busy day for us. We're going to visit the great pyramids and the Sphinx. Our camels will be waiting." He stood and pulled Lynnette's chair out for her to stand.

Lynnette smiled. "You'll have to forgive my husband, Lord Charles. He's on a business trip and I'm on holiday. We're doing our best to combine the two. Dinner was delightful and the cuisine a tantalizing treat to the taste buds. We'll look forward to seeing you again soon.

Lord Charles rose and took Lynnette's hand. "I trust you will have a jolly good tour, I will be in meetings all day tomorrow in Cairo, but we will have plenty of time to get better acquainted on board ship. Enjoy your holiday." He kissed her hand and they parted.

Chapter Fourteen

Camel Confusion

Breakfast was served the following morning on their private terrace with an artist's view of the pyramids that set the stage for a day of adventure. Lynnette appeared in the new "camel riding" ensemble she had purchased in Cairo. Her loose pants in a soft gray color was combined with a silk blouse of creamy-yellow. Around her neck she had wrapped a shocking, bright silk scarf in a color of vibrant magenta. She explained that the scarf would be useful to cover her head should they enter any sacred temples or religious structures, and would protect her delicate skin from the harsh sun and desert wind when needed. This English Vogue look was complete with a colorful parasol.

Sir Reginald greeted her with a kiss and pulled out her chair. "You look as though you just stepped out of a fashion magazine. I've ordered some mint tea. It's perfectly refreshing to start the day, but you can have coffee if you prefer." He was dressed in a standard khaki safari outfit, suitable for camel riding and terribly English, complete with a campaign pith helmet.

"Thank you, my dear. Minnie and I had a delightful shopping spree while you and Thomas were taking care of business in Cairo," exclaimed Lynnette as she gave him the once over, "and don't you look dashing!

"Wait until you see the ensemble Minnie selected to wear. I told her we were going to a pharaoh safari party. I have no idea how that led her to select a pair of emerald green harem pants, which she matched with an Indian-print, silk over-blouse in green, pink and yellow colors, and she topped it off with an egg yolk yellow turban complete with a feather on the front. But she fell in love with it and I couldn't refuse."

Sir Reginald almost choked as he swallowed his tea and coughed. "I'm sure she will look right at home sitting on top of a camel's back. Rest assured, we shan't lose her on the tour. Hopefully we won't meet anyone we know." Lynnette could hardly stop laughing. "Now finish your breakfast while I make a couple of phone calls. Our tour reservation is at 9 a.m. and I don't want to be late.

When they arrived at the ticket hut for their tour, things started to follow the path of no return. "What do you mean you have no camels?" he said with alarm to the man in charge.

"Yes...we have no camels today. You take donkeys to see pyramids. Handsome donkeys. Very calm. Very pretty animals. Walk slow. Comfortable ride," said the young man behind the counter, pointing at the three, saddled and waiting beast of burden.

Sir Reginald was not going to take "no camels" as an answer. He shook his head and took a firm stance—not about to move on. "I specifically reserved three camels for our tour of the pyramids today. The hotel made our reservation weeks ago. We've come all the way from England to Egypt and you stand there and tell me you have no camels."

"Yes...we have no camels today. Reservation in book say you come in two days. All camels busy now. Work caravan with harvest. We have nice donkeys...names Mohamed Ali, Cleopatra, and Bette Davis," he pointed to the donkeys, "she the one with the big eyes. Camels be here in two days. You take donkeys—have nice ride. You ride camel, you walk like Egyptian later," he chuckled at his own joke.

Lynnette had joined him at the desk. "Reggie, dear, we'll take the donkeys. There's no point in arguing with the man. The hotel evidently forgot to change our reservations for the tour. Buck-up, old man, we can ride the camels on the return trip. You take Mohamed, I'll take Cleopatra, and Minnie can ride Bette Davis. She must be the one with the wide-berth to the rear. Maybe they'll have camels in Luxor that we can ride out to the Valley of the Monkeys," she smiled.

"I suppose you're right. It isn't his fault, but I'll speak to the hotel concierge when we get back. Donkeys just aren't the same as camels," he huffed.

"I'm sure any zoologist would agree with you," she grinned and nodded to the man in charge. "We'll take the donkeys, young man, but not at the same price as the camels, agreed?"

"Oh, yes...for you nice lady we make special price, much better than camels. Very comfortable ride. You see."

Meanwhile, Minnie had her eyes on the handsome young man. "I'll need some help getting on the donkey. I've never even ridden a horse before."

His full head of silky black hair bowed to her and he grinned, showing all of his snowy white teeth. "No problem gracious lady. I help."

Once they were in the saddle, so to speak, their colorful parasols offered some relief from the morning sun as individual guides took hold of the reins and walked their little caravan out to the pyramids. Fifteen or so children began running along beside the donkeys begging for bakshish, and hawking their wares of beaded earrings, bracelets, polished stone scarabs, chewing gum, cigarettes, and packaged nuts for a few piasters.

"You buy. You like. Make nice gift for ladies. Ancient sacred symbol—bring good luck." Their voices all sounded alike. They had learned their English phrases well. Dirty faces, with eager eyes and tousled hair, running along in sandals and bare feet on the hot desert sand, taught to smile with their gleaming white teeth.

The young children were forbidden past a certain point and their chatter faded in the background. Their guides stopped for photo opportunities and to offer, in broken English, a story of the history behind the great pyramids. They rested in the shade of some palms and had some cool, refreshing mint tea. Riding a donkey was quite different from riding a horse, and resting in a woven chair was a great deal more comfortable than rocking from side-to-side in a leather saddle. After their tour of the pyramids and the amazing

Sphinx, they headed back to the hotel to freshen up and have a late lunch.

"The reflection of the sun on the sand and the heat generated by their combination made me sweat worse than the donkey." Reginald said, "I could use a shower. How about you, old girl?"

Lynnette was quickly out of her clothes and had already slipped into the coolness of her apricot silk robe, "Men and animals sweat, my dear, ladies perspire. I'll save my shower for later." She was looking through some letters he had picked up at the front desk after his discussion with the concierge about the lack of camels and the mix up of the reservations.

"There's a note here from Lord Charles and one from Sir Thomas. I'll order lunch and we can read them after your shower?"

Sir Reginald was standing in the doorway of the bathroom with a towel wrapped around his waist. His broad shoulders, strong chiseled features and handsome physique for a man in his sixties, topped with a mane of wavy, dark hair lightly streaked with gray at the temples, gave him the appearance of a Greek god. "Minnie wasn't too disappointed about not having a camel ride this morning, was she?"

Lynnette turned her appraising eyes from him. "You must be joking. I don't think I've ever seen anyone so excited about getting on a donkey in my life. Although the handsome young man helping her to mount may have had something to do with it." She rolled her eyes as Reginald dropped his towel and hung it on the open shower door. Lynnette's heartbeat had quickened, "It's easy to make an impression on Minnie and I wasn't sure whether it was the man or the animal." Reginald stepped into the shower laughing hardily about that last comment. Lynnette crossed the room, picked up the phone, and ordered lunch.

Sitting at the table later they discussed the morning's events and read their notes. "It sounds like Lord Charles contacted Sir

Thomas in Cairo. We're to join them for lunch on the barge tomorrow right after departure from Giza." Reginald was reading the note from Sir Thomas.

The note from Lord Charles had been addressed to Lynnette. "How sweet. Lord Charles was most impressed with our company at dinner last night and has paid us a gracious compliment. He thinks I have the makings of a great detective. We're to join him for lunch tomorrow on the barge."

Reginald cleared his throat. "Yes, dear. That's just what I read from Sir Thomas's letter."

"Of course you did, dear. It must be something going around," she answered back with a dreamy look in her eyes, staring off at the pyramids in the distance.

"What's going around?" he asked.

"Repetition, dear. Repetition. Yes...we have no camels. No camels. I'll be hearing that phrase repeated in my sleep tonight."

"Perhaps I can take your mind off of that." Reginald smiled.

Lynnette glanced up from her letter to see his face. "Is that a threat or a promise?" she grinned.

"I've never threatened a lady," he said, staring over the top of his reading glasses.

"Yes...well there's a first time for everything, but I'll take that as a promise," she smiled.

Chapter Fifteen

The Nile Journey Begins

"Hurry now Minnie. We don't want to keep the boat waiting."
It was a perfectly clear morning and Lynnette was excited to begin their journey up the Nile. "Don't forget the extra valise we purchased in Cairo and the packages I added later. I bought something special for Reginald to wear, if I can ever get him to put it on."

Meanwhile Sir Reginald was in the hotel lobby taking care of their bill and sending porters to their room for the luggage. The concierge assured him that the boat would not leave for another hour or more. Passengers and their luggage would be getting off the boat in Giza and that was never done quickly. After all, this was Egypt, where seldom does anything happen with speed.

Lynnette appeared with Minnie in tow and the porter directly behind them. "Sorry we're so slow, but you know how last minute repacking goes. I think we've got everything under control. I do hope the boat hasn't cast off without us."

Reginald led them out to the waiting van that would take them to the docks. "The concierge assured me we have plenty of time, so you can stop fretting." Lynnette and Minnie slipped into the van as the luggage was being loaded. Sir Reginald sat up front with the driver, handing him the information the concierge had given him about which boat and which dock they would be leaving from. It was only a short drive, but the traffic was beginning to get congested.

Arriving with minutes to spare, they saw Grace, Sir Thomas, and Lord Charles on the top deck waving in their direction as they hurried onboard. "Thank goodness we made it. I was so worried we would miss the boat." Lynnette was out of breath as she took a seat and heaved a sigh of relief, fanning herself with a papyrus fan she had bought for the camel ride.

Lord Charles sat next to her as Minnie took her fan and began with rapid fluttering motions to fan Lynnette. She didn't want her mistress to perspire in public.

"There was never any doubt that you would make it. In Egypt, if they say the boat will depart at 9:30 a.m., you can rest assured it will not leave until sometime after 10 a.m.," Lord Charles confirmed. "It's tradition, you know. Let me pour you some soothing, chilled mint tea, it's most refreshing."

The whistle sounded for the third time and the gangplank was removed as the crewman latched the gate. The boat slowly backed away from the dock and into the stream of flowing water traffic. The felucca with their sails fluttering in the morning breeze were passing by in all directions. These small boats had always been the traditional method of transporting food and other goods to communities along the Nile.

Voices could be heard calling back and forth from the boats to people along the river banks. The languages of the different tribes blended together creating a melodic symphony of unusual tones and rhythms. The "voices of the river" as the natives would say.

The canvas awning, stretched across the upper deck, rippled in the warm morning breeze that carried aromas of spices and herbs from the cooking fires at restaurants along the shore. People had gathered to have their first meal as the morning got under way.

The quay was busy with vendors opening their shops and groups of early rising tourists followed their guides' colorful parasols. Ra had brought the sleeping Nile to life and local residents smiled with gleaming white teeth, encouraging tourists and hawking their wares while inviting everyone to try their cuisine. They waved with excitement as the boat glided silently up river.

The cobalt-blue waters of the Nile reflected surface images and movements with the depth of a crystal ball. Fish could be seen swimming against the flowing currents. It was time for lunch and since Lynnette, and Reginald had missed breakfast they were ready to eat. Minnie was going to dine on the upper terrace and watch the world go by in slow motion.

The main dining room on the boat was spacious, luxurious, and comfortable. Their table for five was in a windowed corner where they had a view of the passing scenery and plenty of privacy. Jason Taylor, Reginald's bodyguard was seated across the room. Boris was watching Minnie on the open deck above.

"I've ordered some champagne for our luncheon." Lord Charles announced, as the glasses were being filled by the server, "I want to make a toast to the success of our investigations." Everyone raised their glasses. "To the five musketeers and their journey into unknown territory on a quest to find the missing evidence and solve the mystery at hand."

"To the musketeers!" they said in unison as they clinked their glasses.

"I say, Charles, you certainly have a flamboyant way of making this trip an adventure," Sir Thomas chuckled.

"Every mystery is an adventure, Thomas. We may be on the Nile River for now, but we will soon be on the 'yellow-brick road,' into the Valley of the Monkeys, so watch out for lions and scarecrows wearing gallibayas," he laughed.

"What a romantic way of saying, "Be on your guard," chimed Lynnette.

Grace, who had been silent, added her opinion. "I think what Lord Charles means to say, is that there are hidden dangers ahead that we might encounter, but they will be disguised and not what we would be expecting."

Lord Charles nodded to Grace, "You have a knack for reading between the lines, my dear."

Their food orders arrived and the subject quickly changed to discussions about the cuisine. It was time to enjoy a few stories, and Lynnette was the first to speak out. "Lord Charles promised to tell us more about a female antiquities appraiser from the British Museum and her Italian husband who was a crime inspector on Capri, but now grows grapes in his vineyards in Tuscany. I'm suddenly all ears. Sir Thomas gave us a description of the crime, but I'm more interested in the people who were involved, what their motives were, and who stood to gain from the crime."

All eyes looked with anticipation to Lord Charles. "I did make that promise, didn't I?" he said with a sheepish grin.

Lynnette nodded her head. "And as a gentleman, you always keep your promises. Don't you?"

Lord Charles beamed. "I suppose she's got me there. So let me see, where shall I begin?" He motioned to the waiter for a champagne refill, and cleared his throat.

"Kathy, a most extraordinary woman, was born on a ranch in Gunnison, Colorado where she grew up and fell in love with Mark Stockton, the boy next door, who inherited a huge ranch when his father died. Not long after their marriage, Kathy was widowed when Mark was suddenly killed in a plane crash on their ranch.

"With the help of her dedicated foreman and team of ranch hands, she learned how to successfully work and manage a cattle ranch, but it was not her true calling in life. Her younger brother, who works at the Smithsonian Institute, encouraged her to seek the goals she had originally set for herself.

"Kathy took his advice, electing to return to school and study art history and archeology at Cambridge. Later, she became a leading appraiser of artifacts and antiquities while working as an organizer of exhibitions for the Metropolitan Museum in New York. That's how I came to know her. She helped arrange an exhibition of my collection at the Met Museum and again at the British Museum in London.

"She had just finished dismantling an oriental exhibition at the museum in London when the call came from homicide detective, Mario Regitti, an Italian-American on Capri, with a request to help appraise Ricardo Orcini's stolen items from photographs on hand. Their appraisal value had not yet been established before they disappeared.

Kathy had worked to catalogue Orcini's original collection some time ago and she was due for a vacation. She accepted the detective's invitation to combine work with pleasure, but little did she know that her pleasure trip would lead to a murder arrest and her second marriage.

"So, they met over a crime scene investigation. You see...there may still be hope for Minnie yet," Lynnette giggled.

"Don't tell me you're hoping Minnie finds a husband while we're on vacation and an investigation," Reginald laughed.

"Well, she said in the lift two days ago before we left Cairo, that she thought Boris, the gorilla, was cute and she was making eyes at the man who helped her onto the donkey the other day. As a woman, I notice these things, but far be it for me to gossip about Minnie and her proclivities. Please go on with your story Charles. I apologize for the interruption."

Lord Charles was delighted with Lynnette's comments and gave a hardy laugh. "Women...where would men be without them? However, I do hope you won't lose your ladies-maid and companion before the trip is finished," he added.

"Oh," she said, "no worries there. If there's to be a wedding, it will be in Yorkshire at Mayberry Manor or our place in South Hampton, I wouldn't pass up the opportunity of seeing Minnie walk down the path through the gardens for a June wedding."

"Sounds like you have everything planned," said Grace.

Lynnette grinned, "Minnie and I have talked it over, and all we need now is the groom."

"Splendid," said Reginald, He glanced at Lord Charles. "And now...I believe Charles was in the middle of his story."

"Oh, hardly in the middle, old chap," Lord Charles corrected. "However, I would like to mention detective Mario Regitti. I previously stated that he is an Italian-American. He met his first wife when he was working as a ski instructor in Switzerland.

"She was the only child of a wealthy, widowed wine grower in Tuscany, who died leaving everything to her. She and Mario were skiing when she was caught in an avalanche that separated them and unfortunately she wasn't found in time.

"Mario inherited the Villa Baldini estates consisting of several thousand rolling acres of well-established vineyards. Unfortunately he couldn't bring himself to live there and took a detective position on the Isle of Capri. He left the operation of the villa and the vineyards to his wife's aunt and uncle who had worked with her father for many years.

"That ends the story for now. I feel the need to get some rest and relax after my week of business in Cairo. We'll be meeting some of the Cairo Museum archeologists at the tomb site. I'll fill you in on their details over the next few days."

Lynnette was disappointed. "That can't be the end of your story about Mario and Kathy."

"Oh, most certainly not. That will continue tonight. Shall we meet for sunset cocktails on the top terrace later this evening? You won't want to miss the tranquil views as the Nile twists, winds, and snakes it way through the scenic desert terrain, under the light of a full moon. Until sunset, my friends." Lord Charles returned to his cabin for a short nap.

"I have to admit, Lord Charles can give an in-depth account of the events that took place on Capri. He was more involved than I in the whole case and worked with Scotland Yard to capture the one guard who stole the artifacts. And, on that note, Grace and I will take our leave and follow Lord Charles's example with an afternoon nap. Champagne with lunch tends to mellow one's energy."

Grace nodded in agreement. "We'll see you later. I think a little rest would be good for all of us."

Lynnette and Reginald stood as she yawned and stretched. "I

think I can take a hint. It's time for a little rest. I'm sure it's a combination of the heat, the food, the champagne, and the fact that we were up so early this morning. I better check on Minnie and let her know we will be in the cabin. She's probably still on the upper deck watching all the sailboats in the river."

Chapter Sixteen

Crime Is Everywhere

S ir Reginald and Lynnette wandered up to the top deck, where they found Minnie sitting with Boris having tea. "You really must speak with Minnie about your bodyguard. They shouldn't be seated together."

"Why? What's wrong with Minnie enjoying herself with someone whose job it is to follow her around anyway? Especially when I'm with you and we have Mr. Taylor watching over us. Besides, it isn't every day that Minnie gets to sit with a three-hundred-pound gorilla who appears to enjoy her company. I honestly think that bodyguards often carry their self-distancing to the extreme."

Reginald spread his hands and shrugged his shoulders. "I won't argue with your point of view. But he is supposed to be watching both of you."

"Precisely the point," Lynnette said leaning against his shoulder. "If I'm in the dining room and Minnie is on the observation deck, even Boris can't be expected to be in two places at once."

"Touché." Reginald gave her a short nodding bow. "Shall we go have a little rest before dressing for dinner and cocktails this evening?"

"Good idea, old man. I just need to let Minnie know I'm wearing purple tonight. She'll know which dress I want to have ready. I hate to interrupt their conversation, but it will only take a moment. Just wait here."

Sir Reginald leaned on the railing and watched the scenic landscape along the river flow by. He was reminded of how close Lynnette was to Minnie. She practically treated her like a sister. But then, she treated all of their staff like family. That was how she ran Mayberry Manor so efficiently.

Lynnette rejoined him and he could see mischief in her sparkling green eyes. She was planning something important, but he knew better than to ask. She would tell him at her own chosen time when she had worked out whatever it is. She shook her head to clear her thoughts. "I have to admit that Mr. Rykoff has a personality that tends to grow on you. Perhaps I was too hasty in my judgment of his character and I certainly wouldn't want to stand in the way of Minnie's future happiness."

"Heavens! You don't think it's gone that far do you?" Reginald asked with serious reservations.

"I'm not so sure, but we will give it time, and let nature take its course," she smiled as she hooked her arm in his. "Now, about that nap, old man." They descended the stairs and strolled along the inner corridor.

Returning to their suite, Lynnette was the first to enter and she quickly turned to Reginald. "Something's not right. Someone's been in this room looking for something." Her keen eyes caught items that had been moved and not put back in the same place. Having a photographic memory has always helped her to remember where she left things. "Didn't you notice there was no *click* when you turned the key in the door? It must have been left open."

"I know I locked the door when we left for lunch, but you're right. There was no resistance when I turned the key." Reginald immediately checked the safe in the wardrobe. "The safe is empty! Your jewels are missing!" he exclaimed.

"No they aren't." Lynnette said as she moved about the room putting things back in place. "I gave them to Minnie for safe keeping. But we'd better check her room as well before we sound the alarm and make any report."

"Good show!" Reginald was already out the door and heading for Minnie's room with Lynnette locking the door and following close behind.

"What made you think to leave your jewels with Minnie?"

"A woman's intuition. How many thieves would look at Minnie and see expensive jewelry?" Lynnette said.

Reginald knocked on Minnie's cabin door and it was opened

immediately. "Yes, my lady? Did you need something else?"

"May we come in, Minnie? It's a matter of importance."

"Of course, Miss Lynn. I just got here myself. If it's about Mr. Boris, I..."

"No, no, no Minnie. That's not the problem, at least not for now." She and Reginald stepped into the room and closed the door. "Our room was broken into and they searched the place for something. We need to check the safe in your room to be sure the jewels are still there."

Minnie went to the wardrobe and opened the safe. The emeralds were in their black box and the pearls were in a velvet bag next to them. "They're still here," she said.

Reginald was suddenly alert. "They took the copied documents. The ones Ahmet gave us in Istanbul. The map of the tomb site and the one with all those numbers and times on it. They were also in the safe in our room."

Lynnette smiled and shook her head. "No they didn't. I took them out when I took the jewels out and gave them to Minnie for safe keeping. Sorry, but I forgot to mention it to you."

He looked again in Minnie's safe. "But they aren't here. There aren't any papers in this safe."

Lynnette smiled and glanced at Minnie. "Did you put them where I told you?"

"Yes Miss Lynn. I rolled them up and tucked them into your pantyhose like you said." Minnie turned, pulled open a drawer of the bureau and handed the rolled package to Lynnette.

"Perfectly safe, old man. Obviously the thief is not a woman." She unrolled the garment and handed the papers to Reginald. He handed them back to her.

"Maybe it's a good idea to keep them where they were."

Lynnette grinned at Reginald and without taking her eyes off of him, handed the papers to Minnie "Find a different pair of hose Minnie, I'm wearing these tonight with the purple chiffon dress."

He shook his head. "I just love it when you get that—I told you so look on your face."

She laughed quietly, "Well—At least things are still intact. Nothing was stolen and the room is not damaged. It would be important to mention it to Taylor and Boris, but I hardly think we need to file a report with the boat's captain. Attempted robbery is a rather feeble claim, and no one's been injured."

"I agree, but we need to let him know that someone was able to get into the room and the safe. They must have had keys or knew how to pick the locks." Reginald said. "We'll keep this buttoned down. I don't want to alarm Sir Thomas or Lord Charles without due cause. However, I think I should let the Home Office know about the room search. And of course they'll want to know where the documents were hidden. That could be a bit embarrassing to explain."

"You don't have to give them all the details, dear. Just say that the papers were safely hidden in the room of my maid. We don't want to give away all our secrets. Do we Minnie?"

"No ma'am," she giggled.

"And about Boris," Lynnette added, "don't rush into anything, if you know what I mean. There's plenty of fish in the Nile; so play the game of Go Fish slowly."

"Yes ma'am. I've learned by watching you," Minnie answered.

"I'm not so sure I'm the best example, Minnie. When I was a little girl, my mother used to tell me, 'Don't do as I do Lynn. Just do as I tell you to do.' We'll leave you with that thought and I'll ring when I want to get dressed."

Reginald was smiling as they departed and closed the door. Lynnette tilted her head and gave him a questioning glance. "What are you smiling about? We saved the jewels and the documents. Minnie and I are a team."

"I was just thinking how well you know how to handle your teammates."

"Oh! That's easy. You don't grow up with someone for almost twenty years and not know how they think. Especially someone like Minnie, who is a creature of habit. I can't stop the process of her desires. However, a word of caution will lower the heat and let things simmer for now. Minnie will do what Minnie will do. I suppose she actually has learned by watching me, but I can't take all the credit. Her mother was a strong willed woman, and on occasions, my mother followed her suggestions. So you see, dear, it runs in the family."

"No wonder my mother told me to marry you," Reginald grinned.

"I'm not surprised." Lynnette said as she entered their suite. "Your mother was an intelligent woman. She told me that I would be the wind in your sails, and that you would have a steady hand on the rudder. So far, it's been smooth sailing, wouldn't you agree?"

"Without a doubt," he said, "Without a doubt."

There was a knock on the door behind him. Reginald opened it and found a steward standing there with a letter on a silver plate. "A letter for Sir Reginald, sir."

Taking the envelope, he closed the door. "It's a letter from Sir Thomas. He says their room was searched during lunch today. Nothing was taken." The phone in their suite began to ring and he answered and listened then hung up. "That was Thomas. He wants to meet me in the lounge."

"I'm not surprised," said Lynnette. "This all started on the Orient Express and somehow it's all tied together with the four of us and now Lord Charles as well. The five musketeers have a case to solve and someone doesn't want us getting too close."

"I'm not quite sure how Lord Charles figures into this case, my dear." Reginald said.

"I'm afraid you're forgetting one important point, old man."

Reginald gave her an inquisitive look. "And what would that be," he asked.

"The two missing workers from the excavation site," she smiled.

"Are you...? No you're not—But the mere suggestion implies that you think the sinister Egyptian crook on the train, the baroness kidnapped and now in the hospital, the powdered opium discovered in her compartment, the missing trunk, the documents found by the Turkish secret service, and the search of our rooms on this boat, all have something to do with the museum project in the Valley of the Monkeys.

"Although it stretches the imagination to the limits, the perspective is one to consider, however, that's a lot of loose threads you're weaving together and the web keeps growing. I sincerely hope we'll be able to tangle the spider in the middle."

"Do you want me to come with you to meet Sir Thomas?" she asked.

"I don't think that will be necessary. You need to stay in the room for now and try to get some rest. I'll be sure Boris is on watch and I'll take Taylor with me. They need to know what's been happening and brought up to speed. There's someone on this boat who has an interest in those documents, or a jewel thief who has come up empty-handed, and we need to be on the alert."

"I don't want to frighten Minnie, but perhaps I should put her on alert as well," Lynnette said.

"It might be better to keep Minnie low keyed on these plans. The less she knows the more nonchalant she will be and perhaps that will throw them off the scent. If I were in England I would say, hide Minnie. Servants there have a knack for knowing everything that's going on even before we do. Fortunately, people in other countries don't think of that."

"You had better get on with your meeting. It's not polite to keep Sir Thomas waiting." She smiled and kissed his cheek. "And tell Taylor I'll be wearing purple tonight so I won't get lost in the crowd."

"Lynnette my love, you could never get lost in a crowd. My eyes would find you in a minute."

Chapter Seventeen

Tying Loose Ends

Sir Thomas wasn't waiting in the lounge currently occupied by a few other guests. Reginald asked the steward in charge of the lounge if Sir Thomas had arrived for their meeting.

"Yes sir. If you'll follow me, please." He led the way to the captain's quarters, and knocked on the door. "They're in here, sir."

The captain opened the door and invited him in. Sir Thomas greeted him. "I asked the captain if there was an empty room available for our little meeting, but they are full to the brim. He kindly suggested we could meet here. It's the most private space on the boat other than the loo," he chuckled.

"This is much appreciated, sir." Reginald thanked the captain.

The Egyptian smiled, "I use this room very little. I am in the office, and on deck more often than not. A steward will be outside the door should you need anything and I have ordered mint tea delivered with my compliments." There was a knock at the door. "Ah! That would be the tea. I will leave you now." Tea was delivered and the captain departed.

Sir Thomas seated himself comfortably in the conversation area consisting of two overstuffed chairs, and a small table. Sir Reginald joined him as he poured the tea. "We still need to speak softly. I don't even trust the steward outside the door."

"I didn't mention it on the phone when you called, but our room was searched during lunch also. Lynnette knew it the minute she entered the room. I have to admit, they had plenty of time and were very neat about it. However, they left the safe open. Whoever it was, had a key or knew how to pick locks. The door to the room was not damaged. It was closed, but not relocked."

"Then it had to be the same person who searched our room. The method of entry is identical. We hadn't stored anything in the safe so it was empty. Grace refuses to travel with a lot of jewelry and I keep all our needed papers in my briefcase, which is with me at all times. What do you think they were searching for?" Sir Thomas asked.

"The papers that Ahmet gave us at the airport in Istanbul. You remember, the ones of the map, the code-numbers and other strange number and letter combinations on them. I thought they had been taken, but Lynnette had given them to Minnie for safe keeping, along with her jewelry that I had put in the safe. Fortunately, Minnie's room was not searched."

"I think we need to start at the beginning and work our way to the present putting the pieces of the puzzle together. I sense there's a possibility that Lord Charles and the tomb excavation could be involved," Sir Thomas said.

Reginald nodded his approval. "So, you and Lynnette are thinking alike. She believes that the missing workers are connected with the events on the train for starters."

Sir Thomas had a thoughtful expression on his face as he tapped his nose with his index finger. "She could be right. Perhaps they knew something illegal was happening at the tomb site. Possibly they attempted to blackmail someone and were disposed of before they could point fingers."

"It's a thought," said Reginald. "Something strange is definitely happening at the site. Otherwise, the Home Office wouldn't send me here with two bodyguards. However, the workers have been missing over two weeks now and the police haven't lifted a finger to find them. They made lots of excuses but no results."

Sir Thomas nodded in agreement. "That's true, old chap. And then, of course, there's the business of the baroness, who was arrested for dealing in drugs. We need information from her and we haven't heard from Ahmet. I wonder if she's made any statements as yet."

"I sent Ahmet an inquiry from the hotel this morning before we left. So far, I've not heard back from him. However, perhaps I'll get a response this evening. He did say he would keep us informed and I feel we can trust him. He's not like the Egyptian police." Reginald said.

"Agreed, old boy. Agreed. So that brings us to the room searches today. If someone is after those documents they won't give up until they find them. Where are they now?"

Reginald grinned. "Safely tucked away in a pair of Lynnette's pantyhose and stored in a drawer in Minnie's cabin."

Sir Thomas chuckled and shook his head. "They're probably safer there than they would be in the Tower of London."

Reginald tried to control his laughter. "I didn't want to disturb him, but don't you think we should inform Lord Charles about this meeting?"

"Oh, absolutely, dear boy! He's actually rather sharp when it comes to viewing things from a different angle. And if it has anything to do with the project he's sponsored, it would be only fair that he's informed. Remember... All for one and one for all!" Sir Thomas stood.

"We've uncovered three crimes so far—drug smuggling, kidnapping, assault, and possibly prevented a murder. That's not bad for a week's work. But now comes the difficult task of tying the strings together. If indeed there is any connection with the missing persons at the tomb site that could involve some very important people. We'll need to be discreet with our inquiries and the people we speak with. The less they know what we know, the better. I'll fill Grace in on what we've covered if you'll warn Lynnette. Perhaps this evening, one of us, will have the opportunity to speak with Lord Charles in confidence."

Sir Reginald rose from the comfortable chair, "I'm beginning to regret my idea of a holiday in Egypt to surprise Lynnette. I wish she were safe at Mayberry Manor, surrounded by fog and rain. I know she's excited about being here, but I don't like putting her in danger."

Sir Thomas patted Reginald's shoulder. "Cheer up, old chap. She wouldn't miss this for the world, and with two bodyguards and a protective maid on board, I'm sure she's in good hands. Not to mention that she's an excellent shot and knows how to protect herself.

Now let's give the captain his room back and check on our ladies."

"Speaking of ladies," I've been meaning to ask you why your staff at Penderleigh, from butler to kitchen maid, are all females"

Sir Thomas chuckled as they left the room and closed the door. "To put it bluntly, you have to admit they're prettier to look at. However, I also find them much more efficient than males. After all, women are far more adept at running a house, cooking, cleaning, and making it feel like a home. They make excellent chauffeurs and secretaries. And of course, they take good care of me. I rest my case."

"I think I see your point." Reginald patted Thomas on the back. "And they seem to know where to find something you have lost or misplaced. Lynnette calls it her intuition. I call it witchcraft."

"Well, old boy, you'll have to admit, she makes a very pretty witch. Better hide the broomstick so she can't escape," Thomas grinned. "Maybe they can conjure up a spell and solve our mysterious investigation."

Reginald's face lit up and he said jokingly, "Would you like to make a wager on that last comment?"

Thomas looked surprised. "I don't normally wager on the instincts and abilities of others. It's never a sure thing. However, in this case I'll make an exception. Shall we say five pounds?"

"Why not make it ten? I'll bank on the male intelligence."

"You're on!" said Sir Thomas, offering his hand to seal the wager. "Don't let the skirts fool you."

"And don't forget to bring the documents this evening. I want to show them to Lord Charles. Perhaps he'll have a clue to their connection. It's best to share our information so we are all in the same cart. I'll fill Grace in on our meeting. We have an agreement. She lets me off the leash as long as she knows what I'm doing. Otherwise, she won't let me out of her sight. That's the bodyguard training in her. I actually think she sleeps with one eye open."

Reginald burst into a laugh as they parted. "We'll see you at sunset."

Lynnette glanced up from her chair by the window as he entered their suite and noticed the serious, pensive look on his face. "That must have been some meeting. I just ordered some tea to be delivered. Will you join me and tell me all about it?"

"I thought you were going to lie down."

"Yes, dear. That was after lunch. It's now tea time and I'm well rested. Come, join me."

"Do you mind if I stretch out and relax for a moment? I'll tell you all about it before we meet for cocktails this evening," he said.

"Of course, old man. How inconsiderate of me. You do look as though you could use a little nap. By the way, a wire came while you were out." She handed it to him. "It's from Istanbul."

He opened and read it as he slipped out of his shoes.

Need to talk with you...Stop
More information available on shipping-schedules
and merchandise...Stop
Contact me on private cell number tomorrow.

Ahmet

He handed it to Lynnette as he headed for the bedroom. "I wonder what it means?" she asked.

He hung up his jacket and stretched out on top of the bed. "We'll know soon enough tomorrow."

A knock came at the cabin door. She closed the bedroom door and answered the knock. Tea had arrived. Still carrying the cable in her hand, she sat down to have her tea and contemplate the message. Her mind was churning with various conspiracies.

Shipping schedules? Could that refer to the document with numbers and times? Merchandise? It must have something to do with the missing trunk. Was it artifacts, drugs, jewels or other stolen items to be sold on the "black market?" And, where does the map of the tomb fit in the picture? Questions needed answers.

"All in due time," she said aloud. "All in due time." She could hear Reginald's snoring coming from the bedroom as she sipped her tea and stared at the cable in her hands attempting to put the message and her thoughts in order.

Lynnette reached for a piece of paper and pen on the small writing desk behind her. As she visualized the secret document in her photographic memory, she wondered where to begin. She drew lines forming three columns and closed her eyes. She remembered that column number one was in single digits from one to six.

It occurred to her that they could possibly indicate the days of the week, but then there would be seven. Unless, of course Sunday was excluded, then the six would work. A shipping schedule would normally not include Sundays.

She moved on to the second blank column. This presented a puzzle, but not insurmountable for her imagination. Those numbers appeared to indicate the times in a day. A light clicked on in her brain and she slowly smiled. These numbers corresponded with military times. Thus 1:30 would indicate an early morning time, while fifteen would be at three in the afternoon. Everyone but Americans use military time so that would stand to reason.

The third column of numbers and letters offered the biggest challenge. Were they stock numbers, tracking numbers of shipments, codes indicating locations on a map, or perhaps something else entirely?

Lynnette searched her memory. Somewhere, at some time in the past, she had seen such numbers and letters used. Was it her uncle...no it was her father who had told her what they meant and why they were used.

It was in Dover, and again in Brighton on a summer holiday. They were sailing when she asked about boats and where they got their names. His answer included the fact that not all boats or ships had names, but they all had coded letters and numbers issued by the maritime offices around the world, making it easy to register their movements from port to port or if they got lost at sea. This was an explanation that any eight year old could understand.

Quickly she realized the document was not in code and no cypher was needed. It was no longer a mystery. She smiled as she folded her paper and slipped it into her evening purse for safe keeping. She could wait until cocktail time to let the others in on her discovery.

Chapter Eighteen

Lynnette's Discovery

A giant golden ball of fire began its descent behind the rugged, hills of the stark and distant landscape of the river valley. This part of the desert was not the soft rolling sand dunes of the Sahara. The river had carved a broad deep scar from south to north across the face of Egypt, leaving the fertile valley of rich soil in the center, surrounding it with ages of eroded limestone and sandstone canyons, etched by the rains and wind, with a lonely and desolate beauty of an aged queen on her throne.

A crescent moon was high overhead as the sun disappeared from view and the stars in the sky began to sparkle in the glow of twilight. It was cocktail time on the upper deck and the striped canopy had been rolled back to offer the best views and a soothing, cool breeze captured the tranquility of the evening desert air.

Swaying palms cast their lingering shadows across the flowing Nile as swallows dipped and dived catching small insects for their evening meal. The distant sound of crickets hiding in the rushes kept time with the music floating like a mist on the now black water of the river.

Sir Thomas and Grace were seated at a round table with Lord Charles Marquis, who was speaking with the captain of the boat. "Ah...here they are now," said Lord Charles. "We were just talking about you and your secret meeting while I was napping this afternoon. Sleeping on the job, so they say," he chuckled. "The captain here has offered the use of his private quarters anytime we have need while on this cruise. Abdul Mohamed and I are old friends and have made this journey many times together. Of course, he does it more often than I."

Abdul grinned and bowed. "You are my honored guests. Please enjoy yourselves." He bowed again and began to circulate among the other guests. Lynnette and Reginald ordered drinks and settled in around the rather private table.

Lord Charles was curious about the meeting. Reginald and

Thomas had already briefed Lynnette and Grace. He looked at Reginald, "I understand you have an excavation map of the tomb site in the Valley of the Monkeys. I would like to see it, to see if it is of the site we are working on for the museum. There are numerous fake maps of tomb sites all over Egypt. It's rather a tourist's curio to take back home and show friends. However, I will most certainly be able to verify if it is truly authentic. Perhaps at breakfast tomorrow morning."

"No need to wait until then," Reginald said. "We stopped by Minnie's cabin on the way here and I brought both documents with me."

Lynnette was as anxious as a child with the correct answer to a test. "Reggie received a cable from our friend Ahmet in Istanbul."

Reginald held up his hand and stopped her from saying anymore. "We'll get to that in a moment. First I would like to verify the map, if Lord Charles will help us to do that." He spread the folded document on the table in front of Charles. Lord Charles put on his spectacles and held the map close for a better view.

"That's the site," he announced with surprise. "It's not far from KV22, the area chosen as the burial site by Amenhotep III for his own enormous tomb, part way up the valley. His son Akhenaten also began a tomb in the valley, but later relocated it near the new capital at Amarna.

"The new tomb is thought to be that of Ay, who succeeded Tutankhamun from 1327 to 1323 BC. Due to his unexpected early death, King Tut was buried in KV62—a tomb in the traditional section of the Valley of the Kings.

"The tomb is actually accessed by a dirt road shown here." He pointed to a squiggly line on the document. "It's close to two kilometers up the desolate valley past sheer rock cliffs, capturing the silence and atmosphere once found in the Valley of the Kings. Hidden where you would least expect to find it, and possibly the only reason why grave robbers had not discovered it. May I ask where you came by that map?"

"I'll explain that in a moment. Reginald took the map from Lord Charles. "I assume we are confirmed that this is a map of the tomb where the two workers vanished." Lord Charles nodded his head.

Next we need to address this second document that was found folded along with the map." He handed it to Lord Charles.

"We haven't been able to decipher what all the numbers and letters mean. However, I received a cable from Ahmet in Istanbul and I'm to call him tomorrow. It appears that they could have something to do with shipping schedules."

Lord Charles shook his head, "I haven't a clue. Show me antiquities and artifacts from ancient worlds and I can talk for hours, but you lose me when it comes to numbers."

Sir Thomas and Grace glanced at each other and chuckled, "We know precisely what you mean, neither of us have a head for figures, much less codes and cyphers."

Lynnette slowly sipped her martini and smiled. "I know what it means, if you would care to listen."

Reginald glanced at her with surprise. "How can you suddenly know what it means? I only got the cable this afternoon and we won't learn anything from Ahmet until tomorrow,"

Lynnette leaned forward and placed her cocktail glass on the table and picked up her handbag. "While you were resting this afternoon at tea time, I did some calculations and I'm sure I have made the same discovery that the secret service people in Istanbul have."

Lord Charles was the first to speak. "In that case, my dear, perhaps you would like to share this secret with the rest of the musketeers."

"I would be delighted," she answered. Taking a slip of paper from her small but heavy evening bag, she unfold it for all to see, and began to explain. "The first column is for the days of the week. Sunday is zero, Monday is 1, Tuesday 2...etc. That's why there are only six single digit numbers." She scanned their faces to see if there were any questions. None appearing, she continued.

Column two is for the time of day. Based on military time, the numbers appear from 1 to 12 for the morning hours and 13 to 24 for the evening hours. For example 1:30 would be in the early morning and 13:30 would indicate the afternoon." Again she paused for the dramatic effect. "Are you following me?" she asked. Four heads nodded in unison.

"The next column was the tricky part, but having sailed in the channel and off the shores of Brighton I remembered my dad telling me that all ships and boats are numbered. Some have numbers only, but many have both numbers and letters jumbled together. Not all ships are named, but they all have numbers and are easily tracked by satellite through maritime offices around the globe."

She set back and took a sip of her martini and shrugged her shoulders, "Well...if I'm wrong, I'll be the first to admit it. But what do you think?" She looked at their eyes, set in faces veiled in thought. A moment of silence prevailed. Her own heart was pounding with what she hoped was the truth.

"By George, old girl. Where on earth did that come from?" Reginald was staring at her with questionable pride.

"Woman's intuition," said Grace, raising her glass to Lynnette.

Lynnette nodded to Grace, "I suppose one might say you're right. Especially if one happens to be a woman," she grinned, and raised her martini glass in response.

"Now all we need is confirmation from Ahmet tomorrow," added Sir Reginald. "Do you think I should tell him first or let him tell us?"

"I think it would be interesting to let Lynnette tell him and ask if she is correct. But of course the polite channel of protocol would be for Reginald to listen to Ahmet's news first to save any embarrassment, by all means. Then if she is right, tell him that Lynnette had reached the same conclusions," said Lord Charles. "But, of course, that is for you to decide, Reginald."

"Are we all on a liquid diet or is anyone hungry?" asked Lynnette, attempting to lighten the subject of conversation.

"I wonder if they have camel on the menu," Reginald said, taking the hint.

Lynnette laughed. "Give it up, dear. They don't eat camels in Egypt."

"Oh, but they do," said Lord Charles. "I've heard it's quite a delicacy, though I've never had the stomach to try it. Shall we retire to the dining room below?"

Reginald took Lynnette's arm and whispered in her ear, "You never cease to amaze me."

"That's why you married me," she said with a two martini giggle.

The stars twinkled above in the black velvet of a night sky, and the reflection of a cradled, crescent moon floated on the waters of the Nile, as they descended the stairs to the dining room. Savory aromas of Indian cuisine filled her senses and made Lynnette's mouth water.

"You're not going to order camel, are you?" she asked Reginald.

"Of course not, my love. Remember, they're in short supply," he joked.

Chapter Nineteen

Good News and Bad

eginald and Lynnette had breakfast in their cabin, while reading the English newspaper and Ahmet's wi re over again. "It's almost nine o'clock, I wonder if Ahmet's in his office at this hour?" Reginald mumbled.

Lynnette was dressed in her apricot silk robe and Reginald wore a white cotton robe with the ships logo on it. "He doesn't have to be in his office, dear. You're calling him on his private cell number, remember?"

"Well, I didn't want to disturb him too early," he nodded.

"If I'm correct, Istanbul, Turkey is an hour earlier than Egypt. That would make it ten o'clock his time. He's probably waiting for your call right now. Remember, don't say a word about my theory until we hear what the secret service has discovered."

Reginald placed his call and Ahmet picked up on the first ring tone. "Good morning my friend! I hope you are enjoying the cruise."

"We are," Reginald said. "We got your wire and are anxious to know the latest news."

"My apologies we couldn't speak yesterday, but I am working on two other cases. However, I have some interesting news about the baroness." Reginald turned his cell phone volume up so that Lynnette could hear their conversation. "Although her voice was scratchy after being strangled, she sang like a canary. She admitted to drug trafficking, and implicated the Egyptian fellow, whom she thought was a transfer contact. She was told the drugs were going to Russia and would be shipped from Varna but wasn't expecting the attack in her cabin on the train.

"She said it wasn't the Egyptian who attacked her. It was a white Russian, who had been following her, and was waiting in her cabin with the Egyptian when she returned to the train. She understood their conversation in Russian before she was attacked. They were planning to steal the drug cargo and split the profits. The Russian almost killed her but she passed out; and thinking she was dead he dropped her to the floor.

"The Egyptian must have noticed she was still alive. He drug her, put her in the empty trunk, then beat and raped her at the chateau, and would have killed her, but we got there in time. According to her confession, they thought she was a double agent and wanted to eliminate her. She had outlived her use to them.

"Unfortunately, the second wooden trunk has not been found on the property. Most likely it is already in Russia. The Egyptian admits to nothing and hasn't said a word. We can hold him for a while on suspected kidnapping and assault, but if she doesn't file a complaint we'll have to let him go. There's no evidence against him, unless we can find the missing trunk.

"Meanwhile, the Turkish secret service deciphered the numbers document. It wasn't a cypher but a shipping schedule." His explanation coincided with Lynnette's calculations.

"I'm delighted to tell you that my wife came to the same conclusions, even down to the numbers used to identify the boats."

"That's amazing! But I'm not surprised. She's an intelligent woman. Please convey my congratulations. However, she might be happy to know that the numbers used are all on yachts and larger vessels moving through the Mediterranean, the Black Sea and the Red Sea. We believe the drugs are carried in smaller vessels like the felucca, down the Nile, then transferred to larger yachts and ships whose numbers appear anchored in appointed places at the times indicated and on the dates shown."

"Wasn't Favio Orcini convicted of using his father's container ships for drug trafficking a few years ago?" Reginald asked.

"That's correct. The company was fined and later sold by Adam Orcini, the younger son and playboy who lives on Cypress. He didn't want anything to do with container shipping," added Ahmet.

"Cypress? That's not that far off the coast of Egypt. Perhaps there could still be some connections," Reginald speculated.

"We've kept a close surveillance on the new owners, but they're clean. However, there are numerous villa owners with yachts in that part of the Med. There could be several involved. We're setting up a sting operation once we get the manpower together.

"Meanwhile, I'll keep you posted on any new developments. Please give my regards to your wife and to Sir Thomas and Grace. I don't need to warn you to be careful. I know you will and you have your own bodyguards. We'll be in touch. My work may bring me to Luxor in a day or so."

"We'll be delighted to see you again and thanks for keeping us informed." Reginald disconnected the call. Lynnette was leaning close to him. "I guess you were able to hear the conversation," he smiled.

"Yes, love. It was nice of you to turn the volume up, and now we know even more to tell the other musketeers. This is turning into a novel. I should have brought a larger notebook for our travel adventure. But I'm sure I can find one in Luxor. Now we need to get dressed before everyone begins to wonder if we've been kidnapped or vanished like the workers at the tomb."

"Good heavens, woman! Don't even think that," Reginald voiced with surprise.

"I know, dear. So let's shake a leg. It'll be lunch time before we know it, and I think we are supposed to dock overnight at the next stop. Lord Charles was going to tell us all about the temples we're going to visit. He is absolutely full of knowledge about Egypt's past; but then, why shouldn't he be? He is one of the foremost, noted, collectors of Egyptian antiquities. Come, come...don't dawdle over the paper." Lynnette was practically dressed.

"Don't you need Minnie to help you dress?"

Lynnette chuckled, "Why bother Minnie when I have you to help me? I've been dressing myself for years. Minnie takes care of my clothes and keeps them clean, pressed and mended. Will you zip me up, old man?" Reginald stood and gave her zipper a tug.

She stood studying his clothes in the wardrobe. "Now let's see, what will you wear today for temple viewing?"

Reginald stepped in front of her. "Don't worry, love. I can dress myself. Why don't you ring for the steward and have breakfast removed. I'll be with you in a spot."

~

"Ah! There you are," said Grace. Thomas and Lord Charles were seated on each side of her. They had been watching the multitude of boats motoring and sailing up and down the river. It was like the trains coming and going at Victoria Station.

"Looks like the river traffic has picked up a bit," Lynnette commented.

"It always does when we get close to Abydos," said Lord Charles. It's a big tourist's attraction point. We'll be docking there just before lunch. Then we'll visit the temples of Seti I. Abydos is by far Ancient Egypt's most important burial center. But first we want to hear what news you have from Istanbul. I assume you've spoken with the secret service agent there. Forgive me, but I forget his name."

"Ahmet," said Sir Reginald. He then proceeded to explain their conversation, pointing out all the matching details that Lynnette had discovered with the documents. "It involves a number of yachts and ships, but now they have the registration numbers and will be watching their movements. He mentioned the Red Sea, but there are no ports of entry from the Nile into the Red Sea. If things are being smuggled in that direction, it would have to be by land."

"Lord Charles received some disturbing news this morning," said Grace. Everyone stared at Charles.

"I hesitate to spoil all the good news, but it appears that one of the workers was found dead this morning on the steps leading out of the tomb. He shouldn't have been in the tomb at night, so they are doing an inventory to see if anything is missing. Most likely he snuck into the tomb to steal something and was struck."

"You mean he was murdered?" Lynnette asked.

"No. That's what's strange. There wasn't a mark on him except for the snake bite. They believe it was a cobra. They do live in the desert you know. The man's heart must have been racing as he hurried up the steps of the tomb, pumping the venom quickly into his bloodstream. It doesn't take long without the antivenin to counteract the effect of the poison. That's why I wear high boots when I go hunting in New Guinea and Borneo. However, snakes there can drop out of the trees, so we have to be extra careful and carry the antivenin with us."

Lynnette was curious. "How did the snake get into the tomb?"

"I would wager, the same way the worker did," said Sir Thomas. "Though, perhaps the snake was inside when the worker arrived. There aren't any doors on the tomb."

"Well...," said Lynnette, "on that cheerful note shall we retire to the dining room and have lunch. I want to be fortified for the tour of the temple."

"Splendid idea," Lord Charles smiled. "We should be docking shortly and I've arranged for a special tour with just the eight of us."

"But there's only five of us. Who are the other three?" Lynnette asked.

"If my calculations are correct, there are five of us, one lady's maid and two bodyguards," he answered.

"How did you know about the bodyguards?" asked Reginald.

Lord Charles chuckled. "My dear boy, the Home Office wouldn't dare send a person of your stature off to Egypt to investigate a case without making sure you were protected. If I wasn't already acquainted with Jason Taylor, I might not have noticed him, but the other man is hard to miss, and I've seen him watching Miss Minnie and Lynnette like a hawk. I just assumed they would be making the tour with us."

Lynnette couldn't stop herself from laughing, "You certainly have some tricks up your sleeve Charles."

He smiled. "No tricks to it, my dear. When you've been around the country and are as old as I am, you just have a nose for it." He offered her his arm. "May I escort you to lunch Lady Lynnette?"

She took his arm and grinned. "Charmed, I assure you." They led the way as the others followed behind.

Lynnette whispered into his ear, "Minnie will be so pleased. Thank you for including her."

"My pleasure, my dear. My pleasure."

Chapter Twenty

The Temples

By the time everyone had finished their lunch, the boat had docked in Abydos, where they were met by the private tour director and headed off for the Temples of Abydos, once the epicenter of the cult of Osiris. Here is where the pharaoh, Seti I, built a magnificent temple rising above the river Nile, which he dedicated to this Egyptian god.

Lord Charles gathered his group at the base of the first terrace. "Our guide, Rashid Amari, has agreed to allow me to act as your guide today with his assistance. I hope I'm worthy of this honor."

"You could always teach me a few things," said Rashid in jest. "But I would like to welcome your special guests to our city of Abydos. May your visit here be both pleasant and enlightening."

"Thank you Rashid." Lord Charles signaled for the group to follow him, and with that their tour began.

"Built of limestone and laid out on three levels, this temple was once the epicenter and vortex of cult worship, which made it Ancient Egypt's most important necropolis," Lord Charles announced.

They approached the first terrace which was basically in ruins. The original facade designed with giant stone columns, parts of which now lay scattered and broken, were all that was left.

Charles spread his arms as they gazed at the first courtyard, now a sunbaked expanse of hardened sand. "This area was once an amazing garden filled with fountains and reflecting pools of water, surrounded by tropical plants and exotic flowers. The sheer grandeur of a tropical paradise must have been impressive. Unfortunately, today I'm afraid you'll have to use your imagination."

As they wandered through the various rooms inside, the air was cooled by the thickness of the limestone walls. Lynnette was glad that Minnie had recommended taking a shawl. Lord Charles pointed out the hieroglyphics and delicately detailed stone carvings as he explained their meaning. Everyone was speechless over the era's artistry of vividly colored paintings on the walls and ceilings depicting historical scenes of temple ceremonies.

Massive sculpted columns, eight and ten feet in diameter, lined the courtyards, and chambers, decorated with colorful reliefs, and divided into seven separate temples for the gods Osiris, Isis, Horus, Ptah, Re-Harakhte, Amun, and of course, the deified Pharaoh Seti I.

As they neared the end of their tour, Lynnette tugged on Reginald's arm. "Where did the bodyguards go?" she asked.

He slowly glanced around the temple in which they were now standing and shook his head. "I noticed they disappeared when we were in the temple of Horus, but then I saw them again in the temple of Amun," he whispered. "Possibly they spotted something or someone they needed to check out. I'm sure they're doing what bodyguards are supposed to do. No need to be concerned."

"I know I'm supposed to ignore them," Lynnette whispered, "but it's not easy to do when you look at Boris. I had the feeling we were being followed all morning, but with two bodyguards nearby, is it any wonder?" she said.

Minnie, who stood next to her, couldn't help but hear their whispers, and tapped her on the arm then pointed across the room. Boris had returned, but she couldn't detect any change in his facial expression. He wore his mask of boredom well. A moment later Jason Taylor was standing next to him. All present and accounted for, she thought, but where had they been?

In the meantime, Lord Charles was wrapping up his mono- logue, "By all means, we mustn't miss one of the most important features here, known as the Gallery of the Kings. It's a long corridor depicting the famous Abydos Pharaoh List, recording the names of Egyptian rulers, from the first pharaoh of Egypt, Menes, to Seti and Ramses II. Then, of course, they added 76 revered royal ancestors. For the wealthy pious Egyptians, there was no greater honor than to be buried beside the tomb of Osiris, which we are not seeing today because it is closed. Of course, the names of unimportant or illegitimate rulers were omitted," Charles added with a wave of dismissal.

That was the end of their tour. The bodyguards were waiting outside the exit and moved in tandem with them to the waiting autos. Sir Reginald started to ask Jason about their disappearance, but Taylor put a finger to his own lips, indicating silence. Reginald got the message and nothing more was said. Lynnette had not missed this exchange and knew they would learn later what had drawn the guard's attention.

Once aboard the barge everyone scattered in different directions. Grace and Lynnette decided to rest while Minnie made her way to the upper viewing deck to watch the activity of the sailing boats and people along the river. Boris was not far behind to keep an eye on her.

Thomas and Reginald followed Jason into the dining room bar. The room was currently empty except for staff setting tables for the evening meal and a bartender, who was half asleep. They ordered their drinks and moved to a table in the corner.

Jason was the first to speak. "I didn't wish to be rude back at the temple, but you never know who might be listening in."

"That's quite understood. Perhaps now that we're alone you can enlighten us as to your disappearance in the temple. Were we in any danger?" Reginald asked. "I can't say for sure if there was any danger," Jason said with a shake of his head. "But we realized that two men had the group under surveillance through the first three temples. They tagged us and knew we had spotted them. That's when we split up." He glanced around the room as another couple entered and a waiter delivered their drinks, then continued. "We pursued them slowly, so not to draw attention, but lost them in a large crowd of arriving tourists. They knew we were tailing them."

"Was it anyone from our barge?" Sir Thomas inquired.

Jason shook his head. "No...that is to say, we didn't recognize them. They were dressed in the native Egyptian gallibaya. To be honest, it was their clothing that first caught our attention. Tourists only wear the gallibaya in the evenings and at parties, so they were most likely Egyptian."

Sir Thomas thought it was time to let Jason know about their rooms being searched. "We haven't mentioned this before now, but on the morning we left Giza, both our rooms were searched."

Jason gave a look of surprise. "Why did you not inform us?"

Reginald quickly offered an explanation. "Nothing was taken. The rooms were carefully searched by someone who had a key to the safes and the doors; unless they were seasoned experts at picking locks. Lynnette had given her jewelry and some papers of mine to Minnie for safe keeping. Her room was not searched. However, as nothing was stolen and nothing was damaged, there was no evidence of the search, only our speculation, and any action would have been useless."

"I see your point," Jason said, "but may I recommend that you let us know if anything unusual should happen in the future? The Home Office would be most confused should this search appear in your report and not in ours."

Sir Thomas smiled at Reginald, "We stand rebuked, old chap. You're quite right, Taylor. I might mention that this is the first stop that the boat has made since our departure from Giza. Therefore, the person who searched our rooms must still be onboard."

"Unless, of course, they disembarked here in Abydos. I'll check the passenger and crew list with the captain. Meanwhile, we need to have a signal to let me know if you have something to report or discuss and we can arrange to meet. Touch your index finger to your nose. It's simple and goes unnoticed by most people." He demonstrated.

Sir Reginald chuckled. "That reminds me of the Croydon spy case I worked on two years ago. The code then was to scratch behind your left ear. Unfortunately, Lady Chesterfield had no sense of direction and confused her right with her left. So whenever she scratched we jumped. It was her skin condition that kept us on our toes."

Chapter Twenty-One

Luxor

Day four had arrived and the level of excitement stirred among the passengers onboard the barge as they gathered on the viewing deck to watch the ship's approach into the ancient city of Luxor, also known as Thebes to the Greeks. With a population close to half a million people, the city is often referred to as the "world's greatest open-air museum," with the massive architectural ruins of the Temples of Karnak and Luxor surrounded by the sprawling metropolis.

As they neared the dock, the Temple of Luxor came into view in all its magnificent splendor. It would only be a short walk from the boat to the grand old Winter Palace Hotel, where they would spend two nights in luxury before taking up residence in a tent near the excavation site. Due to the scheduled changes in their itinerary, they had arrived two days earlier than expected and accommodations at the site were limited.

Lynnette was impressed with the old world elegance of the three story cream and white structure of the Winter Palace Hotel with its splendid, horseshoe-stairway entrance and elegant, stately public spaces. Their stay here wasn't on the original itinerary. "Is this a complimentary gift from the Home Office or did someone make a mistake?" she asked.

Reginald smiled as he approached the registration desk. "No, my love. The Home Office had nothing to do with the hotel selection except to allow me to select the accommodations due to the change in our itinerary. It was a suggestion from Thomas and Grace. They're staying here before visiting the tomb site. It appears the camp is rather limited on accommodations. Lord Charles wasn't expected this early and we needed separate quarters for Minnie and the guards. I suppose you could say, everyone has now been put on alert to our investigation, but it couldn't be helped."

"Well...perhaps they needed someone to pull a few strings and put them on their toes. After all, two workers have vanished and one is dead from a snake bite. That doesn't bode well for the museum's reputation for safety in these modern days. I hope our room here has a view and a very large tub in the bathroom. I'm looking forward to a long hot soak before dinner tonight. Meanwhile, we should see the Temples of Luxor and Karnak after lunch." Lynnette never seemed to lack for adventure when traveling. She wanted to experience everything.

"Yes, dear," he answered. As they followed the porter who carried the luggage to their suite. Sir Reginald seemed distracted as he read a telegram from England that was waiting for him on arrival.

"What does the Home Office have to say?" Lynnette inquired.

"They've arranged an interview with the Chief of Police here in Luxor regarding the missing workmen. I have an appointment after lunch."

"Then, might I suggest that you take Sir Thomas or Lord Charles with you. It's always good to have a witness to back you up."

"Lord Charles has gone on to the tomb site. He had appointments to meet with Dr. Herit Kasmut, a new specialist from the Cairo museum, and Dr. Roland Stafford, the British Museum's antiquities curator. We'll meet them when we get there.

I'll see if Thomas would like to accompany me. We'll take Taylor with us and Boris can keep an eye on you and Minnie, with the help of Grace."

"That sounds like a plan. Let's find the dining room. It's time for lunch, and I need sustenance before seeing more ruins today."

Sir Thomas and Grace were already seated in the dining room. They waved for Reginald and Lynnette to join them. "I was beginning to wonder where you two were," said Grace.

"Whether it's breakfast, lunch, tea, or dinner time, you'll always know where to find me," Lynnette chuckled as they sat at the same table.

Reginald looked at Thomas. "I was wondering if I might persuade you to join me after lunch for a meeting with the ENP. I had a cable when we arrived. It appears that the Home Office has arranged an interview with the Chief of Police here in Luxor. It's my understanding that they have been involved with the case of the missing workers at the excavation site."

"I would imagine so since they're the only criminal investigators in the area and the Valley of the Monkeys comes under their jurisdiction. It would be interesting to hear what they have to say and get their point of view on the issues at the site. I'd be delighted to accompany you," Sir Thomas assured him.

Grace glanced at Lynnette. "I trust that you will allow me to join you and Minnie for a tour of the temples. I've seen them before, but that was years ago and I would like to refresh my memory. Besides that, I don't want to be stuck in some stuffy old office listening to an interview with the police. Provided of course that this husband of yours will keep a close watch on Thomas and keep him out of trouble," she grinned.

Sir Reginald cleared his throat, "Grace, my dear, we'll have Taylor with us, so we will be well protected."

"I assumed your guard would be with you. I wasn't worried about protection. Just be sure Thomas behaves and doesn't get himself arrested by the Egyptian police. You know him as well as I do."

After lunch, the two groups split. Lynnette, Grace, and Minnie, under the watchful eyes of Boris "the friendly gorilla," made their way to the temples, while Sir Thomas, Sir Reginald, and Jason Taylor took a taxi to the police station for the interview.

Announcing themselves on arrival, the men were quickly shown to a well-appointed, air-conditioned office. "The Captain will be with you in a moment." Apparently he was on the telephone, as the officer held his hand up to his ear and smiled.

A rather large, dark, mahogany desk, shined to a glossy finish, was the dominating feature in the enclosed square space. Two upholstered arm chairs faced the desk, and the cream colored walls were adorned with photos of the temples in Luxor and the Valley of the Kings. A small bronze statue of the Sphinx reclined on the desk-top as a paperweight. The fluorescent LED cove lighting created an antiseptic atmosphere.

The door opened and a tall swarthy, uniformed man in perhaps his mid-forties, with slicked-back, black hair, only slightly graying at the temples greeted them. "Good afternoon gentlemen, I am Captain Mohamed Kalif Saeed. Please be seated." Taylor located an empty wooden chair by the doorway.

"Thank you. I'm Sir Reginald Whitcomb and this is Sir Thomas Treadwell. We're here at the request of the Home Office in London, to investigate the disappearance or death, of two workers at the excavation site in the Valley of the Monkeys, under the sponsorship of Lord Charles Marques and the British Museum."

The captain sat up right in his chair with a stern look of indignation on his face. "Do you believe these missing men are dead?"

"As a matter of fact no, I don't." Sir Reginald answered. "However, I rather understood that to be your belief and that is why you are not looking for them."

"You understood! And just what persons gave you cause to understand that was our conclusion? The Home Office? And how should they know what I believe? No such statement has been written in any report from this office. It's a dangerous thing to expound another man's beliefs."

Sir Thomas was quick to join the discussion. "Ah! Then you think they may still be alive."

The captain smirked. "Do I? Who says so?"

"Obviously if they are not dead, then they must be alive." Reginald said.

"On that, I am entirely in agreement. You have stated the undeniable truth."

"Don't you believe the disappearance of two men is a strange and mysterious affair?" Sir Thomas inquired.

"Why mysterious, I might ask? Men disappear from time to time, and when they reappear, the explanations they offer, seem to be quite adequate," the captain smiled, shrugged his shoulders, and spread his hands, as if to say, "Who cares?"

"But weren't the circumstances rather mysterious?" asked Sir Reginald.

"What circumstances?"

"I refer to the way in which they vanished," he said.

"And in what way did they vanish?"

'Well, of course, I don't know."

The captain grinned. "Precisely. Neither do I and therefore, I can't say whether it was mysterious or not."

"But their articles of clothing and personal items were left in their tent and no one saw them leave. Don't you feel that that is strange?" questioned Sir Thomas.

Captain Saeed shook his head in disagreement. "Obviously, if they did not take their clothing or personal items, then they must have planned to return. Therefore, if they planned to return, then they have not disappeared, and there is no mystery."

"Then you presume they are still alive." Reginald stated.

"I fail to see your point. If they are alive then it would be impossible to presume they are dead; and if you were certain they are dead, presumption of death would still be impossible. One does not presume a certainty.

"I take no responsibility. I act on behalf of and in accordance with the decisions of the Egyptian Ministry of Interior and have no choice in the matter." He stood behind the desk. "That concludes this interview, gentlemen. I have another appointment."

"Is there any likelihood of further investigation?" Thomas queried as he stood.

"At this point, I would say the case is closed."

Sir Reginald stood and nodded. "Then we apologize for wasting your valued time."

"On the contrary, I trust you have learned how the Egyptian Police force operates with efficiency, in which case, my time has not been wasted. I hope your visit to Istanbul was enjoyable and the cruise up the Nile a pleasant one. The Winter Palace Hotel here in our ancient city is very elegant and comfortable compared to the hot tents at the tomb site. With that in mind, I feel I should offer a word of caution. The Valley of the Monkeys can be a very dangerous place because of its remote location. Good afternoon gentleman."

Sir Reginald couldn't wait until they stepped into the elevator of the police office building. "Well, I must say, that is one Egyptian with a mighty high opinion of himself. Rather pompous, don't you think?"

"Now you know what Grace meant about the Egyptian police. We've had a double dose of negativity, first from Cairo and now here. I would chalk that up to not much assistance," Thomas added.

"What I found disturbing about that conversation was the fact that he knew about our visit to Istanbul, our cruise up the Nile and precisely where we are staying in Luxor." Reginald said skeptically.

Sir Thomas shrugged his shoulders, "He could have gotten all that information from the Home Office when they requested your appointment. No doubt when they asked for his cooperation, he in turn wanted more information on your arrival."

"I suppose you're right, but his last words still sounded like a threat." Reginald mumbled.

"That's the way with the police anywhere. They don't like private investigators sticking their noses into police business. It appears we are on our own to find out what is happening at the tomb site. First, we need to start interviewing the people who are working there. Perhaps Lord Charles can help us separate the wheat from the chaff. The other laborers probably know something, but it will be a cold day in Bermuda before you can get them to divulge any secrets. Meanwhile, I'm sure he was serious about dangers in the desert," Thomas concluded.

"I think you're right about that. I would like to keep Lynnette here in Luxor, but she insists on staying with me at the excavation site. Is Grace coming with you?"

"My dear boy, she won't let me out of her sight. Remember, she's my personal bodyguard. I'm surprised she let me off the leash to accompany you today. I assured her that Taylor would be our shadow today, while she and Boris are guarding Lynnette, and Minnie."

Reginald held the glass door as they exited police headquarters. "They should be back at the hotel by now. It's almost tea time and Lynnette rarely misses tea."

"Then I would suggest we return and join them. You're missing out on touring the Temples of Luxor and Karnak."

Reginald hailed a taxi. "Not really. I visited Luxor before I met Lynnette. This trip was originally for her experience. She'd been dropping hints about a trip to Egypt and they weren't very subtle. I was getting a little tired of eating curry and couscous every week. The Home Office weaseled their way in at the last minute with this investigation. However, as it turns out, I get to mix business with pleasure."

Sir Thomas smiled. "I've always said that's an excellent combination, old chap."

Chapter Twenty-Two

Sir Reginald and Lynnette

After dinner on their first evening in Luxor, Sir Thomas announced that he and Grace would be leaving for the tomb site early the following morning. "They sent a messenger to say that our accommodations would be available, and we were to proceed immediately. Perhaps Lord Charles has become the safari innkeeper," he chuckled.

"More likely they booted some visiting dignitary who had overstayed their welcome," Lynnette added with a smile.

"You're probably correct, my dear," Grace said. "However, he said that the assistant director of the Cairo Museum would be leaving the following day and you and Reginald will have her three connecting tents—an office, a bedroom, and a room for Minnie. He recommended we use the office for our meetings."

Reginald looked pleased. "That will be splendid. I was hoping we would have a place to work in private, and being connected to our quarters will make it more secure and a perfect place for conducting the interviews."

"So, will we see you before you depart in the morning?"

"I'm afraid not, my dear," Sir Thomas answered. "We leave early to have breakfast with Lord Charles at the site, locate our accommodations, and meet the people in charge. We'll check things out and give you a full report on your arrival."

The following morning after a quiet breakfast for two, Sir Reginald, Lynnette, Minnie and the two guards crossed the river to the west bank and made their way to the Valley of the Kings to view the colossal temples of Ramses VII, Seti I and Tutankhamun, plus monumental statues carved from hardened sand and limestone. Numerous tunnels, stairways, and rooms were decorated with detailed scenes of everyday life and the rituals of death in vivid colors.

Hundreds of massive columns stretched into the distance and reached for the heavens, a testament to the architectural design that has survived through centuries combined with the natural destructive forces of nature. The Necropolis dedicated to the kings of Egypt covered a large area next to the Valley of the Queens and was separated by a rocky riff from the Valley of the Monkeys further inland and to the west.

Sir Thomas and Grace arrived at the tomb site for breakfast and were greeted by Lord Charles and Dr. Roland Stafford of the British Museum. "Welcome, my friends. It is a pleasure to meet you," said Stafford. "I trust your journey has been a pleasant one."

Sir Thomas chuckled as he shook Dr. Stafford's large, tanned hand. "That remains to be determined after we've had our breakfast. I'm sure the Lord Charles has filled you in on the strange happenings we encountered while traveling down on the Orient Express. I hope we haven't kept you waiting."

Stafford's large expressive blue eyes twinkled under his almost nonexistent sandy eyebrows. His rugged tanned face bespoke evidence of his days in the sun and his smile was warm and sincere. "It is Egypt, Sir Thomas. One is never late for breakfast until they begin to serve lunch," he joked.

"I'll remember that when they sound the gong at 7 am tomorrow morning," laughed Lord Charles. "I've already finished my exercises and done an hour's worth of paper work. I'm starving, even though you could never tell it to look at me," he said, patting his midsection. "Come, before they sound the call to lunch." Grace and Thomas fell in line and followed him to the mess tent, where workers were in the process of leaving to go back to work.

"Thomas, old chap, I want you to fill me in on our friends Sir Reginald and Lynnette Whitcomb. They're a fascinating couple, but I sense a story behind their age difference." Lord Charles said. "Perhaps you can fill in the blanks. No tittle-tattle gossip, but a background based on facts. I'm sure Dr. Stafford would find it interesting as well."

Sir Thomas looked at Grace and back at Lord Charles. "I'm sure you have looked into some of the information already. However, I'll begin with some history about Sir Reginald which you may not be aware of. His childhood days I will skip. His education was in the top schools, Eton and Cambridge. He was sent to Paris for diplomacy and to Switzerland for economics. His uncle, Colonel Robert Moorland, was a military commander and also head of Scotland Yard for several years.

"Reginald's father served in the RAF and the military police during the war. His first wife and daughter were killed in a bombing raid near Dover. I forget the village name. Carolyn was a volunteer nurse and their teenage daughter lived with her, helping where she could at the rural hospital.

"Reginald's father investigated the bombing and learned that someone had neglected to assign a police guard to warn the hospital of incoming aircraft. A report was submitted but no action was taken—in the end, the report was shelved and forgotten. He later remarried and Reginald was born.

"Young Reginald eventually joined the military police following in his father's footsteps and later became an inspector for the Home Office. He worked on numerous investigations and was assigned a driver because of his rank. This is where Sarah Lynnette Spencer arrives on the scene. She was a volunteer driver for the Home Office.

"Needless to say, he was not expecting a female driver, fifteen years his junior. However, they worked well together and Lynnette was like his right hand assistant, with her intelligent, inquisitive mind and, as women will say," he looked at Grace and smiled, "a woman's intuition.

"She wasn't afraid of hard work and getting her hands dirty. After they were married, it was Lynnette who encouraged Reginald to become a Member of Parliament. At the death of her father, she inherited a rather large estate and country home called Carrolton Manor near Southhampton. Sir Reginald had inherited the

Mayberry Manor estate in Yorkshire near the village of Loxley, and together they share a townhouse in Belgrave Square's embassy row in London.

"Reginald is in his early-sixties which would put Lynnette somewhere in her late-forties. They have no children, but Reginald is from a rather extended family of cousins, nephews, nieces, aunts, and uncles. Lynnette had a sister who died at a very young age.

"They're active in the arts and patrons of numerous London museums and the symphony. I believe I have covered most of the facts. Oh, yes...I forgot, Reginald drinks Scotch and Lynnette is fond of gin martinis. I was wondering if we could supply a bottle of each during their visit here. I'll take care of the brandy. Grace and I enjoy our nightcap, before tucking in," he chuckled.

"I say," Dr. Stafford remarked, "I feel I know Sir Reginald and Lady Whitcomb already."

"Then I'm sure you will enjoy their company," Grace added.

Dr. Herit Kasmut approached their table. "This isn't a social club Dr. Stafford. We all have work to do. Once your friends are settled in I'd like to see you in the lab." She turned quickly and disappeared among the tents, without a word to the newly arrived guests.

Dr. Stafford smiled and rolled his eyes. "The dragon lady has spoken. I must return to my labors, but we will have time to continue our discussion over tea. Meanwhile Dashi," he indicated a young man with a nod of his head, "will show you to your tent." He placed his hands together and bowed. "If you will excuse me."

Dressed in his gallibaya and a turban, he wove his way around the tents, following a pathway in the footsteps of Dr. Kasmut.

Lord Charles glanced around to see who was within listening distance, but saw no one close by. "Now that we're alone, can you tell me how your meeting with the police Captain turned out?"

Sir Thomas held his hands up in defense, "We'll get no response from the local police. They appear to have the opinion that people disappear all the time, and will miraculously reappear at some time in the future."

"So that means they don't plan to offer any assistance." Lord Charles stated.

"Precisely. As far as they're concerned, it's a closed case." Thomas added. "But did we really expect any more than that?"

Lord Charles's voice became a soft whisper. "True. However, there's something else happening in this camp. Something of a suspicious nature, that I can't put my finger on. There was a meeting in the lab area yesterday that I was not asked to attend. I expressed my displeasure to the dragon lady, as Dr. Kasmut of the Cairo Museum is called. She informed me it had nothing to do with me; that it was the business of the Cairo Museum."

"How rude!" exclaimed Grace in a very dignified manner.

"Yes." Lord Charles agreed. "I then proceeded to let her know that anything pertaining to this tomb site was my business since I am paying for this excavation. I said if she had Cairo Museum business to deal with, she might wish to return to Cairo."

"Bravo, old boy!" said Sir Thomas with a smile.

"Well not exactly. I don't believe I'm on her A-list of important people. To be quite honest, I don't think I ever was. But I made it clear that we would start our investigations as soon as Sir Reginald Whitcomb arrives tomorrow, nothing is off limits and we will search every inch of this site for the missing workers and for anything illegal that might be taking place."

"And what was her reaction to that statement?" asked Grace.

Charles chuckled, "It's difficult to say. I think she turned blue in the face, puffed up like an adder, blinked twice, turned around, and stomped off, without a word. I'm afraid Andrew Carnegie would not have been proud of me. I'm probably much better at hosting tea parties, country fairs, and museum exhibitions."

"Don't worry, old chap. She's probably got her broomstick in for repairs in case of a needed quick getaway. I'm sure we will have the full cooperation of Dr. Stafford and his team. He should be the first person we interview. And that boy of his...what did he call him—Dashi? I wonder if he speaks any English."

"Yes sir. I speak good English. Go to school. Top student. Good grades." Suddenly surprised, everyone looked in his direction.

"How long have you been standing there?" asked Grace.

"Long enough to know I help. No one like Dr. Kasmut. Dragon lady, bad medicine. You see. No talk here. I show you tents."

He motioned for them to follow him.

Chapter Twenty-Three

Hell on Earth

It was a short drive into hell. The comforts of home and luxuries of a safari vacation vanished. The dreams of Luxor, Cairo, and Marrakech dissolved like salt in water and were sifted away as the sands of time through an hourglass. From the paved road leading to the Valley of the Kings, Reginald, Lynnette and their party journeyed west on a hard dusty road twisting its way through the harsh landscape like a snake winding its way through this desolate, windblown, sunbaked, rugged, and isolated part of Egypt.

The karst, gnarled, and often grotesque features of weathered limestone cliffs reflecting the rays of the sun and moon, are but silent ghost of an ancient desert that whispers in the wind. A necropolis of ziggurats, sandstone temples, crevasses, and a maze of passageways, dry washes, and rubble strewn, cracked-clay river beds formed by the Nile River centuries ago. Shades of gray, burnt sienna, and ochre paint the scorched earth beneath the robin's egg blue of the clear desert sky.

Vegetation is almost entirely lacking in this uninviting landscape of muted to vivid hues, fading into each other. Inhospitable to wildlife in general except for snakes, scorpions, rats, the desert fox; birds of prey, the ubiquitous hawks, and vultures find company in its environment.

Ridges, fissures and pits, join the skinny ravines that tunnel through hardened mud. As the morning unfolds, eerie, elongated shadows, gargoyle-like creatures of stone begin to march across the desert floor; a sinister army from the depths of hell.

Lynnette and Minnie were fascinated, never having ventured into the wilds of the desert, the scene was captivating. "How can people live in such a cruel environment?" Minnie asked.

"They don't actually live in this part of the desert. This is where the pharaohs built their tombs. They lived along the Nile River where they had a constant source of water and could farm the rich soil." Lynnette instructed.

"Well," she replied, "I'll take rainy old England any day over this ugly land. Our cemeteries are much prettier."

Reginald and Lynnette chuckled. "Don't worry Minnie, dear. The tombs around here were lost to the world for centuries until they were discovered by the English... and of course grave robbers prior to that. When you get back home, you can go visit your Uncle George in the graveyard next to the church, and tell him how fortunate he is to have such a beautiful place for his final rest."

"Thank you. I plan on doing just that and perhaps I can introduce him to Boris while I'm there," declared Minnie.

Lynnette rolled her eyes at Reginald sitting in the front seat with their driver. She gently patted Minnie's hand. "All in due time, old girl. Give it time to blossom. I'm sure your Uncle George wouldn't want you to make any hasty decisions."

She returned her attention to the front seat. "Any idea how much further we have to go? This road just got narrower. Is the driver sure he knows where we're supposed to be?"

Reginald turned and grinned at Lynnette. "The hotel gave him the same directions they did for Thomas and Grace. I know it's an uncomfortable ride, but it shouldn't be much further. Ah, there's a sign up ahead. Perhaps we've arrived."

The tents in the excavation compound soon appeared off to one side of the road and they pulled in to park near other vehicles. The driver stepped out and opened their doors to a sudden burst of heat, as they managed to exit the air-conditioned vehicle.

"How long are we expected to remain in hell," Lynnette fanned herself as the porters unloaded their luggage.

Reginald gave her a rather inquisitive look. "I seem to recall that you were tired of the cool, drizzling, damp, and foggy weather in Yorkshire. You were longing for some place dry and warm. Where is that girl with a sense of adventure? I could have left her in luxury at the Winter Palace in Luxor—should I send her back?"

Lynnette straightened the wrinkles in her linen skirt, wiped the perspiration from her brow, and replied, "There's no need to be sarcastic about it, and most certainly I volunteered. I'm sure we will adjust to our surroundings in time. However, I was simply wondering how much time we will have to make these adjustments." As usual, she was only attempting to politely comprehend her situation. This was not an argument and Reginald accepted her query with understanding.

"At the moment, I don't have the answer to that question." He glanced up and saw Lord Charles and Sir Thomas coming their way. "However, here are two gentlemen who might be able to shine some light on the matter."

"Greetings, and welcome to hell," said Lord Charles with a chuckle.

"Interesting," said Lynnette, "We were just discussing that very subject," she grinned at Reginald. "How do we find our quarters and seek refuge from the heat of Ra?"

"You will come first to the mess tent, relax, and enjoy a cool cup of mint tea while this young man sees to the placement of your luggage." He tapped Dashi on the shoulder.

"Welcome to the Valley of the Monkeys." Dashi said with a bow.

Lynnette stared in surprise at Dashi. "I say...what a handsome young man you are. And you speak English so well."

"Yes, he does," said Sir Thomas smiling at Dashi, "Now if you will follow me, we shall get out of this furnace and under some shade. Grace is waiting in the mess tent."

They joined Grace in the shade of an open tent set with metal tables and folding wicker chairs. "I'm so delighted to see you. There's only one other woman in this camp and she's not what I would call sociable. As a matter of fact, she demonstrated her authority on our arrival and hasn't given us the time of day since. Lord Charles, with a hint of irritation, rather put her in her place and she's been avoiding any contact. She happens to be with the Cairo museum and they refer to her as the "dragon lady."

"I was given instructions from the Home Office to contact the curator of antiquities for the British Museum—a Dr. Roland Stafford," said Reginald.

Sir Thomas glanced up to see Dr. Stafford strolling in their direction and with him were Kathy Stockton and her husband Mario. Dr. Stafford was all smiles with his white teeth and twinkling eyes, set in his chiseled, sun-darkened face. "Is this a private meeting of the English investigation, or might we join you?"

"By all means. You're quite welcome. And perhaps you will introduce yourself and these two charming people with you," said Lord Charles. "I don't believe everyone has met before."

Dr. Stafford made the proper introductions and everyone was seated once again. Lynnette opened the conversation by addressing Kathy. "So, you're the antiquities appraiser who helped solve the murder of Ricardo Orcini."

Kathy blushed slightly. "I suppose you could say I exposed certain aspects of the case, but it was really Mario and his police force that solved the crime. I shared my observations and intuition regarding certain facts and the rest was left to the professional detectives."

Lynnette shook her hand. "Sir Thomas and Lord Charles have explained the murder case to us, and I must say, I hope you will both join us in our endeavor to solve the case of the missing workers here at the tomb site."

Sir Reginald raised his head and nodded to Lynnette. "We've only just arrived and already you're recruiting someone to join forces with us," he said in a jovial tone.

Lynnette shook her head. "Oh no, not just Kathy but Mario too. After all, he's a detective, and from what we've heard, he's a very good detective. That's not to say that you and Thomas aren't trained professionals when it comes to investigations, and you have the assistance of Lord Charles, Grace and myself. Wouldn't seven musketeers be better than five?"

"Make that eight," said Dr. Stafford. "And may we discover the truth. I happen to agree that people don't just disappear."

Dr. Kasmut entered the mess tent. "I see the new guests have arrived. Dr. Stafford and I have work to do if you will excuse us. Please make yourselves comfortable. Should you need to consult me, I'm Dr. Kasmut, and I'm available in my office." She turned and strode off like a marine sergeant, stopped and looked back over her shoulder at Dr. Stafford. "Well, are you coming or not?" She then disappeared into her tent.

"If you will pardon me, I need to inventory the items removed from the tomb yesterday, before they start the cleaning."

"Does she keep the items in her office?" Lynnette asked.

He nodded. "Yes, until they've been cleaned. Then they are appraised, catalogued, wrapped, and stored in the laboratory before shipping them down river to Cairo."

Lord Charles spoke for the group. "I'm sure we will have many more questions to ask you, but we shouldn't keep you from your work. Perhaps we can meet in Sir Reginald's office tent after dinner this evening."

"It will be my pleasure." Stafford bowed and departed. All eyes turned to Lord Charles.

"Come, let's get you settled in. You can take a walk around the camp to stretch your legs and I would recommend a short rest before diner this evening. Tomorrow we will view the tomb and see the objects we've been able to recover. "

At dinner that evening Lynnette surveyed the workers and support staff, but there was one person was missing. "Doesn't Dr. Kasmut eat with the rest of the crew?" she asked.

Dr. Stafford smiled and shook his head. "She always has her

meals in her tent. Rather antisocial I might say. Perhaps she feels it would lower her stature and place of command with the workers. It's really quite amusing and believe me, there are no complaints from the staff," he chuckled.

Lynnette was serious but cautious with her thoughts. "Doesn't that seem rather strange to anyone?"

"I think I know where you're going with this question and I'm with you. How do we know if she's who she says she is?" said Reginald. They looked to Dr. Stafford for a response.

"I checked her credentials on arrival from Cairo. She was a replacement for Dr. Tavvi, the gentleman who was to be here. He had taken ill quite suddenly and was in the hospital. She was sent ahead to prevent any delay on the project."

Lord Charles appeared to be having second thoughts about Dr. Kasmut. "I've worked on several occasions with the Cairo Museum, but I don't recall ever seeing her there. My memory isn't as good as it used to be, but I don't have a problem remembering faces. Names maybe, but never faces. She could be new. They're constantly shifting personnel like most museums, but I know who to contact. I'll handle that first thing tomorrow and find out the answer."

Kathy glanced at Mario. "Perhaps this would be a good time to mention our discovery," she continued. "It has to do with the way they're cleaning some of the artifacts. Mario noticed that only certain artifacts are taken to her private tent before being released to the labs for cleaning. The canopic jars and several of the Ushabit figures are often delayed three or four days before they're sent to the labs."

"It may be nothing. Perhaps she has a different way of doing things and I'm certainly not an expert on the matter, but Kathy has worked at many excavation sites and this didn't appear to be the normal routine. So other than searching her tent, we've been keeping our eyes on her," added Mario.

Sir Reginald wanted to explore another angle. "I'm here because two of the workers have vanished. Dr. Stafford and I discussed this before dinner this evening and I asked him what Dr. Kasmut's thoughts were on that subject." He glanced at Dr. Stafford. "Perhaps you would let our friends know how she reacted when you brought the case to her attention."

"She didn't appear to be interested," he said, "and I quote."

"I don't have time to be concerned with workers who can't do their job. If they're tired of digging and dusting, then who really cares where they are? That is the end of this subject and there will be no more said about it."

"And for the past three weeks it hasn't been mentioned until Lord Charles arrived."

"Grace, my dear, I hope you brought the nutcracker with you. It sounds like we have a tough nut to crack," Sir Thomas added.

Grace chuckled, "It won't be the first time, old man."

Chapter
Twenty-Four

The Tomb

African safari vacations were born in the Golden Age of luxury travel. Lynnette recalled, at the age of eighteen, she accompanied her parents on a safari to southern Africa visiting Botswana and Zambia. She was dazzled by the awe-inspiring Victoria Falls seen from a small plane and the close encounter of game viewing in Zimbabwe.

All the quality creature comforts were available, personal service, fine wine, and gourmet dining. She had experienced some of nature's wildest settings in luxury. However, Egypt was a new and strange experience. Their accommodations consisted of a work tent for Reginald's makeshift office and a smaller attached tent for sleeping on folding beds of metal with a thin mattress.

Fresh river water was delivered daily for the two bathing tents in the compound with overhead showers and a limited supply of water trucked in from the river. A line of portable potties was tucked behind a rock out-cropping away from view, and there were no waiters running around with white gloves and wearing dinner jackets with gold braid.

This was not what Lynnette had expected, but she refused to say so. She would rough it with the others. It would be a new experience and she was tough. Although, she expressed her concern for Minnie, whose tent was next to theirs.

However, Minnie was a trouper. She came from a working-class family and to her, this was camping out in an exotic country and definitely better than sleeping four in a bed with her siblings. "Don't you worry about me, Miss Lynne, I'm here to take care of you. You don't need to take care of me. My tent is bigger than that old shed we used to hide in on your uncle's farm and I haven't seen a spider yet, but I'll be sure and call you if I do."

Lynnette rolled her eyes and smiled. "Yes…you be sure and do that, Minnie."

"And I won't let Mr. Boris visit," Minnie added, "Unless, of course there's an emergency."

"I doubt Mr. Boris will need to be called in an emergency. He probably won't take his eyes off this tent as long as you're in it," said Lynnette. They both had a good laugh over that statement, then left Minnie's quarters to find Grace, Sir Thomas, and Reginald for their tour of the tomb with Lord Charles. It appeared they had already gathered at the mess tent and were waiting for the last two to arrive.

"Ah...here they come!" Thomas said. "I think we can make our way to the tomb now."

"Our apologies for keeping everyone waiting. We had a few last minute things to tend to, but we're here now, and good morning to everyone." Lynnette said as they approached the group.

"No apology necessary, my dear," Lord Charles said, taking her hand. "We shall lead the troupes. This way musketeers!"

The flat dusty trail leading down the valley gave the appearance of leading nowhere. The hills and rocks all looked the same. They turned to the left marked by a small white sign post with numbers on it into an even tighter canyon girded on either side with high stone walls etched by the ravages of wind and rain.

Up ahead a dark hole appeared at the end of the trail. As they came closer to the opening it took the form of a doorway, its large, smooth stones forming a square entry, with a massive stone lintel etched with a bah relief of Egyptian designs resting on the square stone columns.

"The stone door has been removed and taken to Cairo," said Lord Charles, "But there is a photo of it in my tent. I'll show it to you when we return. I've had some lights installed so we will be able to see. Follow me and watch your step, the stairs are a bit steep."

Lord Charles was prepared to be the guide as he began to explain for the others what had been discovered years ago. "WV 23 is thought to be the last tomb constructed in the West Valley and is considered to be the Tomb of Ay, one of the last Pharaohs of the Eighteenth Dynasty of Ancient Egypt."

"I suppose its remote location is one of the reasons it has gone unnoticed until now." Lynnette said.

Lord Charles corrected her. "Oh no, my dear. The tomb was discovered in 1816. However, it had already been broken into and robbed some time before that. It was thought to be that of a noble not a royal, and was closed up and abandoned for the more royal tombs in the King's Valley. When I offered to fund the project, the museum was anxious to see what still remained undiscovered. What we've been able to salvage is of historical value. Jewels and other valuable items disappeared long ago.

"The tomb is known as WV 23 due to its location in the West Valley, also known as the Valley of the Monkeys because of the Twelve Baboons of the First Hours depicted on the west wall within the burial chamber. They represent the first twelve hours after midnight. I'll point that out when we get there."

Reginald wanted to clarify his comment earlier. "If I understand you correctly, there is nothing here that someone would want to steal and sell on the black market. Correct?"

"My dear boy, that statement is false. Of course there are priceless items we've recovered that anyone interested in antiquities from the Eighteenth Dynasty of Egypt would sell their souls to have for their private collections. That is what we are here to investigate and discover; where the missing workers have vanished and did they take anything in the process.

"Now, where was I? Oh yes, foundation markings have not been discovered to date, so it is difficult to be certain who this tomb was originally intended for. Archaeologists say it could have been Akhenaten or Tutankhamun, but the tomb had only just been started when Tutankhamun died suddenly, so he was buried instead in the tomb KV 62, which unfortunately is located in a non-royal area of the Valley of the Kings and had originally been intended for Ay, who at the time, was the Vizier for Tutankhamun."

"I notice there is not much decoration on these entrance walls," Sir Thomas mentioned, "but the rough texture has bits of paint indicating that the surface might have been decorated with murals."

"Quite true Thomas. The scenes would have been of stories in the life of the tomb's owner. They would have shown him with his Ushabit, or attendants who would care for him in the afterlife. It's believed that his successor had the murals destroyed. But of course, there's no proof, so it is just speculation." By now, they had reached the bottom of the second stairway.

"The tomb's design is very simple compared to other royal tombs of this period. It was built on a straight axis with the burial chamber offset to the north-east. After several doorways there's another descending stairway. A second corridor leads to the antechamber which is followed by the burial chamber and a final smaller room or canopic chamber.

"The canopic jars we found were decorated with sculpted heads representing the four sons of the god Horus—a jackal, a falcon, a human-head, and a baboon. They are meant to contain the organs of the deceased which he will need for the afterlife. These jars have already been sent to the Cairo Museum, but I have photos in my tent. Dashi has studied photography and he is quite the professional photographer. The heart is the only organ that remains inside the mummy. This too has been removed and sent ahead for preservation.

"The burial chamber is the only room decorated with scenes of Ay, hunting hippopotamus and fishing in the marshes and a relief featuring twelve baboons, representing the twelve hours of the night. Inscribed on one wall of the chamber is the Book of the Dead. A collection of writings that appeared in tombs as a means of guiding the royal soul on its journey to the afterlife.

"The Book of the Dead is a series of rites, prayers, and myths containing Egyptian beliefs about the afterlife. These writings were first discovered in the burial chambers of the pyramids.

"For centuries, it was assumed these writings were passages from ancient scripture. However, later, when scholars learned to decipher hieroglyphs, they discovered that these texts were magic spells—road maps so to speak, provided for the dead to navigate their way safely through the afterlife."

Minnie held up her hand to ask a question. "Do you mean this is the tomb of a king?"

"Precisely, Minnie," Lord Charles answered, "The Book of the Dead inscriptions secured that belief."

"Then why wasn't he buried in a nice pyramid or monument instead of being tucked away and hidden in a rock wall out in the desert?"

Lord Charles nodded and smiled, "There are several theories about that, Minnie, and I have some books you might like to read when we get back to England. I'm sure Miss Lynnette won't mind and might also enjoy them."

"How kind of you, Lord Charles. Now we'll have a project to work on this winter," Lynnette said, smiling at Minnie.

"And speaking of projects," added Sir Reginald, "we should be getting back to the camp. We have work to begin if we are going to solve the mystery of our missing workers. It's for sure the Egyptian Police aren't inclined to be of much assistance."

Chapter Twenty-Five

Investigations Begin

Back at the camp Dr. Stafford was waiting for them. "I'm going to be busy this afternoon, so I thought you might interview me this morning."

Reginald greeted him. "That sounds splendid," he waved his hand in the direction of their tents. "My office is this way," he smiled leading the way.

Reaching the office tent, he pulled back the flap and Dr. Stafford entered first. "Have a seat," he gestured as he sat behind the desk. "The privacy here is lacking and the thickness of these walls doesn't provide much for top secret information to be discussed. If there's anything you wish to say in private, we can take a long walk this evening after dinner."

"Understood," Stafford agreed.

"When did you begin work on this excavation?"

"Six months ago. Things don't move at a rapid pace in Egypt, as you possibly have discovered."

Sir Reginald nodded his head as he jotted down Dr. Stafford's information. "I have to agree with that statement. Was Dr. Kasmut here when you arrived?"

"Yes. Dr. Tavvi, the assistant curator at the museum in Cairo was originally assigned to work with me. However he was taken ill with a fever before I arrived and Dr. Kasmut had been assigned to take charge in his absence. She appeared to provide all the proper credentials."

"Had you ever met her before now?"

"No. But they move people around at the museum in Cairo, so it is quite possible she had been working in another department. She assumed command on behalf of the Cairo Museum and I never questioned her authority. Is there some reason you are suspicious of her position?"

Reginald hesitated a moment, thinking of what had transpired since their arrival. "I must say, both you and Lord Charles seem to be of like opinions. You indicated her methods to be different from the normal routine at other excavation sites where you have worked in the past. Lord Charles isn't comfortable with her attitude of authority. He feels it doesn't bode well for working as a team."

"I'm in total agreement on that point." Dr. Stafford said in a whisper. "Like I said before, she takes artifacts into her private tent before releasing them to the lab for cleaning and restoration. Sometimes they are kept there for two or three days. When the lab gets them, some of them have a waxy residue that was not there when they were removed from the tomb."

Reginald was curious, "Are you saying these artifacts would not have been treated with a coat of wax when placed in the tomb?"

Dr. Stafford cleared his throat. "If they had been coated with wax to seal them, which is rare, but does happen on occasions, , the wax would have dried and hardened after centuries of being buried in the tomb. However, the artifacts brought to my attention by Kathy Stockton, the appraiser, had fresh residue in some of the cracks."

Reginald continued to take down this information in his notebook, "So I should speak with Kathy Stockton about this observation?"

"That would be my recommendation. Perhaps she might have some idea where the wax has come from," said Dr. Stafford. "We haven't had an opportunity to discuss it, and personally, we haven't been making any wax molds or impressions of any artifacts removed from the tomb. All bareliefs are to remain intact and will not be removed from the tomb. Wax impressions will be made and plaster molds can then be used to reconstruct parts of the tomb for display at the museum. However, that involves a different team of workers. "

Reginald bowed his head in understanding and continued his interview. "With regards to the two missing workers—You said Dr. Kasmut showed no interest in their disappearance, even though they left their personal belongings behind." Reginald recalled their earlier conversation.

"That was the appearance she wished to convey, but it didn't set with me," Dr. Stafford said. "When the workers vanished and we requested the police be called to investigate, she started to act in a strange manner."

"What do you mean by that?"

Stafford gave some serious thought before answering. "It was her attitude towards Dashi that changed. The moon was full that evening and he had been taking some photographs over the campsite with his droid.

He takes photos of the desert landscape and sells them to the tourists. The shadows cast by a full moon in the desert are quite artistic. She was suddenly more upset with him—said he was disturbing everyone in the camp and demanded he give her the droid."

"Did he?" Reginald asked with interest.

"No. But she made him take it home and said he couldn't have it here at the excavation site."

"That's most interesting. I'll keep that in mind. I may have more questions later, but I know you have work to do. Thank you for the information. Will you be joining us for lunch today?"

Dr. Stafford stood when Reginald did. "I can't say at the moment, but thank you for the invitation." Sir Thomas entered the ten as Dr. Stafford left and they greeted each other.

"Sorry I got held up with inspecting the personal belongings of the missing workers. I didn't find much of interest. It appears they were already searched through. If they were hiding anything, it was removed. How was the interview with Dr. Stafford?"

"Most enlightening," Reginald said, still thinking about their conversation. "I believe we need to speak with Dashi."

"You think he might be part of what's been happening?"

"I get a feeling he might have access to more information than we imagine. Unfortunately our next interview is with the 'dragon lady' He glanced up as she entered the tent.

"Sorry, I'm a few minutes early," she said with a sarcastic smile. "I'd like to get this over with so I can get on with the important work." She took the chair in front of the desk, crossed her legs, and folded her hands in her lap. "Shall we proceed?"

Thomas pulled up another chair at the side of the desk. "By all means, let us begin. As I'm sure you must be aware, my agency was hired by Lloyd's of London who is covering the insurance on this excavation. The news of two missing workers is troubling to them, as all employees on the project are their responsibility."

"As they are mine as well," she said stiffly. "People go missing all the time. Don't they ever have missing people in London?"

"Of course they do," answered Sir Reginald. "They have missing people all over the world."

"Then what's the point?" she asked.

"These workers vanished over three weeks ago." he added.

"And you're just now starting to search for them?" she quipped.

Sir Thomas jumped into the conversation. "We assumed the local police had been notified and were checking into their disappearance."

"The local police were notified, Sir Thomas, and they are of the same opinion as myself. The workers will return on their own when they are ready. It happens all the time in Egypt, especially if they're owed any money.

"Their whereabouts is not in my interest or the interest of this project. I have plenty of workers who are doing a fine job. The missing workers will be docked their wages for the hours they haven't worked.

"There are no dead bodies lying around, nothing's been stolen to my knowledge, and no one has filed any insurance claims. End of discussion. Now if you will excuse me, I have work to do." Dr.

Kasmut stood to leave.

Sir Reginald remained seated. "The discussion is not over, as you say. However, we will be looking further into the matter and may have need to call on you again. You may leave."

"Remember, Sir Reginald, of the Home Office, you are here as guests. You have no authority over me. I will come and go as I please. I am a citizen of Egypt." She stomped out of the office.

"That is one very rude woman. Just who does she think she is?" said Sir Thomas, looking like he was about to explode.

"A man," chuckled Sir Reginald.

"That's strange," grinned Thomas, "I could have sworn she was wearing a skirt." They both gave a hardy laugh.

"Were you able to learn anything from the other workers?" Reginald inquired as he stacked his notes and papers on the desk.

"Not much. Dashi attempted to translate for them, but there are so many different dialects it was rather difficult," Sir Thomas explained. "And of course, no one saw anything," he shook his head. "Imagine that on a night with a full moon."

"Perhaps they have trouble seeing in the dark. Thanks for reminding me about the full moon. I want to have a talk with Dashi. Have you seen him around camp today?"

"Yes, I believe he was in the mess tent showing Lynnette and Grace some photos he had taken recently. I saw them on the way over here a few minutes ago. Did you know he's a student of photography?"

"I learned that in my interview with Dr. Stafford today. Maybe I should speak with Lynnette first. She might get more out of him than we can," Reginald said.

"You may be right. He seems to have a way with the ladies. Grace has decided he is a true artist. She thinks he should have an exhibition at a gallery in So-ho. I have a feeling I'll be the sponsor on that one," he grinned.

Reginald glanced at his watch just as his cell phone picked up a signal and jingled. "What a surprise. I thought we were in a dead zone out here."

Sir Thomas chuckled, "Literally speaking, that's where one frequently finds tombs."

Reginald spotted the caller ID as he answered. "Ahmet, my friend, what a nice surprise. Sir Thomas and I just finished with some interviews here at the camp. What can we do for you today?"

"Sir Reginald, I trust I'm not interrupting your vacation, but doing investigative interviews tells me you are hard at work, so I won't keep you long. I have a bit of news I think you will want to hear."

"Do continue, this is a working vacation and we are all ears. Sir Thomas is here with me now. I'll turn the volume up."

"You might be careful that no one else hears this." Ahmet said.

"Understood," Reginald replied.

"The Romanian Police, with the help of INTERPOL located the other trunk from the train. It was full of powdered opium in some interesting containers. I'm flying down to Luxor tomorrow and will come to visit you at the job site, but don't mention my position to anyone, and warn the others.

"I'll fill you in on the details when I arrive. It looks like we're on to a major drug ring that we in the Turkish Secret Service and INTERPOL have been investigating for years. I'll see you tomorrow afternoon around tea time. My best to Lady Lynnette and the others." He disconnected.

"Wonder what that was all about?" Sir Thomas asked.

Reginald shrugged. "Looks like we'll have to wait until tomorrow to find out. Meanwhile, I'm hungry. Shall we join the ladies for lunch?"

"With pleasure," said Thomas. "Are you going to say anything to Lynnette?"

"I think I'll wait until tomorrow. He did say to warn the others not to mention his secret service connections. Best not to say anything to Grace, but I'll leave that up to you, old chap."

"Ah! There's the lunch bell. We're just in time," Thomas said.

The sound of the lunch bell ringing from the mess tent echoed loudly as it bounced off the hard surface of the stone walls on either side of the narrow valley as heat waves rose from the sandy desert floor. A light breeze was welcome comfort in the shade of the tent.

Workers stopped what they were doing and made their way to the buffet line. No time to wash-up. Cleanliness was not a major concern in their line of work.

Lynnette and Grace were strolling slowly into the tent for lunch when they spotted Reginald and Thomas. They met in the buffet line. Sir Thomas was searching the tent for their friends, "Where is everyone this morning?" he asked.

"Well, let me see," said Lynnette as she attempted to recall where everyone was. "Lord Charles had a luncheon engagement in Luxor, so Mario drove him in early. We've been taking a tour through the labs with Kathy, and Dr. Stafford joined us briefly. Kathy was explaining all about the process of cleaning, cataloging, photographing, and storing the artifacts for shipment to the museum in Cairo."

"Did you know that Dashi is a photographer?" asked Lynnette.

"Yes. Dr. Stafford brought this to our attention during his interview," Reginald said.

"He's been working in the lab with Kathy taking photos of artifacts before they're sent to Cairo. It appears he's studied photography and archeology in school. We also learned his father works at the museum in Luxor. He's employed in their acquisitions department.

"Dashi left just now for Luxor to have lunch with his father and fetch more photographs from his dark room at home to share with us this evening. Grace is serious about getting him an exhibition in London's art district. That was him speeding off on the red ATV. So it looks like we are only four for lunch today," she said.

"Sorry I missed him. I wanted to speak with him about his photography. Dr. Stafford mentioned he has a drone and takes photos of the desert at night," Reginald said.

"Yes. We know," Grace smiled.

"How did you learn about that?" Sir Thomas questioned.

Lynnette decided to explain their own interview with Kathy and Dashi. "It's really quite simple. You and Sir Thomas were busy with your interviews, so Grace and I decided we should have a couple of interviews on our own.

"There weren't that many suspects left to investigate, so we picked Kathy and Dashi. Not that I would call then suspects, but persons of interest, who might have information they aren't aware of."

Reginald and Thomas looked at each other then back to Grace and Lynnette seated across the table. Sir Thomas opened his mouth then closed it, when Reginald spoke. "So what did you learn?"

"Quite a lot," said Grace, "Kathy was concerned about some waxy substance on several of the Ushabti figures and the four canopic jars that were removed from the tomb.

"It appears that she and Dr. Stafford were questioning this strange waxy condition and Dr. Kasmut was not happy about it. They told her it would require further study and certain items couldn't be released for shipment until they understood where the substance had come from. She stormed out of the lab screaming all kinds of curses in her native language, causing quite a stir among the workers."

Lynnette turned her head from Thomas to Reginald. "Doesn't that sound strange to you? What I mean to say, is that it doesn't seem like a very scientific response to me, unless she's trying to cover something up."

"Was Dashi there when this took place?" asked Reginald.

"Yes," Lynnette answered. "He rolled his eyes, shrugged, and said he would be back after lunch. I asked him to bring his drone with him and he said the 'dragon lady' had forbidden him to have it at the compound. However, he said he would take it apart and sneak it in. Dr. Stafford offered to hide it in his tent."

"It appears that there are more strange happenings here at the compound than just the missing workers. Perhaps they are all tied together," said Reginald.

"I agree with you," Thomas added. "Let's go over our notes with Lord Charles and Mario this evening before dinner. We can put our heads together and work at things from that angle. Perhaps Ahmet will bring us some more interesting news."

"Oh!" said Reginald, seeing Lynnette's eyes light-up and a questioning look appear on her face. "I almost forgot to mention that Ahmet is coming to Luxor later today and will drop by for a visit this afternoon around tea time, or tomorrow depending on his schedule."

"That's interesting," Lynnette said, thinking about this announcement. "Did he have any more information about the baroness?"

"Reginald received the message before lunch," Sir Thomas whispered. "It sounded like the Romanian Police and INTERPOL found the other trunk hidden in Romania and the baroness has been confessing all she knows. Probably to save her own neck and a few extra years in prison. We'll learn more when he arrives. We can't discuss it any further until he gets here. Mum's the word."

Reginald nodded to Lynnette and Grace. "I'm delighted the two of you have found a way to keep busy in this investigation. You've uncovered a lot more information than I expected."

"See," Lynnette smiled at Grace, "I told you he wouldn't be upset with us poking and probing for answers. Reggie knows I wouldn't keep my intuition candle hidden in the dark for long. We'll learn more when Dashi returns. By the way, according to Dr. Stafford, Lord 'dragon lady.' The person he is having lunch with today works at the Cairo Museum. He'll get him to verify her identity and position on the staff. Grace came up with that idea."

He glanced at Sir Thomas. "Looks like I may lose my wager after all," Sir Reginald grinned.

"What have you been betting on, old man?" Lynnette asked.

Reginald swallowed with a sheepish look on his face. "The ingenuity of the female mind, my dear."

She laughed. "I thought you had learned by now, my love, never bet against a sure thing."

Chapter
Twenty-Six

Don't Move

A fter lunch, the four musketeers went their separate ways. Grace decided to take a short nap. After all, the temperature was well over thirty-six degrees Celsius and English people tend to wilt when it goes above twenty-three. Sir Reginald returned to his tent office to finish writing his report for the Home Office.

Meanwhile, Lynnette stopped in their tent to get her camera case.

"I'm going to join Kathy and Dr. Stafford in the lab so I can get some photos of the cleaning process on the artifacts. I'll be back before tea time. Did Ahmet say when he might arrive?"

Reginald glanced up from his writing. "I don't expect him until late this afternoon. Thomas volunteered to meet him in Luxor and ride out with him, but I reminded him that Ahmet said he would meet us here. I understood he had business in Luxor to attend to first. I say, is that a new camera case?"

"Yes," she smiled, "I bought it in Cairo. It's bigger than my old one and I can carry other things in it at the same time so I don't need a purse."

"Very smart. Nice leather," he said.

"Funny you never noticed it in Giza when we toured the pyramids, but your mind was on the absence of camels." She turned to leave just as Dr. Kasmut arrived carrying a basket and a look of surprise on her face.

"I was expecting to see your husband," she stammered.

Lynnette waved her arm in Reginald's direction. "There he sits at his desk. I'm off to take some photos. Don't work yourself to death in this heat," she said, blowing him a kiss as she departed.

Reginald stood at his desk. "Your visit honors me. Please have a seat." She moved to the chair by the desk and took a seat. "How may I be of service?" As he seated himself he observed his guest closely.

She placed her basket on the floor by the chair. Her eyes were downcast as she appeared to be contemplating what she had come to say. "I'm sorry."

"Excuse me?"

She cleared her throat and swallowed. "I said, I'm sorry. I've not been very hospitable and I don't socialize with the staff, but you are guests of our patron Lord Marquis and I should not have been so rude at our first meeting. I suppose it is the way I have been trained all my life. I come from a family that has had to push their way to the top and it hasn't been an easy climb.

"I have nothing against your investigations into the missing workers. However, I do believe it is a waste of time. The police have already looked into the issue, as I'm sure you already know. They believe there's been no foul play, and I'm inclined to follow their line of thought."

Reginald glanced at the report on his desk and picked up one of the papers. "To quote Captain Saeed, obviously, if they did not take their clothing or personal items, then they must have planned to return. Therefore, if they planned to return, then they have not disappeared, and there is no mystery."

"My thoughts exactly," she said with a forced smile.

"Then you presume they are still alive?" Reginald asked.

"Doesn't that stand to reason?" she asked.

Reginald continued. "To quote the good Captain again, I fail to see your point. If they are alive then it would be impossible to presume they are dead; and if you were certain they are dead, presumption of death would still be impossible. One does not presume a certainty. I take no responsibility."

"If a person is taken by surprise and is unable to return for their belongings for various reasons, does that mean they are alive or dead?" Reginald asked her.

She seemed agitated and nervous but didn't answer the question. "So how long do you plan to continue this investigation?"

"It appears that there is more information developing daily. I have a friend that will be here tonight. I'll need to see what evidence he has brought me before I can answer that question," he stated in a voice of authority.

She leaned forward and pushed her chair back. "I won't stand for more interruptions. We have a job to do in a short period of time and the funds are limited. I came here with apologies. However, I can terminate this investigation with the help of the Egyptian Police."

Reginald wasn't going to be bullied. "I'm afraid not. INTERPOL is now involved."

Dr. Kasmut's eyes widened and Reginald sensed the fear behind them. "We'll see about that!" she stood and stormed out of the tent quickly, almost knocking her chair over.

Reginald sat staring after her. He sensed there was something strange and insincere about her apology. What is she hiding? Could she be involved with drug trafficking? Is she really who she claims to be? If the missing workers were involved in the black market trade, why has there not been any reports of stolen artifacts from the tomb? Why is Ahmet making a trip to the excavation site? All of these thoughts raced through his mind like the Orient Express winding its way through the Carpathian mountain range. His concentration attempted to tie the ends of the web together.

As Lynnette entered their tent, her steps were suddenly arrested by a sight that terrified her. "Don't move Reggie, not even your little finger. Stay perfectly still and don't say anything." She reached into the front compartment of her camera bag and slowly retracted her small pistol.

Her heart was racing. Trying to remain calm. There was a small click as she released the safety and took careful aim. Reginald stared at her with an inquisitive surprised expression on his face, but spoke not a word, as she pointed the gun in his direction. Taking in a deep breath, she slowly released it and pulled the trigger.

Bang! Reginald jumped. "It's okay. You can move now," she said breathing deeply. As perspiration formed on her brow.

Suddenly the doorway to their tent was filled with people who had heard the shot. Jason Taylor was standing behind her, his gun in hand. "What happened? Who fired a shot?" he asked, scanning the tent's interior.

Lynnette lowered her now shaking arm with the pistol. "I did," she said with a sigh of relief. "There was a cobra under Reginald's desk getting ready to strike. The body is still under the campaign desk. I think the head is somewhere over there." She pointed towards a back corner of the tent.

Reginald, now standing next to his wife, put his arm around her, and held her close. "Right on, old girl! Bloody good shot, I must say." He looked at her face, drained of all color. "Are you alright, love?"

She slowly placed the pistol back in the camera bag. "I could use a stiff drink about now." In a fog, she moved to the nearest chair and sat down, still shaking like a palm leaf in the desert breeze.

Grace put a hand on her shoulder. "I'll be right back with a brandy. Don't try to move."

"That's what I told Reggie," she said automatically. "Thank god he listened. The snake's head was hooded and he was weaving back and forth. I read somewhere that meant they were hypnotizing their prey and getting ready to strike," she spoke in a daze.

"Oh...Grace, you might just bring the bottle of brandy, I think we could both use a glass," Reginald called out as she left the tent.

Suddenly Dr. Kasmut pushed her way through the crowded tent entrance, "I heard a shot. What's happened? Was anyone hurt?"

"Everything's under control," Taylor said, as he picked the snake up by the tail, and put it in a basket on the floor by the chair. Placing the basket lid back on, he carried it out of the tent.

"Who fired the shot?" she asked with a look of surprise.

Reginald smiled, "My wife did. She was aiming at me, but missed and hit the snake." Everyone laughed.

"You British people have a strange sense of humor," she said, glancing around the room. "Back to work everyone. The show's over." She left the tent in a huff.

"I wonder if that's the same cobra that bit the worker in the tomb?" said Sir Thomas.

"I don't doubt that would be difficult to prove," Reginald said, "but I have an immense suspicion how it came to be in this tent."

"What? Is someone here trying to discourage our inspection?" Thomas asked with a grin.

"Let's just say, the basket Jason put the dead snake in was an unexpected gift."

"I don't understand," Grace said as she handed a glass of brandy to Lynnette and one to him.

Lynnette's photographic memory clicked. "It was her basket. I saw her carry it in as I was leaving," she hesitated. "You don't think —she wouldn't—would she?"

"It would be hard to prove," Reginald answered, "but she left without the basket, and didn't appear surprised about the snake, other than the fact that it was dead."

"Of all the nerve! Wouldn't that be considered attempted murder?" asked Grace.

"Not without proof that the snake was in the basket. Lynnette and I saw the basket when she arrived, but we didn't see the snake. It would be speculation only. I know she's hostile to our being here and it makes me think that she's hiding something much more serious than two missing workers.

"For now, we play the waiting game. Perhaps Ahmet will shed some light on the issues when he arrives."

"I hear the sound of an ATV approaching," said Grace, "That would be Dashi, back from lunch. Maybe he has some photos to show us."

"Get his attention and bring him in here. I want to ask him

about some photos he took on the night the workers went missing," said Reginald. Grace hurried out to find Dashi.

Lynnette had calmed down as she absorbed the conversations and sipped her second glass of brandy slowly, mulling over the recent events.

Grace entered the office followed by Dashi carrying a large box and had a leather portfolio tied to his back. He smiled. "My drone is in box, we must hide it in Dr. Stafford's tent. I bring pictures you asked to see, Miss. Lynn."

"Miss Lynn?" Reginald asked, raising his right eyebrow.

"Don't get in a huff, old man. I told him he could call me that. It's easier for him. He has the photos taken from the drone on the night the workers vanished."

Reginald stared at Dashi. "How did you know I wanted those photos?"

"Miss Lynn say you need them, so I bring."

Reginald gave Lynnette a questioning glance.

"Miss Lynn?" he asked, directing the question to Lynnette.

She shrugged. "Call it intuition, I just thought you might want to view them along with me and Grace." He smiled and shook his head.

"What would I do without you? First the snake and now the photos."

"What snake?" Dashi jumped, quickly scanning around the tent. .

"It's a long story," said Reginald, "my wife was going to shoot me but shot the snake instead."

Dashi laughed out loud, looking at Lynnette and Reginald together. "Funny joke. You British people have strange humor, yes?"

"Yes," they all chuckled in answer.

"Now let's have a look at those pictures," said Sir Thomas.

Dashi spread several photos out on the desk. The lighting in the tent wasn't the best, but the artistry of the photographer and his subject was amazing. The nighttime desert scenes in black and white were captivating works of sculpture.

Lynnette held one up for a closer look. "I really like this shot, but it looks like something was on your lens."

Dashi took a closer look at the photo. "That is line on canyon floor between ridges, here," he pointed. "Nothing on lens."

Lynnette studied it again. "Can you make a blow up of this part of the photo?" she asked, indicating the line.

"You mean make big? No problem. I do tonight and bring tomorrow. I have, how you say, a dark room at home."

"Dashi, do you have any photos of the workers in the compound?" Grace asked.

"Oh yes, many. You want—I bring them too?" he said.

"That would be splendid. Faces always combine a certain texture and depth in black and white photography. It adds a human touch to the abstract," Grace said. Dashi nodded in agreement.

"Did you understand what she just said?" asked Sir Thomas.

"Yes, sir. She speaks language of art," he smiled at Grace.

"Well, no wonder I don't understand her half the time," said a smiling Sir Thomas.

Grace stood up straight with her hands on her hips. "It's not the language, old man. It's your selective hearing that's on the blink."

Reginald coughed, "And on that note, we'd best get ready for tea. Ahmet could make a showing anytime now. Dashi, take these photos home with you and bring them back tomorrow with the others. Before it gets dark tonight, I want you to take some more aerial photos of the compound."

Dashi shook his head. "Dragon lady forbid me to use drone here."

"Don't worry. Dragon lady can't stop you. She's afraid of me." Everyone looked at him with surprise.

"I'll explain later," he said.

Chapter Twenty-Seven

Ahmet

It was just going on four o'clock when they all gathered for tea in the mess tent. The English are very much creatures of habit. When four o'clock rolls around, it doesn't matter what they are doing—it's tea time. Tea to them is like chicken soup, it's the cure-all, calm-all, for any situation. It's a social time and a time to reflect on the issues of the day.

The large tent was almost empty except for their group seated together. Reginald was explaining his meeting with Dr. Kasmut to bring everyone up to date. As usual, the dragon lady was nowhere to be seen.

"I let her know that INTERPOL was now involved in the investigation, and that I was expecting a visitor this afternoon who was bringing additional information to us. I didn't say who he was, but I'm sure she understood my intent to continue our investigations, and I wasn't going to let her stop us."

About that time, a large, black, SUV entered the compound parking area, followed by a second vehicle and three men got out. As they approached the tent, Lynnette commented. "It's Lord Charles and Mario, and look who they have brought with them—it's Ahmet."

The three men were greeted by members of the group and seated themselves at the table. Lord Charles introduced Ahmet to Dr. Stafford. More tea was ordered and the questions began.

"You're probably wondering how we met this gentleman from Istanbul," Lord Charles said. "To tell you the truth, it was Ahmet that I had my appointment with in Luxor. It turns out that Mario and Ahmet are well acquainted. Both have had several occasions to assist with INTERPOL and Scotland Yard investigations in the past."

"I wonder if you could repeat Ahmet's last name and title?" asked Dr. Stafford. "I didn't catch that in the introduction."

Ahmet's answer was quick and in low tones of his deep voice. "Ahmet is the only name I use. It is a code name with the Turkish

Secret Service. I've grown so used to it, I hardly remember my full name. However, for our purposes the name Ahmet is sufficient.

"Perhaps tomorrow I will introduce you to my close friend and traveling companion who has a villa on the Isle of Cyprus. She is at the hotel in Luxor, so I must return this evening.

"I've some new information to share regarding the baroness and the missing trunk on the Orient Express. I thought, as I was meeting Lord Charles with this information, it would be the perfect time to bring you up to date."

Lynnette was curious. "Have you known Lord Charles very long?"

"Oh, yes," Charles spoke out. "Ahmet has supplied secret service protection for several of my exhibitions at museums in Istanbul, Ankara and even in Cairo. We're old friends."

Sir Thomas wanted to know more about the baroness and the missing trunk. "Did the Egyptian man who abducted the baroness ever make a confession?"

"No." said Ahmet, "However, with the help of local residents, and the Romanian Police, INTERPOL was able to track the missing trunk to an old abandoned farm not far from the chateau where they found the baroness. It was hidden under a mound of hay in the loft of the dilapidated barn.

"At first it looked to be full of small Egyptian figures called Ushabti and several canopic jars made of plaster and painted. One of these had evidently broken in transit and the white powder was discovered to be opium. On closer inspection, these figures were found to contain a hollowed center that was filled with opium in glass containers before being sealed at the base."

"That explains the glass we saw on the floor of the train compartment the baroness had occupied when Sir Thomas tasted the powder and discovered it was opium." Lynnette voiced her thoughts as her photographic mind reached back to their search of the compartment on the Orient Express.

"You mentioned before, that the baroness had confessed to being a drug runner and was trafficking the drugs to Russia, am I correct?"

"That's true, your memory is excellent. Her written and signed confession stated she was to transfer the trunk to someone in Varna. From there it was to go by ship to Odesa then on to Kyiv and eventually to Moscow."

"Did she have a name for this person she was to meet or the place for their rendezvous?"

"Unfortunately, they were to contact her on arrival, but of course, she never made it to the hotel. INTERPOL had been alerted to her arrival and they were waiting for her. She is, after all, on their list of known criminals to keep under surveillance. They knew she was on the train. However, she managed to change her train car and compartment without it being detected. They temporarily lost contact and that was when the Egyptian abducted her."

Grace had been following his story intently. "It appears then, that they were not working together. Evidently he knew she was meeting someone in Varna and had very little time to make his move to silence her and steal the opium. So why take the time to kidnap her after he had found the opium in one of the trunks?"

Ahmet was cautious with his answer. "His meeting at the tourist stop in Sinaia had been planned ahead. He sent a coded wire from Budapest which was later traced to the train station where his people had met him, loaded the trunks, and disappeared to the chateau in the mountains.

"The baroness had been strangled until she passed out, but not killed. She was an attractive woman so he took her for his personal pleasure, possibly intending to kill her later at the chateau and bury her body there. Fortunately we found her before that could take place.

"I contacted Lord Charles because of his project here with the tomb excavation. These plaster figures and jars were obviously copies of Egyptian artifacts coming from a project currently in progress. Genuine artifacts from older excavations are already in museums. It was obvious these were made as a disguise to transport drugs."

"Then, your belief, that it's possible they are tied to this excavation, is why you are here?" Sir Reginald commented as he fit pieces of the puzzle together in his mind.

"It gave us cause to speculate and make some investigations." Ahmet glanced around the compound. "For instance, after my contact with Lord Charles, we made some inquiries at the Cairo Museum and learned that their representative, a Dr. Tavvi, who was assigned to assist here at the excavation, recently died of heart complications." Ahmet paused and sipped his mint tea.

Dr. Stafford spoke next. "We were informed that Dr. Tavvi had taken ill, but were not aware he had passed away. His assistant Dr. Kasmut was already here when I arrived, and seemed to have things under her control from the beginning.

"I didn't agree with all of her rules and regulations, but she gave the appearance of experience and the workers followed her orders. I've worked with Egyptians in the past and knew it was best not to push my authority. But I must say, she's a bit overbearing and at times extremely rude. Not one hundred percent scientific but a taskmaster of the first-class to stay on a time schedule. Nothing was going to slow her down. Not even two missing workers."

Ahmet smiled and nodded his head. "Therein lies the problem."

"Excuse me?" Reginald said. "Exactly what is the problem?"

"She's not who she claims to be." Around the table, everyone looked at each other in a question of surprise, then back to Ahmet.

"Are you saying that she's not with the museum in Cairo?" asked Grace, who was the first to speak.

"Not anymore," Ahmet said. "She worked at the museum for the past three years, but moved to the Luxor Museum last year, where she became involved with a drug ring. You have a young man working here as a photographer. His name is Dashi. He's a spy."

Lynnette appeared shocked. "Dashi? A spy?" Her brain had clicked into high gear. "No wonder he has a drone and takes photos of the compound and desert from overhead. But he's an artist."

Ahmet chuckled at her statement. "Yes, Lady Lynnette, and you'll have to admit, it makes an excellent cover. In reality, he's an intelligence gatherer for his father, who is with the Egyptian Secret Police."

Grace quickly added, "That explains why his English, although broken, is so good. Now it makes sense. He has brought some photos he showed us this evening. One in particular that Lynnette was curious about. If we can find Dashi, perhaps you would like to see those photos."

"Here I am. You want to see Dashi?" he asked with a grin on his face.

"Young man. You have the strangest way of popping up when least expected. How long have you been hiding behind the tent?" Grace asked.

"No hide. I listen. You say Dashi. I hear my name. I answer," he grinned and nodded to Ahmet. "You want see pictures now?"

"Yes, Dashi. That would be nice," Lynnette said.

"I go. Back in flash." Lynnette blinked and he was gone.

Reginald had been quietly fitting the pieces of the mystery together. He was still concerned about how Dr. Kasmut fit into the picture. Were her credentials forged? Had she kept the death of Dr. Tavvi a secret to fortify her placement here? Was it possible that she could manufacture the fake artifacts in her tent? So, what part was she playing in this case? Had she caused Dr. Tavvi's death? All these questions needed answers.

Dr. Stafford stood to leave. "I need to return to the lab. There is still work to be done. We've hidden Dashi's drone in my quarters. Sir Reginald has asked him to take some night photos with the light of the full moon this evening. If he keeps it high enough, Dr. Kasmut won't hear it."

Kathy stood to leave also, "I'll join you. There's more cataloguing to do. However, if you need to make a closer observation of the photos, don't forget we have two large microscopes in the lab. If I can assist with any further questions, please let me know." They departed as Dashi returned with the pictures and laid them out on the table for Ahmet to see.

Ahmet stood and glanced quickly at the photos selecting three or four of them. "I really must be getting back to Luxor. If I am late for dinner, my lady friend begins to worry. Let me know if you find anything unusual in these photos. I'll be back in the morning."

"Meanwhile, what shall we do about Dr. Kasmut?" said Sir Thomas.

Ahmet smiled. "Mario is going to keep her under surveillance. If she gets frightened or suspicious he'll notify us. She won't get far. However, it's best to allow her to think she is in the clear. It will give us the opportunity to learn more," he said. "And now I must be off. Thank you for the tea and conversation."

"But you haven't told us anything about the timetables and the ships. If these figures and jars are being filled with opium and are being moved about, how is all that taking place?" asked Lynnette.

Ahmet smiled. "That question will have to wait until tomorrow. Meanwhile, be on the alert. Things are not always as they appear to be."

Chapter Twenty-Eight

Dashi

Reginald glanced up just in time to see Dr. Kasmut coming across the compound to the mess tent, followed by the compound chef and one of his assistants. He quickly gathered the photos and slipped them under the table, out of sight.

"I trust your tea party is over," she said. "The cook didn't wish to interrupt, but he needs to get these tables cleared for dinner." She glanced at Sir Reginald, "I believe you have an office tent reserved for meetings, which I would suggest you use. I'll be in Luxor this evening, so try not to keep the staff up too late." Without further comment, she turned and headed in the direction of the lab.

Lord Charles and the group retired to the office tent. "I will be delighted when I can tell that woman she is fired," said he, once inside the tent.

"Or arrested," added Grace. "According to Ahmet, she is here under false pretenses and a subject of suspicion. We've not been able to search her tent because she's not allowed us entry and we're only investigators without any legal authority. But I'm anxious to hear what Ahmet has to say tomorrow."

"Meanwhile, we should take a closer look at those photos Dashi took with his drone. Reggie and I could take them over to the lab and use the microscope Kathy offered. It would call too much attention if we all went. And we need to be sure Dr. Kasmut is not there," said Lynnette.

"I go check," offered Dashi. "Come back and tell you."

Lynnette turned her head quickly. "Dashi, how do you manage to be everywhere when needed?"

He grinned, "I'm like cat burglar. You no see me. You no hear me. But I'm there." He vanished in a flash.

"I think Grace and I will retire to our facilities for now. Please keep us posted if there are any new developments," said Sir Thomas.

Jason Taylor and Boris Rykoff had remained out of the spotlight while attending to their job as bodyguards. Jason had also been keeping tabs on Dr. Kasmut at the request of Lord Charles and his friend, the chief inspector at Scotland Yard. His appearance in the tent was quite unexpected.

"I know I shouldn't be here, but there's a couple of things I think you might want to know," Taylor said.

"Speak up, young man," said Lord Charles. "If it's anything to do with the investigation, we are all ears."

"I've been watching the moves of Dr. Kasmut as requested and the lady has been very busy especially late at night. An Egyptian man guards her tent all night. She's rarely absent long enough to allow for a search of the unit. She carries small boxes back and forth from her tent to the lab when the others are asleep."

"What's in the boxes?" asked Lynnette.

"This I don't know. But she takes the boxes in her van when she goes into town. I don't follow her out of the compound, so I don't know where she goes."

"Thank you, Jason. Is there anything else you wanted to report?" asked Lord Charles.

"That's all for now," Jason answered as he ducked out of the tent.

"Dragon lady not in lab. You come," said a voice in the doorway. Reginald still had the photos in his hand as they followed the young man to the lab.

Kathy greeted them, "Dashi said you wanted to use the microscope to get a better look at some of the photos. You can use this space over here." She directed them to an area where the instrument sat on a large clean surface.

"Are you here all alone?" Lynnette asked.

"Not really. Mario and Dr. Stafford are in the attached storage area checking the items to be delivered for shipment to the museum tomorrow. They should be finished shortly, then we'll shut things down. We have a new man on guard for the night. Everything is kept under lock and key."

"Did you say the guard is a new man?" Reginald asked.

"Yes, he's been on night duty since the other guard vanished. That's what prompted the first report to the British Museum. Nothing was missing the next morning, but the guard."

Lynnette was staring at one of the photos under the microscope. "Come take a look at this," she beckoned to Reginald. He moved to see what she was talking about.

"What am I looking for?" he asked.

"The white area in the center is the valley between the darker ridges on each side. What do you see?" she asked.

"I see a dark line. Is that it?"

Kathy stepped closer. "Here, let me adjust the lens for a better view. Dashi is an excellent photographer, but not much of a scientist. He can always make an enlargement if you need." She looked through the scope and readjusted the lens. "It's not much better, I'm afraid. It still looks blurred."

Lynnette waved her hand at Dashi. "Come take a look and see if you can guess what this is. You said it wasn't something on the lens, so give us your opinion."

Bending over the microscope his young eyes focused on the center of the photo. "Camels!" he said.

"What do you mean, camels?" asked Lynnette.

"This small caravan—ten maybe twelve camels," he smiled. "Going north. They move and make line blur," he said.

"What would camels be doing in the Valley of the Monkeys?" Lynnette asked.

"Camels carry harvest—grain and cotton. Take shortcut to Nile port at Qina. Travel at night. Camels travel old routes. Like elephant—no forget the way," he smiled.

"Isn't there a road from Qina to some resort on the Red Sea?" Lynnette asked.

"Yes. Many popular resorts on the sea at Safga and north." Dashi answered.

"Is there a marina there for yachts and boats?"

"Oh, yes. Many rich people go by sea." Dashi could see Lynnette's questions were leading somewhere. "You think drugs go by camel to Red Sea?"

"Let's just say, it's a hypothesis. A possibility that should be looked into. We should mention this to Ahmet tomorrow."

"I agree," Reginald concurred. "However, the river ports at Qina or Abydos could also be a destination point for shipping goods down the Nile to the Mediterranean."

"When were these photos taken?" Lynnette asked Dashi.

"Before you arrive. Maybe one day. Lord Charles was here."

"Hand me that photo of the compound. The one Ahmet selected before he left," said Reginald, "He must have noticed something suspicious." Reginald placed the photo under the microscope and peered through the lens, sliding it around until he spotted something. He motioned to Lynnette. "Take a look at this and tell me what you see."

It didn't take her long to understand what he saw. "When was this photo taken?" Dashi didn't have to look at it to know.

"Night before camels. Dragon lady upset. Say no more photos from air. I fly drone down valley next night—away from compound."

Kathy asked, "May I take a look?"

Lynnette stepped aside. "By all means. You might recognize someone."

Kathy peered through the lens and studied it for only a moment. "That looks like Dr. Kasmut. But what would she be carrying in a box in the middle of the night. It appears she's moving something from the lab to her tent."

"That fits with the movements that Jason Taylor reported to us earlier. Shifting boxes from one place to another," Reginald said.

Mario had been following all of this conversation. "All we need is a search warrant for her tent but we have no authority in Egypt. It would have to be done through INTERPOL or the Egyptian Police. And for some reason, I don't believe the police are interested. We haven't any proof that a crime has been committed."

"Didn't Dr. Kasmut say she would be out of the compound this evening?" Lynnette asked.

"Yes," said Kathy, "That's what gave me the idea to use the microscope tonight to view the photos while she's away."

"Splendid! I have an idea." Lynnette said.

"I know that look. You're planning to do something you shouldn't," said Reginald. I hope you're not planning to break into her tent."

"Of course not. I wouldn't think of breaking in. I'm just going to slip in for a look around," she smiled. "I promise not to break anything." Reginald shook his head and removed his glasses. "You do have a way of spinning my words. Might I remind you that her tent is guarded by a very large Egyptian man?"

Lynnette's grin got even bigger and her eyes glittered mischievously. "That's where I need your help." She looked at Kathy, Mario, Reginald, and Dashi. Your team needs to create a distraction so I can sneak in the back entrance."

"How do you know there's a back entrance?" asked Kathy.

"Grace and I took a long stroll around the compound recently and in the process we proceeded to get lost on purpose. Dashi confessed how he suddenly appears in a tent without coming through the main door. I'm sure her tent has a back entrance."

"Lynnette, love, I can't let you do this. It's too dangerous and I forbid it." Reginald said in a stern voice.

"Reginald, dear, you have never forbidden me to do anything, and this isn't the time to start. This is my idea, I'm the one with the camera, and I know how to take photos without a flash. I promise to be discreet and extremely careful. I truly appreciate your concern, but we are wasting time. Now be a good chap and start a fire somewhere to draw the guard away from her tent. But first I need to change my clothes. Black is better for this adventure."

"Let us know when you are in place. We can create a fire here in the lab without causing much damage," said Kathy. "That should draw everyone's attention to the lab and cause a stir."

"I watch guard. Signal when he goes." said Dashi.

"And what would you have me do?" asked Reginald.

"Make a lot of noise. Rouse the compound residents. Create confusion and leave the rest to me," Lynnette smiled and gave him a peck on the cheek as she left to change clothes into something more suitable for a spy.

Minutes later, she had slipped around to the back of Dr. Kasmut's tent. She could see Dashi standing in the shadows to one side of the lab storage tent. All was quiet and the performers were in place. Suddenly a bright flash came from inside the lab. Followed in minutes by a call for help.

"Fire! Fire!" came a scream from Kathy, followed by more voices, as the compound suddenly filled with people rushing in all directions to put out the fire. The guard hurried toward the lab. Dashi gave the signal and Lynnette disappeared through the back entrance of the doctor's tent.

The fire had damaged two metal trash cans in the center of the tent. Smoke had filled the night air as workers lifted the sides of the tent to allow it to escape, while they fanned the air with palm leaves. "Where's Lynnette?" asked Grace, glancing around to locate her.

"She's on a secret mission. This was a distraction. With any luck, she should be back in our tent by now," answered Reginald.

"So...she did it without me. I missed the espionage," she sighed. "That's one brave wife you've married, old man."

"I can vouch for that statement. Just look at all the extra gray hairs she's given me," he added.

"The proof is in the pudding. Dashi will have to develop the film and bring it back tomorrow. Meanwhile, I think we could all use a brandy while Lynnette tells us a spy story, don't you?"

"I could use a drink about now, and probably more than one when the dragon lady hears about the fire tomorrow."

Chapter Twenty-Nine

Lynnette's Espionage

Lynnette had changed into a completely black casual outfit, her black shoes had rubber soles, and she had wrapped her auburn hair in a black scarf. She carried her smaller camera as she moved cautiously behind the tents, hoping she would not encounter any cobras or other nighttime desert creatures.

Her eyes had adjusted to the darkness and there was a sliver of moon rising in the east this late in the evening. She moved with the silence of a snake, weaving in and out of the darker areas. She could hear voices in low muted tones. The language was not one that she spoke, but she knew that a few people were still awake and moving about.

As she reached the doctor's tent she heard a cough and spotted Dashi lurking in the shadows of the lab tent. She had to admit she wouldn't have noticed him if he hadn't coughed. No wonder Ahmet said he was a good spy.

She waited. Her heart was beating so loudly, she was sure the guard could hear it. Her breath came in slow, deep, rhythms from her diaphragm as she counted the seconds. When the alarm came with screams of "fire, fire," she jumped. All her senses were on alert. Her eyes focused on Dashi hoping for the signal. If the guard didn't respond, the plan would have to be canceled.

Dashi, watched the tent carefully as he saw the guard rush in the direction of the commotion. He waved and Lynnette quickly peeled the back flap of the tent open. The Velcro made a scratching sound as it separated. She realized she had only minutes to capture photos that would possibly contain evidence and facts needed to support their suspicions.

On entering, her attention was drawn to several small boxes stacked on one side of the tent. They were partially covered with a heavy cloth and tucked under a table. She quietly pulled the cloth aside to see what was in the boxes.

A strange smell came from the first box as she removed the lid.

The inside was half full of a sticky substance. Lynnette placed her finger on the gooey surface and quickly withdrew it, leaving a small fingerprint.

Ouch! She thought. That was stupid. Now someone will know I was here. She quickly removed the tops off of more boxes filled with the same substance, took several pictures, replaced the lids, and placed the cloth back over them as it was. Minutes slipped by quickly as she searched for more evidence to photograph.

There were bags of a powdery substance stacked under a table and a large empty bucket nearby that appeared to have been used to mix paint. She wasn't sure it would be important, but took a photo anyway, scooping a portion of the white powder into a rubber glove she had taken from the lab earlier in case she might need it.

Time was ticking away as she approached the large desk with stacks of papers and invoices. Reaching for the main drawer, she discovered it was not locked. Inside she saw a list similar to the one they had discovered on the train in the compartment used by the baroness. It might be identical or possibly be a newer list with different dates, times and ship numbers. Using her photographic memory to compare the two lists would take too long. Click went the camera. She froze in place when she heard a voice close by. Had the guard returned?

She held her breath and listened. It was Dashi's voice. He was speaking to the guard about the fire damage and the alarm. Their conversation was interrupted by a third voice that she recognized as Jason Taylor's.

"Everything okay over here?" he said in a loud voice as he spoke to Dashi. "I was asleep when the alarm sounded. Was anyone hurt?" he continued. "We don't want anyone caught off guard. Fires can be a real danger around all these tents."

"I think all is good," Dashi answered just as Taylor caught Lynnette's figure silently moving in the darkened shadows as she passed the guard who had his back to her.

Lynnette had slipped through the back opening and quietly closed the flap. Had she closed the desk drawer? It was too late now to think about that. People were still milling about as she disappeared into Regiald's office quarters like a cat burglar without making a sound.

Grace had been watching their tent and saw her quick moves. "I'm going to check on Lynnette. She just entered your tent," she said to Reginald.

He breathed a sigh of relief, "Thank god! Tell her I'll be there in a minute and give her a Scotch. I'm sure she'll need it. I'll let the others know her mission is complete."

Lynnette was sitting in the office chair, perspiration beaded on her forehead and her hands were shaking. "Welcome back Sherlock," smiled Grace as she entered the tent.

"Watson, old friend, where were you when I needed you?" Lynnette attempted to joke in return.

"How about a Scotch, old girl? I think you've earned it," Grace added.

"Well, we can't count the evidence until it's developed, but I'm confident we've got the goods on Dr. Kasmut. She might try to destroy the evidence, but we have it on film. At least I know where the sticky substance on the artifacts comes from. If you want my opinion, she is making molds of the ushabti figures and possibly the canopic jars, and other artifacts, but that doesn't answer all the questions. What use is she making of them?"

Lynnette pulled the twisted lab glove containing a scoop of the powder in it from her pocket and handed it to Grace. "Maybe Thomas can identify what this powder is. She had bags of it covered with a cloth. It could be the plaster she uses to fill the molds."

Reginald and Thomas entered the tent followed by Dashi, Kathy, Mario, and Lord Charles.

"My hair is going to start falling out if you keep pulling stunts like this," Reginald exclaimed as he embraced Lynnette. "I need a Scotch." Grace poured him a glass and handed it to him. He held Lynnette at arms-length in front of him as his eyes scanned every inch of her body. "Are you okay, old girl? You look kind of blanched."

She smiled, "It's just the black clothing against my white skin. I'm fine. Where is my partner and amazing photographer?" she said, searching the faces in the room.

"Here I am," said Dashi grinning.

She handed him her camera. "Guard this with your life. How soon can you develop the film and be back here tomorrow?"

"I be here by noon," he said, reaching for the camera.

"Don't break any speeding records and don't get stopped by the police. If they get those photos, we might never see them again."

"No problem," Dashi smiled, as he dashed out of the tent.

"I think we've caused enough excitement for one night," said Lord Charles. "Shall we all turn in and leave this couple alone? Tomorrow's another day and we still have a case to solve."

"Before you all leave," Lynnette quickly spoke, "I just wanted to thank you for your help this evening. I couldn't have done that on my own. It's 'one for all and all for one.'"

She suddenly found herself in Reginald's arms again. He kissed her forehead and held her tight. "How did I ever deserve a wife like you? Where do you get the nerve to pull such tricks as you do?"

She smiled as her head rested against his chest. "They're not tricks at all. They're well-coordinated, systematic plans, and you really should read more Agatha Christie books. As for nerves...I get that from my father, but it's your confidence in me that makes it happen," she paused, "ready for bed, old man? I'm exhausted."

~

Sunrise came early the next morning, but not for Lynnette. Her dreams had kept her awake half the night as she saw herself being taken away in handcuffs by Egyptian police and locked away in a cell without any windows. They promised her she would never see the light of day again. She hadn't begun to relax until almost dawn, when the light of day assured her it was all a dream.

"Cup of tea, old girl?" said a familiar voice. She squinted through heavy eyelashes, stretched, and pushed herself up into a sitting position.

"Where am I?" she mumbled.

Grace smiled and handed her the cup. "You're still in bed. We didn't want to wake you. You needed your rest after last night. Thomas, Reginald, and Lord Charles are lingering over breakfast. Would you like me to bring something to you?"

Lynnette gave her a sheepish glance, "I don't think my stomach is ready for food just yet, but the tea will settle it." Her mind raced back to the previous evening's events. "Has Dashi returned with the photos?"

Grace shook her head as she poured herself a cup of tea and turned to sit in the chair by Lynnette's bed. "It's only ten o'clock. He said he would return before noon and I'm sure he will."

Lynnette set her cup on the small table by the bed, swung her feet over the bedside to the wooden floor, and started to rise. "Where do you think you're going?" asked Grace.

"I don't want to miss the meeting. If I'm not there it might look suspicious. I know I left a fingerprint in the tent last night and I can't remember if I closed the desk drawer," she said.

Grace folded her arms across her chest. "Might I remind you, that you have a photographic memory, right?"

"Right," Lynnette nodded.

"Then what was your picture of the desk when you last saw it? Was the drawer closed or open?" she asked.

Lynnette closed her eyes and thought for a moment. "The drawer was closed."

"Good," said Grace with a smile, "In that case, your brain is still functioning and there's nothing to worry about."

"I know, but there's still my fingerprint in that sticky goo," said Lynnette.

Grace shook her head. "I wouldn't give it much thought. The way things are going around here it could be weeks or even months before anyone will find it or even notice it. Trust me."

Reginald appeared in the doorway. "I say, is this a private conversation or can a concerned husband join in?"

"I was just leaving," said Grace placing her cup back on the tray she had carried in. "Have you released my husband?" she smiled.

"I have no control over your husband," he spread his arms and shrugged his shoulders. "When I last saw him, he was strolling to the lab tent with Dr. Stafford to survey the terrible damage from last night's fire." He grinned.

"Good. Then I know where to look." Grace left the tent.

Reginald sat beside Lynnette on her bed and put his arm around her. "How are you feeling, love?"

"Still a little tired. Have I missed anything?" she asked, sipping her tea.

"Only a true confession," he said.

Her eyes blinked in surprise. "Who confessed to what?"

He chuckled. "Your bodyguard, Jason Taylor. He knew you were in Dr. Kasmut's tent last night. He watched every move you made from here to her tent and back. Did you know he was watching?"

She nodded her head. "I knew someone was watching. You know how I sense these things, but I thought it was Dashi. He was my lookout, so naturally he would be watching me. But when the excitement was over, I heard Dashi talking with the guard outside the tent to let me know he was back on duty. Then I heard Taylor's voice, rather loud, as he spoke with Dashi. They were both attempting to warn me and cover any sound I might make leaving the tent.

I'll be sure and thank him and his watchful eyes."

"I had a message this morning from Ahmet. His business is keeping him in Luxor this morning, but we should see him late this afternoon. He's bringing his lady friend from Cyprus to meet you and Grace, and will fill us in on the other case."

"I had better get myself together before Dashi returns. I have a feeling that young man is more than he appears to be and I'm a good judge of character. He's hiding something, but I can't put my finger on it."

Reginald smiled. "Well, Ahmet said Dashi is a spy."

"Ahmet's an amusing person, but I'm sure he was saying that facetiously. No...it's something else. However, I'll find out his secret before we leave."

"A truer statement was never spoken." Reginald chuckled.

Chapter Thirty

Deceptions

Minnie Sparks had been most upset when she couldn't find Lynnette in the crowd during all the commotion of the fire last night. Boris sat with her afterwards to try and calm her down. Once she learned that Lynnette was safe the subject seemed to take a different turn.

"I promise you, Minnie. When we get back to England I'll find another job and we'll get married." He wiped the tears out of her eyes with his thumb.

"You mean you'd give up being a bodyguard and traveling all over the world just for me?" she asked with a sniff, dabbing her nose with his handkerchief.

"Well, I wouldn't want you to be worried about me like you are with Miss Lynn, when I'm off guarding someone in Spain or Africa. It wouldn't be right now, would it?"

She leaned into the muscular arm he had around her shoulder. "That sounds like a plan, only there's one problem. I have to get permission first."

Boris gave her a quizzical stare. "I thought you said your family was all gone. Who has to give you permission to marry?"

"Why, Miss Lynnette, of course. She's the only family I have, but I'm sure she'll be happy for us. And of course, she'll need to find my replacement. But we can discuss all the details when we get home to England. Meanwhile, I need to get back to the tent in case she needs me." She gave him a peck on the cheek and scurried off to do her job. Boris blinked, shook his head, and followed in her direction. After all, Minnie was under his protective eye on this trip.

The sound of an ATV could be heard coming up the valley road with a trail of dust flying behind it. Dashi had arrived. He hurried from the parking area as Dr. Kasmut's white van pulled in behind him. He waved at Sir Reginald and quickly disappeared, as he hurried to the lab tent with a large envelope tucked in his shirt.

Dr. Kasmut rushed through the compound stalking behind him

and followed his footsteps into the lab. She didn't appear to be in a pleasant mood and her voice could be heard loud and clear. "What was the meaning of passing me like that? You almost ran me off the road," she screamed. "Are you just now coming in?" she huffed.

"Yes ma'am," he said.

"If you weren't an assistant working for Dr. Stafford, I would fire you right now. Don't you ever do that again, is that clear?" He nodded without a word.

Out of the lab she stormed and marched directly to her own office. Reginald and Lynnette entered the lab a few minutes later, followed by Grace. Thomas was at the tomb with Lord Charles.

"What was that all about?" asked Grace, who had been inside her tent and missed seeing all the action.

Dashi grinned. "Dragon lady, she no like me much." He chuckled out loud.

"Have you got the photos?" asked Lynnette.

He gave a quick nod and reached for the envelope he had hidden under the oilcloth cover on the table. Lynnette emptied the package of photos and spread them out to take a look. Kathy moved to the lab entry, "I'll keep watch in case she decides to make a return visit. But I'm anxious to see the shots that interest you. The scope is there if you need it." She stepped outside the tent to chat with Mario.

Taking one of the photos, Lynnette showed it to Reginald. "This is the shipping chart I found in her desk. We need to compare it to the copy we got from Ahmet. This one might be new and more up to date." She slid it under the microscope and took a closer look. "Yes," she confirmed. "There are several changes in timing and in the ship numbers. This is not what I remember seeing. We need to get a copy of this to Ahmet as soon as possible."

Lynnette searched the room for Dashi's face. "I hope you made copies of these photos," she said.

He nodded. "Yes copies are in the envelope."

Grace held up a different photo. "What on earth is this? It looks like jelly in a box."

Lynnette took the photo from her. "I don't know what it is, but I put my finger into it and left a fingerprint. There were several boxes under a table covered with a cloth. The bags of powder were stacked next to them."

Dashi was standing close by. "To the naked eye it appears translucent, but to solve the conundrum of the mold boxes taken in your two photos, that is known as molding-wax. It requires a special formula using wheaten flour because it is lighter than mineral powder and more tenacious. It's used to reduce the stickiness of the wax and a rolling pin is used to smooth the wax.

"The wax must be warmed gently under a low heat in order to get a clear impression of the object to be copied, but leaving it firm enough to keep its shape in a half-inch layer of plaster.

"Molding-wax is often used at excavation sites to preserve copies of artifacts in case of damage in shipping. A thin coat of oil is used on the exposed portion of the plaster plate reserved for the mold, which in turn leaves a residue that is then removed in the final cleaning process."

Lynnette stood with her mouth open, but not a sound escaped. Grace blinked, as a slow smile crossed her face, she cleared her throat. "You just said a mouthful without one word of broken English." Dashi blushed and bowed his head.

"Where did you learn to speak English so well and why have you disguised your ability to do so?" Lynnette asked, still in a daze.

"I attended university in America. My father sent me to study archeology, but I also studied a more artistic curriculum with photography, and because I enjoy reading mysteries, I took some classes in forensic science."

Lynnette shook her head in disbelief. "You are a hidden candle whose light has just been revealed, and I'm more than impressed.

Ahmet was right. You, young man, are an intelligence spy."

"Not really. I work with my father to catch forgeries of artifacts. In this country, there are many. However, I don't believe I fooled Kathy or Lord Charles for very long, and when Lady Grace made her statement about understanding my photography and its place in the artistic world, I almost blew my cover with my answer when Sir Thomas, asked if I understood what she had said."

"And how old are you?" asked Grace.

"I'm twenty-seven and have three university degrees. For all intents and purposes, you have not heard any of my confession and it must remain a secret if I'm to complete my assignment here."

"May I be so bold as to ask what your assignment is?" said Sir Reginald.

"We believe there are fake artifacts coming out of this excavation. The molding-wax is a clue but not proof or evidence. As I explained just now, it is used at many tomb sites in Egypt. The drone photo of the camel train could be valuable if Ahmet can find out where they are distributing their cargo and what the cargo is. So much goes undetected here in the desert. Our goal is to prevent the production of fake artifacts, or substituting fakes for real antiquities which are then sold on the black market." Dashi answered.

"I'd say you have your hands full," commented Reginald. "Not to mention finding missing workers."

"With all due respect, sir, that assignment is not mine. However, if I can assist, I'm happy to do so."

Reginald glanced at Lynnette and Grace, then faced Dashi. "In that case, I would like to invite you to attend any of our future meetings with regards to the missing workers. You might find them interesting and perhaps helpful with your assignment."

Lynnette smiled at Reginald. "What a simply marvelous idea, my dear. However, I believe Dashi has already attended several of our meetings, and it's quite obvious that he did so in secret and without our knowledge. He's proven, in our favor, to be talented in the art of deception and intelligence. It's only fitting he should be welcomed into our group of musketeers." Dashi smiled, his skin so darkly tanned, they couldn't see him blush.

Lord Charles stepped into the lab tent. "There you all are. Sir Thomas and I just returned from the tomb and were looking for you. Anything happening I should know about?"

Lynnette stepped next to him and took his arm. "I think you might be interested to see the new evidence we've discovered in the photos Dashi has developed from my recent undercover work," she smiled. "Reginald and Dashi can fill you in on the details. Where did you leave Dr. Stafford? I have a few questions I'd like to ask him."

Lord Charles glanced at Grace. "Sir Thomas was looking for you. You might wish to go find him." He turned to Lynnette. "I last saw Dr. Stafford in a heated conversation with Dr. Kasmut in front of her tent. However, I didn't wish to eavesdrop so I came on over here."

Dr. Stafford entered the lab shaking his head. "That woman has got to be exposed for the fraud that she is and the sooner the better."

Reginald asked, "What has she done now?"

"I wanted to tell her that Lord Charles has decided it is time to seal the tomb until arrangements can be made with the Cairo Museum to staff and reopen it to the public.

"However, she accused me of breaking into her tent while she was away. She threatened to ruin my reputation and work with the British Museum," he stated. Everyone was stunned.

"Of course, she didn't know I was in Luxor last evening. I was told not to give her that information. I even saw her, but she never saw me having dinner with Ahmet. As you know, I didn't get back here until after the fire in the lab had been contained." His eyes went to each person in the room and a grin appeared on his face. "I'm still in a quandary as to how that got started."

Lynnette had a guilty look on her face. "Well, you see..."

"No, no," he held his hand up to stop her confession. "There are some things I don't need to know, as long as the only damage was two trash cans containing a highly flammable substance." he nodded with a grin. "Now, we need to get back to work and wrap things up as quickly as possible. And your people," he addressed Sir Reginald, "may continue their investigations."

Lynnette needed one more question answered. "So what did you tell the dragon lady?"

Dr. Stafford smiled. "As politely as I could, in my state of anger, I told her it would be a cold day in hell when she could destroy my reputation," he paused. "I then told her to take a long walk off a short pier."

"Bravo!" said Lynnette. "You're all heart Rolland," she grinned.

Chapter
Thirty-One

The Web

When a spider spins his web, he begins building by attaching support cables in numerous directions, which he then carefully connects in a circular motion creating a spiral effect. He continues to check for strength and gradually tightens all the lines to be sure he can, not only capture his victims, but that his labors are secure enough to hold them tight.

Ahmet's mind was going over his research papers after his meeting with Dr. Stafford and Dashi last night. There was no mistake that the photos taken by Lynnette were undeniable evidence that Dr. Kasmut was involved with drug trafficking and the shipping scheme currently being researched by the Turkish Secret Service and INTERPOL.

It was obvious that the British Museum antiquities curator had no knowledge of Dr. Kasmut's involvement in securing a method of transporting drugs out of Egypt and smuggling them to other countries. Ahmet's intelligence web of secret agents covers a large area of Asia, the Mediterranean and all of the countries that border the Black Sea. In many circles, he was known as 'The Spider King.' He had worked hard to achieve his position and risked his life on many occasions. Intelligence was his game and he knew how to play it and win. Patience was a virtue he had learned as a child.

Ahmet, now in his fifties, was still unmarried, and a handsome man of means with influential friends. His dark wavy hair was mostly silver and his chin-strap beard, sculpted to perfection, was speckled with gray and accented his strong, square jaw. Ahmet's dark eyes shined like onyx surrounded by a sea of white as he gazed across the room at Laura Clark, the love of his life,

Twenty years ago Laura had been an internet technician working on the computers at the Turkish embassy when they met. She married, had two sons, and built her own billion dollar international business computer networking company all in ten years' time. Her husband, a US secret service courier, had faked his own death at the hands of Syrian rebels, and attempted to extort $50,000,000 from her in ransom payment. However, her first love, and good friend, Ahmet, had stopped that crime from happening. She now owned a villa on the island of Cyprus where she and Ahmet spent much of their time together when possible.

"I'm anxious to meet your English friends at the new tomb this afternoon. I hope we will be there early enough to take a tour before they lock it up for another ten years. You know how slowly things progress here in Egypt," she said.

"That's true," he chuckled, "everything except crime."

Laura crossed the room, bent down and kissed him on the cheek as he sat at the desk with documents in his hands. She glanced at the papers scattered across the surface of the desk. "I suppose you can't escape work, even while we're on vacation together."

"I promise," he said, "we'll go back to the villa and spend the next month together before you leave for the states. Are the boys coming over with you when you return for the winter holidays?" he asked.

She tapped him on the head with the palm of her hand. "You're trying to change the subject and I'm not going to let you. But, yes, the boys will be here for December. However, I want you to think about retirement. You're not as fast as you used to be and shouldn't be doing the work of a field agent. You promised two years ago that you would work behind a desk. I don't want to lose you to a stray bullet and neither do the boys."

He placed his arm around her as she stood next to him and pulled her onto his lap. "As soon as I can wrap up this case, I promise I will consider retirement. I would like nothing more than to spend the rest of my life with you and the boys."

"Then I guess I can't ask for more than that. Let me know when you are ready to leave the hotel, but be sure we get out to the Valley of the Monkeys in time for a tour of the tomb. It will be nice to meet

Lady Lynnette and Lady Grace. At least I won't be the only woman there. Of course, I'm not including the 'dragon lady,' as they call her."

Ahmet chuckled at her last comment. "I don't think you need to worry about meeting her. I doubt she will show her face if she knows I'm there. We've met before under similar circumstances. I sent her to prison on a case of fraud fifteen years ago.

"My guess is, that she has already packed things up and is getting ready for her escape. Sir Reginald let her know, without mentioning my name, that INTERPOL and the Turkish Secret Service had become interested in the missing workers. If I were a gambling man, I would venture to bet that she saw my face flash before her eyes."

Laura glanced at him with a look of concern. "She doesn't carry a gun, does she?"

He laughed. "She probably does, but she never was a very good shot. She missed me once before and I don't think she's had much time for target practice in prison."

"Very funny, but I'm not laughing." He could tell that she was dead serious and her soft face was suddenly like stone. "These drug people are tough and ruthless," she said. "They stop at nothing. You've made so many promises, I know I can't ask for something you have no control over. So, please be careful," Laura sighed as she held him tight, not wanting to let go.

Ahmet wrapped his arms around her, "You were a foolish woman to fall for a man in the secret service, twice." His strong hands caressed her back and her cheek rested on his chest.

"I should have listened to my heart and stayed with my first choice, but our lives were on different courses and our own needs and beliefs pulled us apart. That was then, but this is now and I won't let you go this time," Laura whispered.

Ahmet picked her up in his strong arms and carried her back to the bedroom in their hotel suite, kicking the door shut with his foot. He wasn't in any hurry to leave. Patience was a virtue he was proud of, and time was a luxury he had learned to enjoy once Laura had returned to him.

~

The tendrils of the spider's web reached all the way to The Home Office at No. 2 Marsham Street in London, where the Home Secretary and senior Minister of The Crown, the Right Honorable Lord John Henry Templeton, was in the middle of a conference.

"Gentlemen and ladies...I received a report this morning from Her Majesty's investigator, Sir Reginald Whitcomb, who is in Egypt at the tomb site excavation in the Valley of the Monkeys near Luxor, which is currently being conducted by the British Museum with assistance from the Cairo Museum," he announced.

"Isn't Lord Charles Marques funding that project?" asked committee member, Lady Sylvia Albright.

"Correct, your ladyship." Lord Templeton continued, "From this report, I understand that Lord Charles is also at the site. As you may remember, two workers were reported, by Dr. Stafford, to have vanished almost three weeks ago. According to this report, they've not returned and their bodies have not been found. The local police, as Sir Reginald states, were not interested to investigate their disappearance," he paused. "Lloyd's of London has insured this project on behalf of the British Museum and requested our assistance to procure information with regards to any possible criminal activities at the site. Their concern, of course, is that there has been foul play."

"So what does Sir Reginald have to report?" asked Sir Harry Foster.

Lord Templeton glanced over the top of his bifocals. "I was just getting to that part." He cleared his throat, a frown on his face as his eyes scanned the members around the table. Both men and women sat quietly waiting. There had already been more than enough interruptions and they could see that Lord John's patience was wearing thin. His personal assistant handed out copies of the report to each member.

"As you will see for yourself, this is no longer a simple case of missing persons. It appears there are investigations which have uncovered a drug ring that deals in trafficking and distribution of opium." He paused, once again looking over his spectacles, as he judged the reaction on each member's face, while allowing them to read further.

"Sir Reginald Whitcomb from this office and Sir Thomas Treadwell of the MIA intelligence agency, became involved when the disappearance of a well-known passenger happened while they were traveling on the Orient Express through Romania en route to Istanbul."

Sir Anthony Bellingham, one of the older members of the committee and a bit hard of hearing shouted as he shook the report in his left hand. "Oh, for Christ sake! Don't tell me the Baroness Von Karlsberg is back out on the circuit again. Is there no way we can keep that woman locked up?"

"Well, it appears that she was the one who vanished, but is now in the custody of INTERPOL. Perhaps the third time is a charm," chimed Lady Sylvia.

Lord Templeton, head of the Home Office committee, attempted to continue with the report. "Upon arrival in Istanbul, the Turkish Secret Service took over the investigation, which in turn, due to the various countries involved and the scope of the crime, caused INTERPOL to join the investigations. From this report, we are looking at kidnapping, attempted murder, robbery, falsifying of antiquities, and drug trafficking." One of the members gave a long whistle.

"Exactly!" said Lord Templeton. "We've stumbled onto Pandora's Box."

"Or a rather nasty can of worms," said Lady Summertrees.

Lord Templeton tapped his gavel on the marble palate to quiet the mumbled conversations of his colleagues. "The point is..." he said as everyone stopped talking and began to listen. "The point is, we need to decide if we are to recall Sir Reginald and allow the Turkish Secret Service and INTERPOL to continue their investigations or let him continue on the mission he was assigned to do, possibly placing his life in more danger than we had anticipated. I understand his wife is traveling with him."

"Lady Lynnette? What's she doing on his assignment?" asked MP Margaret Turnbridge from the opposite end of the table.

"Sir Reginald and Lady Lynnette had planned a holiday to Egypt. We voted to take advantage of his time there to look into the disappearance of the two workers as requested by the museum. I believe you were absent at that meeting. It was supposed to be a simple project of inspection not a full blown international criminal case," Lord Templeton stated.

"Has he requested to return to London?" MP Tylor Morgan asked.

"No...he has not," Templeton answered.

"Is his investigation of the missing workers tied together with this drug ring and the other crimes?" Morgan queried.

"From his report, there's no indication or evidence to that effect. He appears to speculate that there could possibly be a connection." Templeton added, "However, in my personal opinion I fail to see how one involves the other."

Morgan continued. "Then I move we allow him to complete the job he was sent to accomplish. If there are no claims made and no workers bodies are discovered by the end of this week, I'm sure that the lawyers for Lloyd's will have those contingencies covered in their contracts. He does mention a death by snake bite, which of course was an accident, and restitution to the family would be covered.

"If, on the other hand, he should request to return to London, then by all means, he should be allowed to return. If he wishes to send his wife back to England, while he remains in Egypt, that too should be arranged,"

"Spoken like a true solicitor. Thank you Morgan," said Templeton. "We have a motion on the floor. Do I hear a second?"

"I second the motion," said a voice somewhere in the room. The vote was taken and approved.

Templeton tapped his gavel. "I will send Sir Reginald a wire immediately with the offer of an option to return. It never hurts to keep the gate open," he said. "This meeting is adjourned."

Chapter Thirty-Two

Meeting in the Tomb

It was two o'clock in the afternoon when Ahmet and Laura arrived at the WV23 compound in the Valley of the Monkeys. Lord Charles was the first to spot their SUV coming up the road to the parking area. He hurried out to meet them, "Welcome to the tomb of Ay," he said in greeting. "And this must be the lovely and beautiful Mrs. Laura Clarke I've heard so much about." He took Laura's hand and kissed it. "Charming. Simply charming."

Laura turned with a raised eyebrow and smiled at Ahmet. "Have you been spreading rumors again?" she laughed.

"Your reputation precedes you, my love." He spread his hands in surrender.

"You are too kind sir," she said to Lord Charles.

"Not at all. Not at all. I have a good eye for beauty, but usually it is 2000 years old or older," he chuckled. "Come, let me introduce you to some of my friends. They've been waiting to meet you." They followed him into Sir Reginald's office tent where Laura met Lynnette, Sir Reginald, Grace, and Sir Thomas.

"Ahmet has spoken of you all and I feel as if I already know you, but it's nice to match a face with the name," Laura smiled as she shook their hands.

Lord Charles, appearing to take charge, cleared his throat to make an announcement. "We were about to make a final tour of the tomb before sealing the newly installed metal doors, until it can once again be properly opened for tourists; which will probably take a while knowing how time passes like a desert tortoise in Egypt. I've seen snails that move at a more rapid pace." Everyone laughed at his comparison.

"I was hoping you would allow me a preview tour of the tomb," said Laura, "I would be so honored."

"May I also suggest that Dr. Stafford, Kathy, Mario, and Dashi join us?" suggested Ahmet.

"What a splendid idea!" Lord Charles agreed. "We'll make it a celebration tour."

Ahmet grinned. "There might be more to celebrate than you think, Lord Charles." All heads turned in his direction.

"Is that an indication that you have more news for us?" asked Lynnette.

"I'll explain more once we're in the tomb and away from prying eyes and ears," he said.

"Then we must be off with haste before our imagination gets ahead of us," said Grace.

"I'll go find the others," said Dashi as he rushed off.

"That boy would make an excellent cat burglar. He must walk on air. I never know when he is in a room until he speaks," admitted Lynnette, to everyone's laughter.

Joined by the others, the group, led by Lord Charles and Laura walked slowly in the narrow, afternoon shadows cast by the karst landscape to avoid the heat of the sun. Once inside the tomb the temperature dropped as they descended the steep steps to the main chambers. Lord Charles explained how the tomb was discovered years ago, but never excavated until the funds could be found to sponsor the project. Laura was impressed.

Once they were in the burial chamber with the carved sarcophagus in the center of the room, everyone turned not to Lord Charles, but to Ahmet.

"You can whisper in this chamber if you wish," said Lord Charles, "and no one will miss a word," he nodded.

"Thank you," Ahmet bowed. "I wanted everyone present to hear this news at the same time to avoid any misunderstandings, and it makes life easier for me to say this only once," he smiled. The space fell silent with anticipation, not a word was spoken. Expectations filled the air and the beating hearts and heavy breathing of eleven people echoed in the stone chamber as their shadows in the soft lighting reflected on the cold walls. The pin was about to drop and all their senses were alert.

"With your help, we have been able to consolidate information on a major drug ring here in Egypt." He paused to allow that statement to register. "INTERPOL, the Turkish Secret Service, and the Egyptian Secret Police have been aware of their existence for some time, but our efforts to track information on them has proven unsuccessful until now."

"I assume you must be referring to our involvement with the incident on the Orient Express," said Thomas, who was most astute and preferred to see things in a chronological order.

"Exactly, Sir Thomas. It was your intelligence in the discovery of the missing baroness and the extraordinary detailed search of her compartment on the train that opened the path which led us into even further investigations.

"Following Lady Grace's observation of the trunks being removed at the station in Romania and the departure of the Egyptian man in the same vehicle after the disappearance of a known female criminal, we began to make certain connections with previous inquiries that had led to nowhere.

"Lady Lynnette's keen eye for detail was remarkable by noticing the broken glass and white powder on the floor of the train compartment, plus the fact that there were no trunks or suitcases found to belong to the baroness, provided even more threads to the web.

"Sir Thomas tested the powder, which he accurately declared to be opium. INTERPOL and the Romanian Police were then able to locate the chateau in the mountains, with the help of the villagers in the countryside, where certain vehicles, such as a Range Rover SUV, are rarely seen. They apprehended the Egyptian man and found the baroness still alive, abused, drugged, and chained to a bed in one of the rooms."

"That poor woman," said Laura.

Ahmet chuckled. "Laura and I don't normally discuss my work. It's an agreement we've had since we first met. All of this is new to her."

"Sorry," she whispered as she glanced around at the others.

"Please, don't be. His work is also new to some of us as well," Lynnette smiled.

"As I was saying..."Ahmet continued, "It wasn't until they found the second missing trunk, buried under a stack of hay in an old barn, full of opium filled glass containers, hidden inside fake Egyptian artifacts, that I remembered your trip to Egypt and the missing workers at the excavation of a new tomb."

"That's when you contacted me," said Lord Charles.

"Correct. I knew if anyone would know about a new tomb being opened in Egypt, it would be you. I knew you had been in Cairo on business and the museum helped me track you down."

"Is that when you began to suspect that the missing workers might have some connection with the contents of the trunk?" asked Grace.

"You read my thoughts exactly, Lady Grace, but it was the visit that Sir Thomas and Sir Reginald made to the Cairo Police Department that started to make noticeable waves on the Nile. Corruption is not always easy to spot when the waters are calm."

"So, how did Dashi become a spy for the Turkish Secret Service?" asked Lynnette.

Ahmet grinned at Dashi and indicated with a nod that he could answer. "I don't work for Mr. Ahmet," he said. "I work for my father who, as an undercover agent at the museum in Luxor, is with the Egyptian Secret Police. When the workers went missing, he was able to have me replace the photographer who was here at the site. There are things I'm not at liberty to speak of just now, but they have connections to the missing workers."

"Which brings me to the subject that Lady Lynnette mentioned only yesterday about the timetable and the shipping documents found on the train and the most recent photograph of a similar document found in the desk of Dr. Kasmut," Ahmet continued, "We have an updated document with the numbers on the ships involved. The times and dates with regards to their exact locations will take some skillful coordination which is currently being processed under the watchful satellite eyes of the Global Marine offices."

"So where do the camels fit into the picture?" Lynnette asked. "I'm referring to the photograph that Dashi took of the Valley of the Monkeys from his drone on the evening that the workers were reported to have gone missing."

"Ah yes, the small caravan transporting cargo at night." Ahmet replied. "Did you know that camels have three eyelids? One is used for night vision and to keep the blowing sand out of their eyes. Their pace is normally slow, but they have memories like an elephant when it comes to following traditional routes, which allowed us to intercept them and gain the information needed to expose the opium supplier.

"We discovered they were carrying hollowed out plaster casts of artifacts made here in this compound. Once we had Lady Lynnette's photos from Dr. Kasmut's tent, it didn't take long to add that string to the web. The glass vials were filled with opium, at a warehouse in Qina, then inserted in these plaster figures, sealed and painted before being boxed and delivered to the ships for distribution down the Nile to the Mediterranean or over land to the Red Sea, again by camel train."

"Amazing," said Kathy.

"Extremely well planned and coordinated," added Mario.

"Thank you," came a voice from the corridor outside the chamber. Dashi, standing by the entrance, recognized the voice and quickly slipped behind the carved stone door as the dragon lady entered with a gun in her hand.

"I was wondering where everyone had disappeared to. Is this a private meeting or can anyone attend?" Her voice was cool and sarcastic as she glanced at Ahmet. "Haven't we met before?" she paused, "don't bother answering. I never forget a face. Especially one so handsome."

"So it was you who planned a way to smuggle drugs out of Egypt?" Lynnette asked.

"I wasn't responsible for planning everything, but I played my part. I had plenty of time sitting in prison to plot and scheme. That's what people do when they're locked behind bars. The mechanics of the operation were managed by several others. I can't take all the credit. However, this man here," she pointed the gun at Ahmet, "gave me the time I needed to hone my education." She stared into his eyes. "Did you really think you could catch me again?" she laughed.

Ahmet stood in front of Laura. "You won't escape from here. There's roadblocks at the end of the valley and at the entrance to the Valley of the Kings. Even the river crossing is covered."

She laughed. "You don't really think I was planning to drive out of here, do you?" she asked.

About that time they could hear the low thrum of a helicopter arriving. Dr. Kasmut gave a sarcastic smile, "It sounds like my friends have arrived.

"My apologies for interrupting your meeting but I wanted to say goodbye. We won't be meeting again. The tomb will be sealed on my departure and no one will find you before I have disappeared.

"Like the workers we had to get rid of, I will simply vanish. But before I go..." she stared at Ahmet with fire in her onyx eyes, as if she was on drugs; her head weaving from side to side, like a snake ready to strike. "You shot me once and I haven't forgotten that. It's time I paid you back." She raised the pistol just as Dashi's arm came down across hers, causing the pistol to drop as it fired, echoing loudly in the chamber.

Mario rushed from the other side and together they held her tight. Sir Reginald carefully picked up the gun and placed it on the sarcophagus, Ahmet borrowed Lara's neck scarf and gently wrapped the revolver in it. He smiled as he stared at Kasmut.

"You won't get out of here alive," she said with a menacing grin as she squirmed to be released.

"Oh...I think we can manage that. Your partner in crime has already been arrested as he was about to board a flight from Luxor to Cairo then on to Brazil. It might interest you to know that he had only a single one-way ticket. Did you seriously think he was going to take you with him? I don't suppose it pays to be the one left holding the bag full of evidence."

All the color had drained from her now ghost-like face. The grin had disappeared and heavy lines creased around the jowls as her facial muscles began to sag. He hadn't planned for her to go with him. She was the decoy. The distraction for his escape.

"Murder, attempted murder, drug trafficking, and forgery. Anything else you want to add to that?" Ahmet asked her.

"I didn't kill anyone," she hissed. "He took care of that, and I hope he hangs."

"Sir Reginald, will you check the entrance and let me know if the police helicopter is waiting."

"Right'o, old man."

"That was some confession," said Sir Thomas, He tapped his breast pocket. "I hope my small pen recorder was able to capture all of it."

Laura, Grace, Lynnette, and Kathy all looked at each other in surprise and back to Ahmet. "You mean you had this planned in advance? How did you know she would come looking for us here?" asked Lynnette.

"Where else would she look if she couldn't find us in the compound? Someone was bound to tell her where we had gone. We purposely made a show of coming to the tomb," said Dashi.

Ahmet smiled at him. "I would call it female curiosity as reasoned by male intuition." They nodded to each other and grinned.

Lynnette huffed. "I suppose there's no getting around it, Grace. We've been outsmarted by male intuition." They all began to laugh, except for Dr. Kasmut, who was now wearing handcuffs and a look that could kill, if she had the chance.

Reginald, hearing their laughter as he returned gave everyone a strange, inquisitive, look. "What did I miss?" he asked.

"Only two more confessions," chuckled Sir Thomas. "We'll fill you in later."

"I'll count on that," he said. "Meanwhile, the helicopter is ready, sir, provided this party is over."

"On the contrary," said Ahmet with his arm around Laura. "This party has just begun."

As they filed out of the tomb, Lord Charles turned back. "I really must find that bullet," he said to Lynnette, "It would be strange for the archeologist to discover it when they reopen the tomb, not to mention, terribly confusing."

She took his arm. "I'll help you," she agreed. "We wouldn't want to change history now, would we?"

Chapter Thirty-Three

The Truth

The large police helicopter was waiting at the walkway lead-ing to the tomb of Ay. Six officers guarded the entrance while two others stood by Ahmet's awaiting vehicle. The action was over and the rein of the dragon lady had come to an end as the criminal was loaded into the chopper. Dust swirled in the air and the rotors mad a loud clapping sound as they rose into the air and headed north.

"Where will they take her?" asked Lynnette.

"First to the Interpol offices in Cairo," answered Ahmet. She'll be placed in a cell under their close supervision until their trial date is set. Then they'll be separated and placed in the prison outside of Cairo. And now we must depart for Luxor and a meeting with the Egyptian Secret Police." He took Laura's arm.

"But you haven't told us the whole story," said Grace, "Who was her partner in crime?"

Ahmet smiled, "That information will have to wait until the party this evening," he grinned. "Meanwhile, Interpol has reserved hotel accommodations for all of you at the Winter Palace. You're invited as my guests to dinner this evening in a private dining room. An invitation will be waiting in your suites with all the details. And now we really must be on our way. You have packing to do and a tomb to seal. Dr. Stafford and Lord Charles will manage those details with the remaining workers. It's time to fold your tents and steal away into the night like the nomadic Bedouins of old. Your cars with drivers will be arriving shortly."

Laura waved goodbye as she ducked into the coolness of the waiting SUV and Ahmet joined her in the back seat. The chauffeur put the vehicle in gear and they vanished in a cloud of dust down the sandy road exiting the Valley of the Monkeys.

Lynnette glanced around at the faces of her comrades as they stood like frozen pillars of salt. "So…now we play the guessing game until this evening," she remarked with a huff. "Someone here must know who her partner in crime is."

She studied each person carefully. "Lord Charles?"

"Sorry, my dear. I haven't the foggiest."

"Sir Thomas?" she continued.

"I could only hazard a queer guess at this time and wouldn't want to accuse the wrong person without further evidence. However, at least our mission here is complete. We have her confession that she knows who murdered the two workers. Lloyd's, of course won't be too pleased about that issue," Thomas said. "However, when you're in the business of insurance, those things happen."

"Grace." Lynnette appealed to her friend. "What can you come up with?"

"As you say, old girl...it's a guessing game. Perhaps it would be best if we finished packing and headed into Luxor for a late lunch and an afternoon nap. I think at the dinner party this evening you will have the answer to your question,"

"Oh poo, Grace," Lynnette said with an air of disappointment. "We're supposed to figure this out before they do."

"Grace chuckled, "I'm afraid, my dear, you missed the point. They already have the answer."

Lynnette was not quite ready to give-up. "Reggie. You have a guilty look on your face. You can't hide it from me. You know something we don't. Spill the beans or no dinner for you tonight, old man."

Sir Reginald contemplated before he answered. "Lynnette, my love...the only hint that I can offer, is what Ahmet told us when he set his plans in motion here at the compound. He said that a certain person had been suspected of corrupt behavior for quite some time and that Interpol had that person under surveillance.

"He wouldn't give me a name without confirmed evidence. That, of course, is highly regular and I totally understood. Now...I think we should finish packing, unless Minnie has done that for us." He chuckled. With a resigned sigh, Lynnette shook her head and followed him to their quarters.

Kathy, Mario, Dr. Stafford, and Dashi were busy boxing equipment up in the lab, which would be picked up by the trucks and delivered to the museum storage warehouse in Luxor. All the artifacts were in safe keeping at the Cairo Museum, where they would be on exhibit at the same time as Lord Charles's private Egyptian Collection in December.

Goodbyes were put aside for now. They would all be together at dinner this evening and there would be time for parting words later.

Lynnette, Minnie, and Reggie were the first to depart. Minnie had taken care to pack everything. Boris Rykoff and Jared Taylor followed them out of the rugged Valley of the Monkeys and into Luxor, their job was not yet complete and Boris was feeling a bit nervous about his future meeting with Lynnette. There was something she wanted to settle with him before leaving Egypt.

As yet, she had not informed Sir Reginald of her plans. She had every intention of keeping it a secret until they were on the plane back to London. Reggie would not be able to escape the conversation while seated next to the window and she was sure he would be in full agreement by the time they landed at Heathrow.

Lynnette knew he would be busy making notes to include in his report to the Home Office and his full attention would be distracted. She knew also the art of managing her husband.

Sir Thomas and Grace were next to leave as Lord Charles saw them off. "Well, old chap, we helped to solve another crime. This is becoming a habit of enjoyment," he chuckled. "Wait until I tell Elizabeth back at home. She's currently at her sister's summer place in South Hampton where I'll join her on my return. However, we'll see you late for the winter season in London. She always enjoys your company."

"It will be our pleasure. Grace and I will see you at dinner this evening. Don't get locked up in the tomb, old man," he said with a smile, slipping into the seat beside Grace.

"No worries there, my friend. Dr. Stafford, Kathy, Mario, and Dashi will keep me out of trouble. Lynnette and I found the bullet and casing in the burial chamber." He opened the palm of his hand to show the proof. "At least we won't make waves with the course of history. I'm adding them to my private collection of mystery artifacts," he chuckled—closing the limousine door as he waved.

The trucks were loaded with all the equipment and the tents had been dismantled. The tomb was now sealed with electronic signaling devices connected to the Museum security offices in Luxor by satellite. Lord Charles joined Dr. Stafford, Mario, and Kathy in his stretch limo. Dashi followed them out on his ATV behind the caravan of trucks. The Valley of the Monkeys fell silent once again as the rumble from the trucks slowly died in the distance. The coyotes, the cobras, the desert rats, tortoises, and scorpions would once again reclaim their territory until the tourist's future invasion became a reality.

~

It was almost time for dinner. The invitation was for eight o'clock. Sir Reginald was in his white dinner jacket and black bow-tie. He was sitting at the desk in their complimentary suite making notes for his report when Lynnette entered from the bedroom, wearing a full-length, pure-white, off-the-shoulder, flowing chiffon evening gown. Her emerald necklace and earrings sparkled in their platinum setting on her deep, healthy tan.

"Holy Mary!" cried Reginald. "I've seen an angel," he said as he stood and kissed her on the forehead. "You're going to knock'm dead tonight."

She chuckled, "I certainly hope not. There's been far too much death on this trip and too close for comfort. Now put down your pen and let's be off. You know how I hate making a grand entrance after everyone else has arrive." He obeyed her command and they left for the dinner party.

They met Grace, dressed in a midnight blue cocktail dress with a beaded top, and Sir Thomas, looking dapper in his tux, as they crossed the main lobby and entered the restaurant together. They were shown to a private dining room where several others were already gathered.

Dashi introduced them to his father, who had known Ahmet for many years. Kathy was standing next to him in a bright lemon-yellow cocktail dress and Laura looked cool in her refreshing ice-blue harem ensemble. The men were all in evening attire, even Dashi, who was smartly dressed in his white blazer, black jeans, a black V-neck T-shirt, and loafers. The contemporary artistic touch.

A single round table with seating for twelve stood in the center of the room with a magnificent colorful floral arrangement at its center. Once everyone was seated, Ahmet began his speech.

"Ladies and gentlemen, I would like to take this opportunity to thank all of you for your assistance in bringing to a close one of the baffling cases of drug trafficking that Interpol, the Turkish Secret Service and the Egyptian Secret Intelligence Service have been attempting to solve for over a year. This is probably news to you, but believe me, you have helped to capture the spiders in their own web of crime.

"It all began with a mysterious woman on the Orient Express that caught the eye of an intelligent and inquiring Lady Lynnette. Not only did the strange actions of this woman capture your attention," he said watching Lynnette's reaction, "but your suspicion that she was afraid and attempting to hide from someone on the train was proven to be true.

"The Egyptian man was a former convict and a paid assassin, hired to kill the baroness and steal the shipment of opium that she was transporting. Hired by none other than her partner and former lover—a man of high rank here in Egypt, and a person whose position should be above suspicion. But then, things are not always what they seem to be.

"We've been watching the moves of this individual with much interest for quite some time. Unfortunately, there was never enough evidence or information to follow through with any charges."

Ahmet's eyes fell on Sir Reginald. "He was extremely clever and covered his involvement at every turn, until you arrived from the Home Office and stirred the hornet's nest with your questions about the missing workers."

"Is it possible that you're speaking of a certain member of the Egyptian Police in Luxor?" asked Sir Thomas.

"Of course he is," Sir Reginald said nodding his head. "We should have suspected a cover-up with his less than professional excuses and the way he attempted to make it sound like a normal occurrence."

"You are both correct. Captain Mohamed Kalif Saeed, of the Egyptian Police, was running the drug shipments with the help of his current mistress, Dr. Kasmut, whose real name is Rashida Hassan. They became acquainted when he was a guard at the Cairo prison where she was incarcerated.

"It was Saeed who developed the plan for shipping the opium out of Egypt. And once the excavation of the tomb in the Valley of the Monkeys began, he arranged to poison Dr. Tavvi and replace him with Dr. Kasmut, who had been schooled in the art of molding wax and plaster casting."

"So that explains the disappearance and reappearance of the canopic jars and Ushabti figures," Kathy suddenly realized. "She was making molds to be filled with glass containers of opium."

"I wanted to share this information with you last night, but I was sworn to secrecy after our meeting with Ahmet," said Dr. Stafford.

"That is the truth," added Ahmet. "We couldn't afford for information to be spread by accident. The fewer who knew, the better our chances were to obtain the facts, and confessions we needed to wrap this case up." He glanced at the doorway and received a nod from the hotel manager.

"It appears our dinner is about to be served, so perhaps we can continue with questions while we eat. Please enjoy your meal. He raised his glass of wine and made a toast. "To all of the musketeers. Thank you for your diligence, intelligence, and perseverance."

As he sat down, Lynnette, who was seated on his left gave him a curious glance. "Please pardon my being so bold, but aren't you Muslim?"

Ahmet smiled, "How could you help but notice?" he asked placing his wine glass on the table.

She paused before her next question, then continued, "Aren't Muslims supposed to refrain from drinking alcohol? I believe I read that somewhere."

He chuckled as he raised his glass of red wine." I'm what you might call an "MM"—a Modern Muslim. It's true, we are not supposed to drink one drop of the evil alcohol." He tipped his glass and put his finger in the wine. "So...we reach in and find that one drop of evil alcohol on the tip of our finger, and toss it out," which he did. "Then we can drink the rest." He grinned at the look on her face.

"Well," Lynnette said with a chuckle, "I suppose that's most convenient."

"Works every time," he smiled.

Thirty-Four
Farewells

Lynnette was up early the following morning having her coffee by the window of their suite overlooking the Nile River and waiting for Reginald to join her. He had finished his morning shower and stood in the doorway of the bedroom dressed in a white hotel robe and drying his wet hair with a white, Egyptian cotton towel, as he watched his charming wife stare out the window.

"How long have you been up?" he asked.

"Oh...long enough to watch the sunrise on the Valley of the Kings, and to get Minnie started with packing. Most of the luggage was never unpacked after we left the compound except for our evening clothes and what we will wear on the plane today. Will you join me for coffee?"

"I'm sure I would enjoy it, but I need to get dressed. We have a quick meeting downstairs with Ahmet," he said, disappearing into the bedroom.

"Why didn't you say so? I'll need to dress too," Lynnette said standing in the bedroom doorway.

"No, no...The meeting is just for Sir Thomas and myself, to go over what he will need from us, depositions, reports, and so forth," he said from the bathroom combing his hair in place.

"Perfect," Lynnette said, handing him his shirt, "that will give me the opportunity to have my meeting with Minnie and Boris in private. I was hoping you would be here, but we can fill you in later." He reached for the tie she held in her hand and began to form a knot.

"Lynnette, dear, I hope you're not going to make a fuss about their little holiday romance. Boris seems to be a rather likeable chap and Minnie...well, you know Minnie better than anyone."

"Don't be so concerned," she smiled while straightening his tie, "I'm sure that Minnie and I can handle the details like two intelligent English women do."

"That's what worries me," he cracked a grin with a questioning look.

She kissed his cheek and gave him a pat on the ass, as he slipped on his jacket. "Off you go to your meeting, old man, and be sure to tell Ahmet what a wonderful time we had at the dinner party last night."

Reginald shook his head. "You've already told him a dozen times last night, but I'll be sure to pass along your message once again."

~

Ahmet was waiting in the coffee shop. Sir Thomas had not yet arrived. He stood to greet Sir Reginald. "Please, have a seat, Thomas won't be joining us as they have an early flight to Paris this morning. Apparently, Grace had planned to do some Christmas shopping before they returned on to England," he chuckled. "However, I've made copies of everything for both of you and depositions can be sent by special embassy courier. All the instructions are there." He handed Reginald two packages.

"I wanted this meeting to express my gratitude and to let you know it was a pleasure working with you and your charming wife on this case. The sting operation on the ships is under way as we speak. Drugs are being collected, ships are being confiscated, and the drug traffickers are being arrested. This is the final case of my career, and the one I am most proud of. It has taken a long time to snip the threads of this web and put these spiders behind bars where they belong. Your wife was instrumental in making this happen. I'm sure you will pass my compliments on to her should I not see her before you leave.

"Ordinary women's brains are pretty much made from a single mold, like a batch of pottery. But Lynnette's brain was a special order."

"What you mean," Reginald said, "is that she has a great deal more intelligence than is given to the rank and file of humanity."

"No, I don't." Ahmet shook his head. "It isn't a question of quantity at all. It's a different kind of intelligence, Ordinary people have

 ---

to reason from visible facts. But Lynnette doesn't. She reasons from facts in her imagination that tells her they exist even when others don't see them.

"Rather like a portrait artist who can paint a likeness of your face just by looking at the back of your head. She sees beyond the known facts, and blends that reasoning with the confirmed information she has at her fingertips. You're a most fortunate man to have found a mate with both talent and beauty."

"Here, here. I agree with you most hardily, but it's best not to let her hear you say that. I wouldn't be able to get her swollen head on the plane," he chuckled.

"I do hope you will come visit us on Cypress. Laura and I will both be retiring to the villa. We plan to do some traveling in the near future. I've included our contact information in your envelope."

"Lynnette and I would be delighted to accept your invitation and you must come to England and visit us on your travels." He glanced up to see Lord Charles heading their way.

"Gentlemen, what a refreshing morning. I feel like I've walked half the quay along the Nile." His face was a bit flushed and his breathing heavy. "Mind if I join you for a spot of tea?"

"By all means," said Ahmet, standing to greet him as he signaled the waiter to bring more mint tea.

"What's next on your agenda when you leave Egypt?" Reginald asked Lord Charles.

"Well, to tell the truth, Emily is going to stay with her sister at Summerfield Manor near Brighton. She and her husband have a lovely estate there. As for me, when I leave here, I will be off to South Africa and on safari in Botswana and Zimbabwe then off to do some bird hunting on Madagascar. We have friends, Lord and Lady Chillingsworth, who have vineyards in the hills outside of Cape Town, so I'll spend some time there before returning to Cairo in December for the opening of my exhibition and the grand addition of the artifacts from the tomb of Ay.

"Emily wants to spend Christmas at Summerville Manor before we return to Menton Abbey for New Years. Perhaps you and Lynnette will join us for New Years. I'll have Emily send you an invitation. We have plenty of rooms and we'll invite Sir Thomas and Grace. Kathy and Mario have already agreed to come. It would be great fun to sit around the dinner table and regale our guests with our tales of catching drug lords and shooting cobras." he laughed.

"I'll speak with Lynnette about it," Reginald said, "I'm sure she would be delighted to accept. Your reputation for hospitality is extraordinary."

Lord Charles blushed as he chuckled, "I don't know that I can take much credit for that, old chap. I leave all that up to Emily. Hosting events at the abbey is her forte. I try to do as I'm instructed. And now I see my valet, Stevens, is waiting in the doorway. The car must be loaded and I have an early flight to catch back to Cairo and on to Johannesburg. Gentlemen, it has been an exciting experience and a great pleasure," he nodded in parting.

~

Sir Reginald had said goodbye to Ahmet and was passing through the elegant lobby when he saw Kathy and Mario waiting for their airport transportation to arrive. "Well, my friends, I assume you are off to Italy. It must be grape harvest time in Tuscany."

"It's getting close," replied Mario, "but we're off to Paris first. Kathy wants to spend a week in the Loire Valley. Their harvest has already started, and I am on the board of major European Wine Growers, so there are a few meetings to attend."

Kathy stood next to her husband. "The doorman has indicated our car is waiting," she relayed to Mario. "It was an adventure working with you and Lynnette at the compound. I only wish we had more time to get better acquainted. Please tell her I hope our paths will cross again in the future under less trying circumstances," she chuckled.

"I'm sure they will," Reginald said as he walked with them to the entrance, "As a matter of fact, we have been invited to Menton Abby for New Years. I understand you will be staying there as well."

Kathy's face lit up with a smile. "That's marvelous! We will look forward to seeing you there. Our best to you both," she said as they departed.

~

Meanwhile, Lynnette was having her own meeting upstairs with Boris and Minnie.

"I must say, Mr. Rykoff, you are a surprising individual. Minnie tells me that you have asked her to marry you. Is that correct?"

Boris swallowed a lump in his throat, glancing at Minnie and then back to Lynnette, before he answered. "Yes, ma'am. I know it would be proper to make this request to a family member, but since Minnie has no family, she said it would be best to seek your blessings and permission."

Lynnette gave him a reassuring smile and nodded her head. "And, she is quite right in making that suggestion. You see, I have known Minnie most of my life, and she is like family to me. I wouldn't want her to make any rash decisions. Although, when it comes to matters of the heart, I'll admit I'm not an expert. However, I would expect Minnie to consult me and request my council." Boris nodded, but remained silent.

"It's important, as they say, that we are all on the same page, so to speak. So you will understand if I need to ask you a few questions." Boris nodded with a confident look of compliance.

Lynnette's eyes shifted quickly from Boris to Minnie and back. "Is it your intention to remain employed as a bodyguard for the Home Office?" she asked.

Boris was prepared for this question. Minnie had warned him that Lynnette would not be pleased with the travel and dangers involved in his working conditions. "I realize that the profession of bodyguard is not one for a married man. Minnie and I have already discussed that, but I'm sure I could find another kind of work and would be happy to do so to please Minnie." Lynnette smiled at Minnie with reassurance.

She too had given this conversation much thought. "You have only known Minnie for the past three weeks, which I will point out, is a very short courtship." She paused just long enough to see the look of concern on Boris's face, then continued her speech. "Of course, there will need to be a period of engagement to consider."

"Oh, yes!" said Minnie, having previously had this discussion with Lynnette when she mentioned Boris's proposal. "That will give Boris time to find another job and a place to live in London."

Lynnette smiled. "Well, let's not put the cart before the horse. I have an idea that might work for everyone concerned." She studied Boris's face and physique as if seeing him for the first time. He wasn't really as much a gorilla as his first impression had made on her. As a matter of fact, he had a rather aristocratic face, with chiseled features and a stern jawline. His blue eyes and sandy hair were very Germanic and his small ears laid flat against his tilted head.

"I..." she contemplated her next question. "Tell me, Boris, do you know how to drive an automobile?"

"I drove a tractor on our farm and driving is a Home Office requirement for all bodyguards," he smiled. It was the first time Lynnette recalled seeing him smile—rather pleasantly.

Lynnette watched them both as they sat holding hands. A mischievous grin appeared on her face. "I'm going to suggest an engagement period of nine months. That's rather short considering, but I don't wish to torture Minnie more than is proper to wait.

"Sir Reginald's chauffeur is getting married next June and has given his notice of intent to leave our employment and move to Kent with his new bride."

"You have a plan. I know that look I see in your eyes," said Minnie.

"Of course I have a plan, Minnie. However, it will involve convincing Sir Reginald, but I think he will see the advantage once I've explained the reasoning behind it.

"We will hire Mr. Rykoff to fill the position of chauffeur if he is willing. That will make it possible for you to continue working for me. You can move into the chauffeur's cottage and have your own gardens. It will also give Reginald a personal bodyguard. Not that an MP needs one, but it can't hurt the way things are going in Parliament these days."

She glanced at Boris. "What do you say, Mr. Rykoff—nine months, marriage, new job, your own cottage, less stress and a happy wife to share it with? You will be a part of our family."

Boris was surprised to say the least. It took him a moment to comprehend how Lynnette had put it all in a nutshell. Minnie was grinning from ear to ear as she gazed into his blank face. "If that's what Minnie wants, then I'm pleased to accept the offer," he smiled.

"Yes—well, let's not get too excited," said Lynnette. "We still have Sir Reginald to consult."

"You can always tell him it would be like Sir Thomas with Lady Grace. She's his wife, chauffeur, and bodyguard all in one," said Boris with a smile.

Lynnette chuckled. "Well, not quite," she said. "I'll still be his wife, but I think he'll get the picture. Leave it to me. It looks like Minnie and I are going to have a garden wedding to plan for next June at Carrolton Manor. Now, off you go—I need to find Reginald and explain our plans. Perhaps I should wait until we are on the plane for Heathrow. He won't be able to go very far with a seatbelt on and I'm sure I'll have his agreement before we land."

The End

Author—D.G. Heath

D.G. Heath lives in the Yucatan. In his former life, he was an interior designer, private secretary, real estate broker, fashion model, and owner of the Rancho de San Juan Country Inn and Restaurant near Santa Fe, New Mexico for 22 years, receiving numerous awards in the hospitality industry.

Books

- **D.G. Heath Mystery Collection —Volume I**
  Double Martini / Web of Intrigue / Codes and Confessions

- **D.G. Heath Mystery Collection—Volume II**
  A Person of Interest / Accent / Vortex

- **D.G. Heath Mystery Collection—Volume III**
  The Viper's Nest / Accidentally Complicit

- **Tales from a Country Inn**

- **The Art of Imagination**

- **Bedtime Stories and Other Tales**
  Adelaide Literary Magazine

- **The Cappuccino and No Time for Tears**
  "Fiction, fantasy, travel, humor, suspense, mystery, and romance are tools that stir the imagination."

Author's Interview

D.G. Heath

Q. After working in hospitality for more than twenty years, what made you decided to become a writer when you moved to the Yucatan?

A. I was told I needed to find an outlet for my creative energy. I had suddenly stopped working 24/7 and became an email junky, writing to friends back in the US, who suggested I should write a book with all the stories I could tell about the strange things that happen when you run a country inn and restaurant.

Q. Is that what prompted your first book, Tales from a Country Inn?

A. Actually I started to write a memoir about my adventures in life and realized the most exciting part of my life was during the time I was an innkeeper. So from memory, I pieced together actual happenings and events that would give my readers a 'Uniquely Difference Experience' about operating a B&B. It was twenty-two years of laughs, love, and a learning curve, that I wouldn't trade for anything.

Q. What made you decide to write mystery such as your second book, *D.G. Heath Mystery Collection,* and what methods do you find work best for you when writing?

A. I've always enjoyed reading mysteries and watching TV shows about mystery, such as *Law and Order, Castle* or *CSI*. I suppose you could say I'm a 'plot driven' writer. Inspiration comes first, either from something I've seen, heard, or read, that caught my attention and stirred my imagination. Giving an old plot a new twist is also a challenge. I draw my characters from people I know or have met. At 77, I've met a lot of characters in my life and my memory is still in good working order.

Q. What was your reasoning for putting three mysteries in one book rather than writing each as a separate book?

A. Television mysteries are usually about an hour long. The plot runs fast and the viewer is not lost. I didn't want to lose the plot or my reader's attention when weaving my Web of Intrigue. Suspense is something you weave into the web off and on to be sure the reader is still with you. I don't always know how my mysteries will end, but once I get there, I go back and fill in the blanks—characters and scene

> "Traveling adds to the spice of life and definitely to a writer's perspective. To experience is to know. To remember is to be in control of that experience."

descriptions, add clues where needed, blend in the five senses when possible, and rewrite, rewrite, rewrite—like separating the wheat from the chaff. I want my readers to be able to read a story to the end and not fall asleep before they get there.

Q. Your third book, Art of the Imagination, offers working suggestions for advancing a person's writing skills, by using techniques that helped you get started. What prompted you to write this book?

A. I needed a lot of help when I started writing at 70, and no doubt I still do. I had an English teacher who once said, "Those who can...do, and those who can't...teach." I admit, I'll never be a best-selling author, because I write for pleasure—my own and that of my readers. But life is full of surprises.

Q. Why did you select mystery as the genre for your writing talents and is there any connection to your travels and past life?

A. Traveling adds to the spice of life and definitely to a writer's perspective. To experience is to know. To remember is to be in control of that experience.

Q. Final question...what is the hardest thing you have learned about writing?

A. Finding a good editor...especially if a writer is self-publishing as so many are now days. I have an excellent publisher and I couldn't have published six books in three years without his guidance.

www.ingramcontent.com/pod-product-compliance
Lightning Source LLC
Chambersburg PA
CBHW050502260626
47157CB00004B/1152